# Mistress

*of the*

# Storm

# Mistress

*of the*

# Storm

*A Verity Gallant Tale*

## M.L. Welsh

David Fickling Books

A DAVID FICKLING BOOK

David Fickling Books and the colophon are trademarks of David Fickling.

Visit us on the Web! www.randomhouse.com/kids

Educators and librarians, for a variety of teaching tools, visit us at www.randomhouse.com/teachers

*Library of Congress Cataloging-in-Publication Data*
Welsh, M. L.
Mistress of the Storm : a Verity Gallant tale / by M.L. Welsh. — 1st American ed.
p.    cm.
Summary: After a stranger gives an ancient book to unpopular, twelve-year-old Verity Gallant,
she and her newfound friends, Henry and Martha, uncover secrets stirring in
the harbor town of Wellow and use them to face a powerful, vengeful witch.
ISBN 978-0-385-75244-2 (trade) — ISBN 978-0-385-75245-9 (lib. bdg.) —
ISBN 978-0-375-89917-1 (ebook)
[1. Books and reading—Fiction. 2. Friendship—Fiction. 3. Witches—Fiction.
4. Family life—Fiction. 5. Sailing—Fiction. 6. Fantasy.] I. Title.
PZ7.W46854Mis 2011
[Fic]—dc22
2010018721

Printed in the United States of America
June 2011
10 9 8 7 6 5 4 3 2 1

First American Edition

*This book features many sisters but I have only one,
and so it is dedicated with love to Caroline.*

*People ask me if I miss it. If I miss the adventure of smuggling. And the truth is, I do. I miss the thrill of the chase – I miss picking my way through the rocks, riding out a south-westerly as it batters the coast. Ours were skills that few could master – part practice, part secrets passed down through the generations, and part sheer hellcat daring.*

*We were natural businessmen. It all came so easily to us: arranging finance; transporting goods; bartering with suppliers; charming . . . those who needed to be charmed. We loved every part of it. We loved the freedom money buys: with enough currency, no door in the land is locked to you. We loved our fine houses and rich clothes. We loved knowing we were as wealthy and powerful as any real Gentry.*

*Do I regret it? I regret where it took me. I regret what I lost as a result. And if the exchange were mine to make, I'd swap every last penny of profit, every thrilling chase, every porcelain-skinned lady for the chance to tell the story anew.*

# Book One
# AUTUMN

## Chapter One

Wellow library was quiet. Verity expected it to be quiet. She came here all the time and always had the run of it. Which is why it came as a shock to see a giant of a man kneeling on the floor, in tears.

Wellow is famed, of course. But it is remote too – a far-flung outpost of this great land we call Albion. And he was the most exotic man she had ever seen. Verity knew it wasn't polite to stare, but she couldn't help it. His skin was so dark it had a sheen of blue to it. Though hunched on the floor, he was clearly tall – well over six foot – and handsome, with high cheekbones, wide full lips and almond-shaped eyes. His clothes were equally foreign: a long velvet coat made of squares of chocolate brown, burnt orange and bottle green covered a white linen shirt and moleskin trousers. His boots were leather with soft flat soles.

Books were scattered on the floor all around him. In his lap lay a large red volume; his head was bowed over it as silent tears ran down his face. His hand clutched a tiny peg doll carved from a dark shiny wood. It was covered with a few scraps of faded material which might once – a long time ago – have been brightly coloured. An air of unutterable sadness hung over him. Verity's presence didn't seem to have registered at all.

It was like finding a panther in your sitting room. Something so vital, so alive, was never meant for the dust-filled air of Wellow library. Verity was filled with an overwhelming urge to comfort the stranger. Without thinking, she took a step towards him . . . And broke the spell. He looked up as if the world had come into focus.

His cheeks were wet and his gaze direct. Slowly he took in everything about her – and more slowly still, the faintest and saddest of smiles appeared. He sprang up from the floor, clutching the book, and ran past Verity to the front door. With one swift push he was gone.

Verity stared in astonishment at the spot where he had been. Miss Cameron, the librarian, continued with her indexing at the entrance. Verity came to life. Running after the man, she burst through the double doors and chased him down the street. More than anything in the world she wanted to know who he was.

Wellow library sits at the junction of two cliff-top paths. One leads to the harbour. The visitor chose the other, running down the narrow track to Steephill Cove.

'Wait,' shouted Verity, sprinting. 'Please wait.'

Below them on the shore lay the fishermen's boats, their nets gathered in the bilges. Verity was going so fast she had to grab the iron railing every few seconds to steady herself.

The stranger didn't slacken his pace in the slightest. He was on the shore now and heading for a small rowing boat beached there. He untied it and started pushing it out towards the sea.

Verity raced down the last few steps and across the sand. She stopped and stood on the beach, salt water gently soaking its way through her shoes, and called out one last time: 'Please wait.'

Finally he looked up. Lost for words, Verity realized she didn't have one good reason for chasing this man all the way down the cliff. Not one good reason. Just an overwhelming sense that it was important to do so.

'You can't . . .' she started. 'Take books from the library . . . without signing for them.' Her cheeks burned pink with embarrassment. Surely she could think of something better to say than that?

The man looked with surprise at the book clutched in his hand. To Verity's astonishment he laughed. A rich melodic sound.

'Understanding the rules. Yes, that is very important.' Staring at her for a second, he appeared to make a decision. He took something from his pocket and placed it on top of the book, passing both to her. 'The storm is coming,' he said, as if this were an explanation, then turned back to his task.

Verity stood on the shore. Clutching the book under one arm, she examined her other gift. It was a round wooden ball, clearly very old. The surface was smooth from handling, and polished to a rich sheen. It looked a bit like a nut, with a joining seal along one side. Verity shook it. It rattled. She put it in her coat pocket.

She turned the book over to read its title. *On the Origin of Stories: A Disquisition* by Messrs R. Hodge, Heyworth & Helerley. Embossed on the red leather cover was a golden globe. She opened it and read the Foreword.

*All things were created at the Lord of the Sky's word* [it said]. *All things were made by him, and without him nothing had life. But once he created our world, it was wild and untamed. And his people suffered greatly at the hands of the elements.*

*So He of the Sky said, 'I will give each element a Keeper, to control them and protect my people.' And he read out a story of their beginning: of four sisters whose duty it was to control the elements. It was a joyous event, and as he spoke, the words fell from the sky. Each place where they landed around the world became a sacred one of special powers, so when a story was read aloud there, it would become true.*

Places where stories could become real? Verity thought of the many, many tales she'd read in her short life, and was enchanted. She looked through the rest of the book. It appeared to be a journal or catalogue of some kind. Why had the strange man run all the way down the cliff with it? And why had it moved him to tears?

It was windy, and clouds were skidding across the sky.

Verity noticed that the large, fast-moving one above her looked like an old woman.

Hundreds of years ago people believed that such visions were signs of things to come: portents, they called them. These days, with our sophisticated scientific understanding, we know this to be untrue. And most of the time we are right.

But now the storm was coming. And it would change Verity Gallant's life for ever. Even though she – like a caterpillar wrapped in its chrysalis – knew nothing of it.

Long after the other members of her family had fallen asleep that night Verity was still awake, reading the red leather-bound book from cover to cover.

At first she told herself she was simply looking to see if there was something else tucked between the pages: a written note, some scribbled comments – anything that might explain the interest of the man in the library, or tell her why he had given it to her.

The entire book was about one of the four sisters mentioned in the Foreword: the Keeper of the Wind. The authors had travelled the whole world, it seemed, and each time they came upon a reference to her – be it in folklore, or a manuscript, or even in the architecture of a building – they noted it down.

As the hours passed, Verity grew ever more captivated by the book; or, to be precise, by its heroine. A woman whose ability to terrify only seemed to make her more fascinating. Verity completely understood why the authors had been obsessed with her.

*She was the most beautiful of the four* [she read, in an early chapter], *as if the Lord of the Sky had finally perfected his work in her. She could charm the moon itself from the night sky. Grown men would kill for the promise of her smile. Women fought for the sunshine of her attention. She could make a stone laugh if she chose to. She could draw tears from a mountain.*

(Vellum manuscript, Nordic region, believed to be a precursor of *Tales of Wiser Times*)

Only when dawn started to break did Verity realize she had read the whole thing from cover to cover. And was still none the wiser.

The next morning Verity could be found in the kitchen, buttering toast. She surreptitiously rubbed her eyes and stifled a yawn. What had possessed her? How could she have spent a whole night reading *On the Origin of Stories: A Disquisition* by Messrs R. Hodge, Heyworth & Helerley?

Her sister, Poppy, was busily wolfing down breakfast, consumed by thoughts of her audition for the Christmas revue.

'So *exciting*,' she chattered as Mrs Gallant looked at her proudly. She was such a pretty little girl: petite in every way, with fair hair, clear blue eyes and a sunny charm that people instantly warmed to.

'I'm sure they'll be delighted to have you,' her mother encouraged. 'It must be terribly difficult to find cast members with your looks and talent.'

Poppy glanced across the kitchen. 'You should try too, Verity,' she urged. 'Shouldn't she, Mother?'

Mrs Gallant looked uncertainly at her elder daughter. 'There's no harm in trying,' she agreed hesitantly.

Verity knew her mother didn't mean to be hurtful. Still, as her old friend Alice had often said to her: *Not everything in life turns out as we would like.*

Nor should it, Verity reminded herself. It just seemed a little hard sometimes to be tall for your age – and sturdy – with long brown hair that strayed from its clasp in an unruly fashion. To be the exception that proved the rule in a family of slender blondes.

Verity did not match the rest of the Gallants. Her solemn little face with its pink cheeks and charcoal eyes wavered constantly between very pretty and very plain. But it wasn't just her looks. Like all good parents, Verity's mother and father had lined up the full range of appropriate activities for their daughters: horse-riding, piano lessons, dance classes, choir practice . . . the list ran on and on. Poppy seemed to love them all, and Verity didn't want to be ungrateful, but sometimes, when she was walking down the hill, she caught herself looking out to sea and wishing it was possible to pick herself up in the air and fly away. To feel the wind in her hair, and dirt on her face.

*Not everything in life turns out as we would like. But things can change.*

Verity's father – a tall, fair man – entered the room, already absorbed in a new manuscript which had just been delivered. Mr Gallant edited books for a living and spent most of his time at home in the study – a room Verity loved.

'Sleep well?' he asked his elder daughter.

Verity perked up. Perhaps her father might be able to throw more light on the matter? This was a little optimistic: Verity's parents rarely discussed any subjects other than school and ladylike behaviour.

'I was wondering—' she started.

'Good, good . . .' Mr Gallant said, benevolently rubbing the top of Verity's head, clearly not listening at all.

Seeing her husband, Mrs Gallant began to clear her throat. 'Now, girls,' she announced in a carefully cheerful tone, 'we have some news for you. Rather an event actually.'

Verity wondered what she could possibly be about to announce that would make her so anxious. Her mind raced with possibilities. Were they planning a journey perhaps, or a long voyage? She drifted off for a second: would they be going by sea, or maybe even by car?

'. . . so you'll have another little sister, or brother,' her mother finished, smiling tentatively. 'Isn't that nice?'

'It's wonderful,' declared Poppy, running to give her a hug.

The words dragged Verity's focus unceremoniously back to the here and now. Her face filled with confusion.

Mrs Gallant sighed. Why was her elder daughter always off in a dream world? 'We're expecting a baby, Verity,' she said.

'I . . .' murmured Verity uncertainly.

Mr Gallant smiled and patted her arm fondly. 'There's nothing to worry about,' he reassured her. 'Isn't that right, Felicity?'

'Of course . . .' said Mrs Gallant brightly.

Verity found herself staring at her mother's fingers, which were anxiously twisting and untwisting a tassel from the tablecloth.

'There's nothing to say we'd have three girls in a row . . .' her mother finished.

'We agreed, Felicity,' insisted Mr Gallant, 'that superstitious nonsense has no place in a modern household.'

Verity's mother avoided her husband's gaze. 'I'm sure it will all be fine,' she said.


Verity ambled slowly towards Priory Bay College, a few yards behind a group of girls from her year: all slim, all pretty, and all allowed to choose their clothes on the basis of fashion, not practicality.

The school sat at the top of Wellow's overcliff and could be approached by a number of paths that ran through its surrounding parkland. As the imposing gothic towers of a more recent extension came into view, scores of children could be seen trudging towards it.

Verity, meanwhile, battled with her own internal struggle. Her mother was having a baby, and she wasn't sure how she felt about it. She was used to things as they were. What would a baby be like? Would it cry all the time? In truth, Verity didn't see the appeal of babies. They seemed to keep everyone awake at night, and she was fairly sure there was sick involved. They took up quite a lot of time, didn't they?

Was it wrong to feel sad – more lonely still – at the idea that there might be yet another person in your home who was better at getting on with people than you were? Was it shaming to be jealous of a baby that hadn't even been born yet? Why couldn't she just be pleased for her parents like Poppy?

A strong gust of wind buffeted her. Verity buried her hands deep in her coat pockets and gripped the strange wooden ball. She shook it. It was oddly comforting. Was it a rattle of some kind? A thought occurred to her: if Mother was having a baby, then their family would get bigger. She smiled. That would be fun.

Two large boys loomed on the horizon: George Blake and his brother, Oscar. Jostling past Verity, George grabbed her bag. The girls in front giggled as he raced ahead brandishing his prize.

'Give the bag back, George,' chanted one, Bella, in a tone that clearly implied this was the last thing she thought he should do.

'You are mean,' chimed in her friend, Amanda, batting his shirt flirtatiously.

The most popular, Charlotte Chiverton, moved to

Verity's side and nudged her. 'Aren't you going to ask for your things back, Gallant?'

George Blake was obviously very pleased with himself. He walked backwards, opening the bag, investigating its contents and grinning ear to ear.

'Sure there's nothing you want to keep?' he asked as he extracted Verity's things. 'Pencil case? No. Exercise books? No. *Three* bags of sweets,' he exclaimed, pulling out his latest find. 'Tut, tut, Verity. No wonder you're so hefty.'

Verity blushed as the girls pealed into chimes of laughter.

'And what's this tatty old volume?' he continued.

Verity's heart jumped anxiously. Not her book . . .

George opened the front cover to inspect it. Tapping the library form glued inside, he shook his head in mock disapproval. 'Past the return date, Verity,' he scolded. 'How are you going to maintain your reputation as the world's biggest swot when you're making silly errors like that?'

The girls shrieked with delight.

Tired of this particular game, George threw the book over his shoulder and thrust the bag into Verity's hands. 'Cheer up, Gallant,' he told her. 'Might never happen.' Then he ran off, giving her skirt a quick parting flick. She fended him off with an anxious flap of her hands – which just made everyone laugh all the harder.

As her tormentors headed towards the school gates, Verity bent over to pick up the red leather-bound book and dusted it down. In the distance the girls' giggles rang out as the two brothers tauntingly slapped their hands at each other. 'Not my books, not my books,' she heard Oscar simper.

Verity knelt forlornly on the grass and began to put the rest of her belongings back in her bag. She could feel a familiar pricking in the corners of her eyes. Staring hard at the ground, she concentrated on not crying. A new peal of laughter prompted her to look up. Charlotte was leaning on Amanda, the two of them bent over in mirth.

Verity's chest squeezed with misery. Uncontrollable hot tears streamed down her cheeks. She had never felt so out of place and alone.

At the edge of the park an elderly man stood watching. His once handsome face was lined and scored but his blue eyes burned. He looked troubled. As Verity began to walk dispiritedly towards the school gates, he appeared to make a decision. Turning round, he headed for the town.

Verity's day hadn't got any better by the afternoon, when she found herself sitting on a gym bench, filled with quiet dread. She hated games lessons. She hated the cold, damp changing rooms for a start. But she also hated trudging up and down muddy fields in winter. She hated being stuck in some rubbish position on the pitch. She hated indoor athletics. She hated cross-country runs in the rain. But most of all she hated the way she felt standing there on her own, shivering from the cold: the last person to be chosen for any team.

'Ready, girls?' boomed the head of games as she strode in. Mrs Watson wasn't just heavier than the other teachers; she also seemed to be taller, wider, and somehow . . . denser. A heated discussion had been taking place amongst the rest of the class. And now an envoy was dispatched to communicate with her:

'Charlotte's bailing out of Sunday's sailing match. And it's our first against the Whale Chine girls.'

'I have to,' insisted the same girl who'd witnessed Verity's humiliation that morning. 'Mother says it's this weekend or never for shopping and I've simply *nothing* to wear.'

Verity listened with half-hearted interest as she pulled on an ugly games sock in a particularly virulent shade of blue. She wondered what it would be like to look forward to a shopping trip. Mother's store of choice was Dereham's: a small, dour emporium that took a Puritan approach to girls' clothes. Mrs Dereham believed that apparel should have purpose.

'Gallant,' Mrs Watson announced. 'Gallant can take Chiverton's place.'

Verity froze with shock. She'd never sailed before. She'd never even set foot on a dinghy.

'*Gallant?*' howled one particularly incensed member of the group, backed immediately by a chorus of disapproval.

'Don't see why not,' said Mrs Watson. 'Can't believe we've never fielded you before. Probably been out on the water with the family.'

A fleeting vision of her parents trying to manoeuvre a dinghy on the open sea flashed through Verity's mind. She stifled a giggle. Laughing was not going to help. 'I won't be much use to the team,' she agreed. 'Couldn't someone else fill the place?'

'You'll be fine, girl,' Mrs Watson replied, to Verity's dismay. 'May be a little below your standard, but it's a day out. Tactics session Friday at the club – four o'clock – don't be late.'

'*Below her standard?*' snorted a frustrated classmate.

'Verity can't *sail*,' moaned another girl.

'Verity isn't good at *anything* sporty,' said a third.

The accusation stung, but Verity nodded her head earnestly in agreement. 'It's true. I can't,' she said.

For the first time ever, she saw something like astonishment on Mrs Watson's face. 'Can't sail?' she repeated. 'Verity *Gallant* can't sail? Extraordinary.'

Verity felt slightly disgruntled. Lots of people couldn't sail, she reflected to herself. She didn't see the need to make such a fuss about it.

'Well, you can crew anyway,' Mrs Watson continued, to a collective groan of disappointment.

'Really?' asked Verity. She'd never been deliberately chosen for anything before.

'Absolutely,' confirmed Mrs Watson. 'Apparently the wind will be getting up so we could do with some weight.'

# Chapter Two

The next day found Verity on the well-worn path to school once more. And once again the sizeable figures of George and Oscar Blake emerged in the distance. They looked . . . purposeful. Verity's heart sank. She knew this did not bode well.

'Heard they're using you as ballast for the sailing team,' sneered Oscar as he wrenched Verity's bag from her futilely folded arms.

'What do you think you're playing at, Gallant?' demanded George, taking the stolen item from his brother and proceeding to extract its contents again.

The girls from yesterday had spotted this latest incident and were on the scene already. 'You're going to bring the whole team down with you,' agreed one crossly.

'This season is make or break for us,' added a second. 'The school's reputation is at stake. Do you really want that on your head?'

George had Verity's hockey kit now. A rare glimmer of original thought found its way into his mind and he grinned . . . then, with one deft movement, threw her skirt up into the branches of a nearby tree. The watching girls shrieked with delight.

Verity gasped in horror. 'I need that,' she protested.

George prepared to launch her shirt in the same direction, then bellowed and dropped the bag in shock. Verity looked at him with a start. The top of his head was covered in a mess of mud and leaves. His audience exploded with laughter. Only as he swung round did it become apparent that the creator of George's new head-wear was a small sandy-haired boy, growing smaller still as he disappeared off into the distance.

'Henry Twogood,' bellowed George, running after him at full tilt. 'I am going to kill you.'

Verity picked up her bag and smiled. One of her tormentors giggled as she made her way past. 'Lucky you, being helped out by Henry *Twogood*,' she mocked.

*Better than not being helped at all*, thought Verity to her-self as she stared upwards at the lost skirt, stuck now on a branch from which she would never be able to dislodge it.

Lunch time found Henry Twogood joining the queue for school dinner. Ahead of him the usual pleas could be heard:

'Just the *tiniest* bit of cabbage please.'

'A really, really, really, really *little* scoop of swede thanks.'

In response the dinner ladies continued to ladle out overcooked vegetables in equal and unchanging portions.

Henry moved past them to the dessert section. 'Hi, Mum,' he muttered.

Mrs Twogood beamed as she looked up. 'Hello, cherub,' she replied.

Henry flinched. 'Mu-umm. *Please*. Not in school.'

'Sorry, love.' She put a slab of bread pudding on his tray.

Henry glared at it. 'I thought we agreed,' he said. 'No more cakes, no more pies and no more bread pudding.'

Mrs Twogood looked down in dismay. 'Force of habit,' she confessed. 'Saw that George Blake chasing you across the grounds this morning,' she added conversationally.

'Glad to hear you sounding so breezy,' said Henry. 'Wouldn't like it to bother you.'

Mrs Twogood gazed at her son fondly. 'I think if you can handle all six of your brothers, one Blake boy should be fine.'

Henry raised his eyebrows to concede the point. 'He was picking on Verity Gallant,' he explained, looking a little self-conscious. 'I didn't think it was fair.'

Mrs Twogood smiled and surreptitiously added another slice of pudding to his tray. 'Why don't you go and see how she is?' she suggested. 'Could be a bit shook up.'

Henry looked pointedly at his mother and removed both the contraband items.

As the end-of-day bell rang at Priory Bay, Verity made her way despondently towards the school gates. It had been an even more hideous day than usual. Her fellow classmates had complained bitterly at being lumbered with her for an important sailing match. And to make things worse, Mrs Watson had refused to let her off hockey even though there were no replacement skirts in the lost property cupboard.

'Gym shorts will be absolutely fine,' she'd boomed firmly.

Verity shuddered at the memory of seventy long freezing minutes on the playing field dressed in what for all the world looked like a large unflattering pair of pants. She'd got so cold she'd ended up running about to keep warm and inadvertently scored two goals – which just made her team-mates all the more furious.

Verity didn't hear her name being called at first. Her mind was busy replaying the hideous embarrassment of it all. Only when Henry eventually caught up did she snap out of it.

'Oh, er . . . hi,' she mumbled awkwardly.

'So, are you all right then?' he repeated for the fifth time. As an enquiry, it had lost the intended casualness after the third attempt but he supposed it would have to do.

*All right?* Verity was so focused on her own personal world of self-loathing she immediately assumed he must be talking about the playing field incident. Had it really got round school that quickly?

'I couldn't get my skirt back out of the tree,' she snapped. 'I didn't wear them on purpose.'

Henry looked confused. 'I, er . . . I just meant

after George Blake this morning. Was your bag all right?'

Verity felt terrible. He'd only helped her out a few hours ago and she'd forgotten already. 'Sorry. I thought you were talking about something else . . . I had a pretty bad games lesson this afternoon.'

'Oh.' Henry's face filled with sympathy. 'I hate games,' he offered. 'Never get chosen for any of the teams, hate cross-country running and standing around in the freezing cold.'

Verity smiled. 'Yeah, it's rubbish,' she agreed.

'I could walk you home if you like,' he volunteered.

She looked up in surprise.

Henry looked embarrassed. 'You know, in case George Blake is hanging around.' He looked down at the ground, clearly expecting a no.

Verity didn't particularly want to be around anyone at the moment but: 'I have to drop in on a family friend . . .' she started. Henry looked resigned to a refusal, so she relented: 'But if you don't mind meeting her, then that would be nice.'

Henry beamed. 'No, that's fine.'

Together they made their way across the park.

'So they made you play hockey in your underwear?' he asked.

Verity's family friend, Alice, lived near the school at the top of the uppercliff: Wellow's most desirable area. Verity's mother and father approved of their weekly meetings because they assumed (wrongly) that the time was spent reading improving texts and making small talk.

As Verity and Henry turned into Alice's road, he blew a low whistle to indicate his approval. 'Priory Avenue? Very nice . . .' Each house was different to the next, but all sat in their own grounds, with trees and shrubs aplenty to shade the windows from view. 'Though I could take it or leave it . . . Having your own bedroom is probably very overrated.'

'Do you share a bedroom then?' asked Verity.

'Yeah,' he sighed, booting a stray stone. 'With my brothers Percy and Will.'

'With two other brothers?' Verity could have kicked herself for sounding surprised, but Henry didn't seem to mind.

'I know. It's rubbish: I've got six brothers. Me, Percy and Will are the closest in age so we share one room. Bertie and Fred get the other because they're older. Charlie and Frank left home a couple of years ago. And you've got one sister?' he asked.

Verity nodded.

'It's funny how people from the same family can be so different,' said Henry – an early display of his talent for not thinking before he spoke. 'Poppy doesn't seem at all like you – she's so—'

Verity smiled wryly and interrupted. 'Likeable? Pretty?'

Henry looked uncomfortable and a little defiant. 'Blonde. I was going to say that she's very blonde. Whereas, of course, you're not.'

Verity nodded slowly and came to a halt, indicating a particularly unkempt house. 'This is it,' she said.

Like many other houses in the road, Alice's boasted an ornate wrought-iron veranda, and like some, it had an air of genteel decline. But none of its neighbours managed to combine both to such effect.

The front door swung open vigorously. 'Verity, my dear, you're going to have another sibling.'

Verity was slightly taken aback. How did Alice know already?

'Is your mum expecting?' asked Henry.

Verity nodded.

'Don't dawdle, come on through,' instructed Alice. Henry was astonished at the speed with which someone so old could move. She shot back down the hallway with great purpose.

Henry pushed his way past a coat-rack laden with clothes and crammed in every orifice with walking sticks, umbrellas, shooting sticks and an apple-picker; past a large glass cabinet of stuffed animals, all dressed, disconcertingly, as mermaids. On the opposite wall hung a large selection of hats balanced precariously on the over-filled hooks. By the entrance to the sitting room stood a very large and battered Noah's Ark and a collection of old and battered jugs, balancing on a mirrored hallstand. Every spare inch of wall was covered in pictures: framed maps, photographs, oil paintings, portraits, prints and sketches.

Henry was fascinated. 'Look at all this amazing *stuff*,' he exclaimed. 'Is that a statue of the Sumerian god Enki? And a Greek tableau of naiads? It looks quite old – I'm surprised you were allowed to keep it.'

Alice looked slightly taken aback – and amused. 'You know a lot for someone so young,' she observed.

Henry looked abashed but couldn't control his urge to stare. 'I have a good memory for things,' he explained.

He turned his attention to Alice while a bemused Verity looked on. The old lady's pink, inquisitive face was deeply lined and scored, but out of it her blue eyes shone in a way that was more alive than anything Henry had ever seen.

'So who is this young man, Verity?' asked Alice. 'Are you going to introduce me?'

Verity shrugged off her coat. 'Alice, meet Henry Twogood. He offered to walk me home because . . . well—'

Henry sensed that Verity didn't want Alice to know that people were picking on her. 'I heard you had good cakes,' he interrupted. 'I'll go a long way for a cake.'

Alice laughed and extended a very pale hand. It was surprisingly supple and strong.

Verity had moved into the kitchen and was boiling a kettle for tea. Henry continued to gaze about him.

'You can have a look if you like,' offered Alice as she took a seat. 'It's been a long time since anyone was interested in my junk.'

Henry didn't need to be asked twice. 'Was this your Gypsy Moth?' he asked, picking up a photo of a younger Alice next to a bi-plane in full leather flying kit. 'Is that how you collected all these things? By flying to different places?'

'I have been to a lot of different countries, yes.'

'What a collection. I don't know how you had time to fit it all in.' Alice just smiled. 'So, do you remember the Gentry?' he asked, opening a tin filled with pebbles.

'*Henry*,' shouted Verity from the kitchen, shocked into remonstration. 'It's rude to make assumptions about a lady's age.'

'It's all right, Henry,' Alice reassured him. 'Of course I'm quite old enough to remember the Gentry.'

'Did you ever see the famous Rafe Gallant, Verity's grandfather?' he asked.

Alice looked troubled. 'Verity's parents don't talk much of their history. I'm sure you can understand why.'

'Rafe who?' Verity called out from the kitchen as the kettle whistled energetically on the stove.

Alice ignored the question. Leaning forward, she began to interrogate Henry. 'So you're at Priory Bay too?'

'Yeah, I won a scholarship last year. Mum took a job as dinner lady so we could qualify for places.'

'Sounds like some of the pupils can be quite hard work.'

Verity peered round the door with a brown and orange knitted tea-cosy in one hand. 'I'm fine, Alice,' then, turning her attention to Henry, 'Would you like tea?'

Henry nodded, while Alice went on regardless, 'Do you see much of Verity?'

He considered his reply, but without waiting for an

answer, she continued, 'She could socialize a little more, don't you think?'

Shooting Alice a reproving glance, Verity returned with a tray laden with teacups and saucers, a teapot, milk, sugar, spoons and cake. She knew her elderly friend meant well, but this was embarrassing.

'Alice's date loaf,' she said to Henry, deliberately changing the subject. 'Which is particularly good.'

After the tea and cake had been distributed, Alice, Verity and Henry settled into comfortable chat about whatever took their fancy: Constantinople, the melting point of magnesium, why certain kinds of biscuit always drop off when you dunk them in hot drinks . . . Henry would never have thought that taking tea with an elderly lady could be so entertaining.

Suddenly, out of nowhere, Verity remembered the man in the library.

'Something rather unusual happened the other day,' she started. Reliving the strange event, she pulled the book out of her school bag to show them. 'It's a kind of journal. The authors travelled the world collecting stories related to this one character.

'. . . *until one day the eldest daughter had to leave for a while. And when she came back only the youngest remained. Where her two sisters were she wouldn't say. Not telling. The youngest just smiled. Then, finally, she burst out laughing. And that's when the oldest sister knew she was lost,*' she read out from a chapter entitled 'Oral Tradition'.

Verity looked up excitedly, desperately hoping the other two would think it just as fascinating.

Henry took it from her and flicked through the pages. 'The man who gave you this was tall and dark, unusually dressed?' he asked.

'Yes.' Verity nodded. 'And he told me the storm was coming. Isn't that strange?'

Henry frowned at her. Alice had said nothing up to now. Her porcelain skin looked pale. 'Goodness me. Is that the time?' she said. 'Verity, dear, I have an appointment at the old people's home. I mustn't disappoint them.'

Henry looked confused. 'At the old people's home? But don't you live he—'

Verity interrupted before he could finish his sentence. 'Alice goes there to *visit* the old people. She reads to them.' Her gaze dared him to question the logic of that sentence.

'Gives them such pleasure, dear things,' Alice chipped in cheerfully.

Bustling around the room, she crammed a half-empty packet of biscuits, some wool and a paperback book with its cover missing into a bag that didn't appear to have space for anything more.


The next day after school, pupils were milling around outside Priory Bay's gates, catching up with each other before going home. Verity and Henry ambled slowly towards the entrance.

'Alice is brilliant, isn't she?' said Henry.

Verity nodded. 'She's amazing,' she agreed.

As if summoned by this compliment, the subject of their conversation appeared at the wheel of a shiny green car. Dressed in a jaunty tweed flat cap, she lurched erratically up over the kerb and came to an abrupt halt inches from Verity's toes. In a cursory nod to safety, she tapped the horn.

'*An MG two-seater,*' gasped Henry. Verity thought he might explode with excitement right there and then. Eyes popping out of his head, he darted around the vehicle, gazing in admiration at first one feature and then the next.

Alice looked rather pleased. 'Your mother said you'd be here,' she shouted at Verity over the noise of the engine. Verity smiled, wondering where else she might be on a school day. 'Something about a tactics session? Give you a lift, if you like.' Noticing Henry, she added, 'Room for one extra if we squeeze.'

Henry grinned: there was no way he was turning down a ride in Alice's car. Without waiting for an answer, he jumped in after Verity and happily closed the door. 'This is a flat radiator model, you know,' he clarified.

'Good day at school?' Alice enquired at full volume as they sped down the hill to Wellow's sailing club.

Verity and Henry shrugged.

'Glad to see you're getting involved with the school sailing team. Do you good,' she went on.

'Who knows, with Verity onside we might actually win something,' said Henry.

Verity laughed. Why would he assume that? 'I don't know the first thing—' she started to explain.

'Bit of news actually,' Alice interrupted as they hurtled along at breakneck speed. 'I have to leave Wellow for a while. Something rather urgent has turned up.'

Verity looked at Alice with concern. 'You're going away? But why? Where?'

Alice's eyes were troubled but she brushed the questions aside with a wave. Turning to Henry, she looked at him intently. 'I was hoping you'd be able to keep an eye on Verity while I'm away. Keep her out of mischief.'

Henry beamed at her. 'I will.'

Alice smiled back warmly. 'That's settled then. She's bound to be all right with a big strong lad like you around.'

Henry puffed himself out a little at that.

Verity stepped nervously through the sailing-club door and straight into a hall that smelled of stale beer and pipe smoke. On the yellowing walls hung a motley collection of framed photographs, mounted pen-and-ink cartoons and assorted sailing paraphernalia, including a brass navigation light and a life buoy. A fishing net was tacked to the ceiling, with a number of green glass floats hanging in the sagging folds.

In the far corner was a small group of girls. Verity's heart sank as she spotted the venomous Miranda Blake, sister to George and Oscar. Thin and small, with a pinched face and slightly bulbous eyes, Miranda was utterly poisonous. Even the girls who picked on Verity at Priory Bay were grateful that she attended the all-girls Whale Chine.

Spying Verity, Miranda called a halt to the conversation. The hall fell silent as she made her way with absolute confidence over the wooden floor. She studied Verity disdainfully, from her wind-blown hair to her coat, which was buttoned askew, then leaned towards her ear.

'Do your parents find you terribly disappointing, Gallant?' she murmured, with the faintest of lisps.

Verity flinched. Inside she felt the pain of a truth spoken out loud. Worse still, there was no sign of her fellow pupils. She wondered if she'd got the wrong time or place, or both.

'They're in the Protest Room,' said Miranda, nodding her head to indicate a door to the left. 'Scraping the barrel a little, aren't they?'

Verity's fingers brushed against the curious wooden ball in her pocket. She turned it around in her hand and was aware that she didn't feel intimidated any more. 'I hear they were holding out for a skinny midget who'd get blown overboard at the first puff of wind' – Verity stared levelly at the other girl – 'but now they've got me.'

Miranda smirked, acknowledging Verity's humour in a manner calculated to chill to the bone. 'The storm is coming, Gallant,' she whispered as Verity passed by. 'But your family shan't rule the roost this time.'

Miranda Blake too? What *was* this storm? Her burst of defiance over, Verity realized all at once that she was pretty close to tears. Pulling herself together, she pushed open a second door labelled PROTESTS and concentrated on facing the next group of adversaries.

Over an hour later Verity left the club, breathing a sigh of relief that her ordeal was over. She hadn't understood a word Mrs Watson was saying, or any of the peculiar diagrams on the blackboard – which were apparently depictions of dinghies, starting lines and buoys. Looking up, she smiled at the sight of Henry waiting patiently for her on the low wall, a paper parcel in his hands.

'Cheesy chips,' he offered.

Verity took her package with thanks and opened it to investigate. This wasn't a foodstuff she'd ever come across before.

'The trick with cheesy chips,' Henry explained authoritatively, 'is to make sure the chips aren't too hot when the cheese goes on. That's what keeps it . . . cheesy.'

Verity tried one. It was surprisingly good.

Henry nodded gravely. 'The food of kings.'

Verity sat down on the wall next to him. 'Miranda Blake said the storm was coming,' she said as they ate. 'She seemed quite pleased about it.'

Henry snorted. 'Typical Blake,' he said, waving a chip dismissively.

'Why is everyone so excited about the weather?' asked Verity. 'Is it going to be particularly bad?'

Henry looked at her, chewing thoughtfully. 'Your

parents really don't talk much about the Gentry, do they?'

Verity frowned. What did that have to do with anything? 'Not a lot,' she admitted. 'I think they see it all as slightly vulgar.'

Henry laughed. 'That's one way of putting it,' he conceded. His chips finished, he scrunched the paper into a ball and threw it with pinpoint accuracy into a wood-slatted bin. 'Come on,' he said. 'If we hurry we'll just about get to the headland in time.'

Verity stared at him in alarm. 'In time for what . . .? I have to go home,' she insisted. 'My parents will be wondering where I am.'

'Do they know how long a tactics session lasts?' Henry asked her.

'No. I don't suppose they do.' Verity had never deliberately stayed out late in her life.

'Come on then, or we'll miss it. You get the best view from up there.'

'The best view of what?' asked Verity, scurrying after him, overwhelmed with curiosity now.

'This way,' said Henry, pointing to an alley. 'I know a short cut.'

## Chapter Three

The town of Wellow lay still and expectant under a silent sky. Above the bay, its houses clung to the curved cliff-face. The small white fishermen's cottages clustered round the harbour. Further up, the stone villas grew larger and more ornate as they ascended. At the top, the Manor dominated the skyline to the west, while to the east was Priory Bay College.

The weather was changing. In the distance the sky was a bruised black. An overwhelming sense of calm and peace cocooned the town. The air was close and warm. No trees rustled. No birds sang. The atmospheric pressure had dropped and it felt like a promise of hopes to be fulfilled.

A lone gull flew across the downs towards the headland – here, the wind blew clean and fast and straight – swooping down again to the ocean, which stretched all the way to the horizon. The salt spray was fresh and cold, the rolling sea flecked with specks of white. Without warning the greatest smuggling ship of all time crashed into view.

The *Storm* was coming.

She cut through the bright green ocean like a knife. The waves beat at her pristine wooden hull as she towered above the water. She was colossal – three hundred feet high and two hundred and twenty-five long, her deck a quarter of an acre. She made her presence felt like a living thing. She didn't just dominate the view, she gripped your attention and held it by the throat. She was awesome and magnificent, so vivid that she seemed to put everything around her out of focus.

The sounds of deck, hull and masts straining – of loose blocks and sheets slapping and smacking and banging – rang out; the crash of the prow as the *Storm* ploughed head-on into the churning waves. Sea water washed over her deck and drained back in torrents of foam. Her crew worked furiously – dirt-stained, sun-brown and wind-beaten, each one a master of his particular skill. The weather was getting worse now, but they just whooped and cat-called all the more, flying in defiance of the sea.

In Wellow harbour a crowd had gathered on the quay. Word had spread – as it always does. A gaggle of spectators stood awaiting a first glimpse. A hush had fallen.

The *Storm* was coming. And it would change Verity Gallant's life for ever. But while she knew nothing of this, there were those in Wellow who were alive with anticipation. And they were drawn to the quay like children to a piper.

Jasper Cutgrass – only child of loving parents Cyril and Iris

Cutgrass and officer of the Preventative Men – waited there patiently, oblivious to the shoves and buffets of the surrounding crowd. His was not a popular or well-paid career, but Jasper had never seen that as sufficient reason not to take pride in his professional appearance. From the gleaming buttons on his jacket to his lovingly polished, if more than a little worn, boots, Jasper shone with the enthusiasm of a man whose life revolved around his employment.

He could scarcely believe he was actually here. But he wouldn't have missed the *Storm*'s return to Wellow for anything. From the minute he'd heard she was expected, he'd known he had to bear witness. He knew her arrival would bring enlightenment. And she was bringing the weather with her too, just like the books said.

The heavens opened, and rain started to pour down on the crowd. Out at sea lightning struck. The *Storm* rounded the headland and the crowd let out a gasp.

'The most famous of the Gentry fleet,' Jasper breathed to himself. 'The *Storm*.'

He stood on the quay and gazed out in awe through the drenching rain. His woollen coat had soaked up so much water it must have been twice its usual weight. It was maddeningly uncomfortable. But Jasper Cutgrass didn't give a damn. This was the happiest day of his life.

Villainous Usage had also been helplessly pulled to the quay, in no little part by the iron will of his parent, Mother

Usage. The Usages were the kind of family the people of Wellow crossed the street to avoid. As his mother elbowed herself a clear view of the *Storm*, Villainous trailed silently in her wake, his verminous eyes darting from observer to observer. Nobody bothered protesting: they were mesmerized by the scene taking place before them on the open sea.

It had been a wearing day for Villainous. The rent man had turned up just as Mother was putting her key to the door. And some interfering busybody in the baker's had the effrontery to offer her a job washing laundry. He just thanked his lucky stars the *Storm* was finally coming back to Wellow. At last he could resurrect the family business, the source of their former good fortune.

As Mother sighted the fabled ship at last, her face took on an unaccustomed look of genuine happiness. Her greasy chins wobbled with emotion. Villainous winced as she gripped his arm in excitement. 'She's here, son,' she crowed triumphantly.

Villainous gazed at the *Storm* with reverence. He had never got beyond the basics of sailing (too cold, too wet and too much like hard work for his liking) but he knew enough to understand that the crew of the *Storm* were masters of their art. Like hounds of the sea they bayed and bellowed as they worked the vessel, clearly loving every thrilling minute of this battle with the elements.

Mother turned to her son gleefully. He had never seen her so jubilant. 'This is where our fortunes change,' she promised, stroking the shiny arm of his coat affectionately. Villainous' weasel-thin face was set in a rictus of anticipation. The sight of his haphazard dentistry was unnerving, but Mother patted his cheek happily. Her son enjoyed the momentary affection while it lasted.

Standing under the overhang of a quayside building, Isaac Tempest – an old man now – watched the *Storm*'s arrival with his seventeen-year-old grandson. Two generations, both unable to resist the *Storm*'s call.

Placidly Isaac packed his pipe with tobacco. Lighting it, he drew hard until a cloud of sweet vanilla smoke surrounded them. His grandson stared out to sea, covetously admiring the skill shown by the crew of the *Storm*. His family were steeped in sailing. Without their talent and daring the Gentry could never have established their empire. But the crew of the *Storm* were more legendary still.

'Don't need to make such a show of it, do they?' he finally blurted out in a disgruntled outburst.

His grandfather hid a smile. 'They can't resist the sport,' he said. His clear blue eyes crinkled mischievously. 'Not sure many young men could, if truth be told.'

At the top of the headland Verity stood next to Henry and stared in wonder. The rain was so heavy it was like a sheet of water – dragging on their eyelashes, creeping into their mouths, running up their noses. Verity's hair was plastered to her skull but she scarcely noticed.

'That's why everyone is here,' Henry shouted over the wind, pointing down to the quay. 'The *Storm* is incredibly famous, and she hasn't visited Wellow since the Gentry disbanded. No one knows why.' He grabbed Verity's arm and pointed to the upper deck behind the mast. 'Is that the man you met in the library?' he asked.

Verity gasped. It *was* him. The tall stranger.

'His name's Abednego,' said Henry. 'He's the captain of the *Storm*. Must be terribly old now.'

The man looked ageless. Holding his place on the quarterdeck – the control centre of the ship – he shouted out the occasional order while the crew whirled in frenzied activity around him. His stillness made him seem, if anything, all the more commanding. It was as if they had worked as a team for so long they no longer needed mere words to communicate.

In the hands of a less skilled captain, the *Storm* would have been pitching about like a cork on Wellow's perilous lee shore by now. There was so little sea room; no margin for error.

'He's searching for the spot,' yelled Henry. Verity didn't understand. 'There's only one place where the *Storm* can anchor on this piece of shore,' he explained. 'Abednego's looking for it.'

Aboard the *Storm*, a crew member swung a long rope – marked with cloth and leather strips and weighted with a waxed piece of lead – into the sea. After pulling it up to determine whether the sea bed was of sand, shingle or rock, he threw it back in again. Now at last he seemed to have found what he had been ordered to seek out. The word went back to Abednego.

The captain gave the command to reduce sail. The euphoric cries of the wild-eyed crew were deafening: they scrambled up the precarious web of ratlines and shrouds that gave access to the rigging, and set about furling the sails. They balanced on the yards that extended from the masts – hundreds of feet above the sea – terrifying in their fearlessness.

The *Storm* slowed down. With skill and care Abednego steered his vessel into the wind, to the point where she could do nothing but stand still. He gave the order, and the best anchor was lowered on the starboard side – the crew letting out just the right amount of chain to hold her fast.

As the anchor bit into the sea bed, the *Storm* snapped to a halt, then slowly settled to point in the direction of the tide. Like an angry child who has finally run out of steam, the foul weather stopped just as abruptly as it had started. The wind ceased howling through the rigging. The merciless noise of straining wood, the slapping and banging of loose sheets and blocks ended. The churning waves that had washed the decks subsided back into a steady rolling mass. Only the rain continued to pour down relentlessly.

In the harbour the stunned crowd cheered and applauded. Above them, on the downs, Verity and Henry began to make their way back to town, skidding and slipping on the water-soaked ground. The harbour buzzed with the bustle of crewmen starting the formidable task of provisioning. Verity couldn't help glancing over her shoulder at the *Storm*. Like many others in Wellow, she was irresistibly drawn to the magnificent galleon. Little did she know that the *Storm* would bring change – rippling out in a circle like the wind from a terrifying explosion. Verity may not have understood what she had seen, but there was no doubt that she would be amongst the first to feel its effects.

## Chapter Four

Home at last, Henry walked into the Twogoods' kitchen and slipped off his sopping wet coat. The room was hot with cooking and every window was covered with steam. For a few seconds his arrival went unnoticed, giving him an opportunity to surreptitiously grab a tea towel and dry his hair – a move that would have earned him a sharp smack on the head if it had been spotted.

Around the kitchen table four of Henry's brothers jostled with his father for the best seat. Mrs Twogood lifted a large casserole pot out of the oven. Placing it in the centre of the table, she started dishing out the food. Fierce argument broke out almost immediately on the subject of portion size – fairness thereof.

'He's got loads of stew. And three potatoes. I've only got two.'

'At least you've *got* yours – there'll hardly be anything left for me at this rate.'

Mrs Twogood carried on with her task, ignoring them all.

Slipping into the available space, Henry joined them. His mother put a plate piled high with food in front of him – to howls of complaint.

'Henry doesn't need all that food.'

''S not fair, Mum. Why's he got the best portion?'

'Got to keep his strength up,' she replied equably. 'Growing boy like young Henry.' She smiled fondly at her youngest son.

'Growing sideways,' joked Bertie, winking at Henry, while Fred made a dive with his fork for one of his potatoes.

'Saw you walking home with your *girlfriend*, Henry,' chipped in Will, the second youngest, to his sibling.

'Oh, that's nice, Henry,' said Mrs Twogood, perking up. 'Verity Gallant, was it?'

'She's not my girlfriend,' said Henry, squirming un-comfortably in his seat and fending off an attempt from Fred on a second potato.

'*Henry's got a girlfriend, Henry's got a girlfriend,*' chanted Percy and Will.

Their younger brother glowered unhappily down at his plate. 'She's *not* my girlfriend.'

Mr Twogood – who had already started on his food, despite a disapproving glance from his wife – looked up from his plate. 'Steer clear of the Gallants. No good ever came of 'em.'

'Oh, Daniel,' chided Henry's mother.

Henry looked pained. 'Verity's not like that, Dad. Is she, Mum?'

'Seems very nice to me, Dan. Always says please and thank you – which is more'n you can say for most of 'em.'

'Once a Gallant, always a Gallant, that's all I'm saying.'

Back now in the comfort and warmth of her home – no one seemed to have noticed her uncharacteristically late appearance – Verity stood by her bedroom window, watching the rain batter the glass, heavy droplets of water colliding and merging in random paths. She pressed her face against the cold pane and gazed at the lights of the *Storm*, anchored out at sea.

Verity's bedroom was in the eaves of the roof, which made her ceiling low in places but gave her lots of nooks in which to pile all the books she had gleaned from charity shops and jumble sales. Something about the room being so high up made it feel cut off from the world and safe. Verity liked to sit by the arched window and look down across the rooftops to the ocean.

She fished the wooden ball out of her coat pocket. So the tall stranger from the library was the captain of the *Storm* . . . But why had he given this to her? Why hand the book to her? Holding the ball up to the window for added illumination, she tilted her head to look at it once more. The doorbell jangled. Torn from debating her mystery, Verity frowned. A visitor at any time of day was unusual in the Gallant household.

Turning back to the red leather-bound book, she ignored the muffled clamour of voices two floors below.

*. . . but this time she chose to tell a tale of terrifying cruelty: for she was running short of youth and vitality. She spoke of how each would be sacrificed; that she would feast greedily on their blood, sucking every last drop from them – heedless of their pain – so she might have longer life. And from then on it was a bitter blessing to bear a third daughter. From then, the joy of her arrival was mixed with worry and fear.*

Verity shivered and then jumped at the sound of her mother's voice calling up to her from the bottom of the stairs. She sounded startled. Reluctantly Verity put down the book and went to the window. She peered down, trying to get a glimpse of the unannounced visitor.

The light from the hall streamed out onto the dark street, but all she could see past the pillars of the portico was a shadowed figure whose cloak trailed down almost to the ground. Further down the street, Verity could make out a number of silhouetted men approaching her house, each with a heavy box or case on his shoulder.

Her mother called up again. 'Verity. Could you come downstairs please?'

Tucking the wooden ball into the pocket of her pinafore, Verity hurried down the first flight of stairs: *her* stairs – no one else ever used them. Jumping down the two steps of the corner turn, she remembered to adopt a more seemly gait for the final, more impressive, flight with its red runner and brass rods.

At the bottom, in the hall, her mother was looking up at

her with a mixture of confusion and anticipation. Beside her stood the cloaked figure. A woman. She was directing a swarthy man as he manoeuvred a large trunk through the doorway.

'Verity,' her mother repeated slightly distractedly, 'have you seen your father? I can't think where he's gone . . .'

Verity shook her head politely, then stood quietly waiting to be introduced.

Mrs Gallant ran a hand nervously through her hair. 'So unexpected . . . What a day for surprises. Your father's, er . . . the, er . . . wife of your father's father . . .' Clearly a little lost for words, she eventually trailed off into complete silence.

The figure turned to face Verity at last. Tall, with a slender figure, the elderly lady before her had obviously once been stunning. Even now she was still very attractive. She towered elegantly over Verity.

'I am the wife of your grandfather,' she said. 'And you will call me Grandmother.' Her mouth twitched into a smile, but her pale blue eyes were distant. They reminded Verity of the stuffed shark in the maritime museum. She gazed in silent astonishment at the latest development in a thoroughly unusual week. She didn't have a grandmother. What was this lady talking about?

'Yes. Grandmother,' agreed Mrs Gallant, seizing gratefully on the *mot juste*. 'Of course. Your grandmother has come to visit. Isn't that nice?'

Was it Verity's imagination or did her mother sound unsure – as if she were trying to convince herself?

'Apparently it was all arranged some time ago,' she added brightly. 'I wonder where your father's got to . . . So odd – I'm sure he was in his study just a moment ago.'

But the old lady wasn't listening. Bending over, she grabbed Verity's face with her cool, dry hands, staring into it intently. Verity forced herself not to pull away, looking instead at the old lady's features: the perfectly straight nose, the high cheekbones, the delicately arched brows, the soft white hair that looked stylish rather than old. Verity shivered, as if a chill breeze had passed over her.

The visitor stood up, and without further comment swept past, her interest at an end.

Verity regained enough composure to close her mouth, reminding herself that it was still rude to stare, even if this person was the grandmother no one had ever told you about. Unconsciously keeping several steps behind, she followed the imposing visitor into the sitting room.

Their mysterious relative had the assured self-possession of the naturally good-looking. Her clothes were clearly of the highest quality and there was an air of privilege about her. She looked like a woman who wasn't used to people disagreeing with her.

The woman to be known as Grandmother continued to direct the various men who were now bringing a stream of cases and boxes into the house. She was used to commanding respect, Verity observed. Fear, even. 'Not there. Keep that one upright. This will do very well on the table.'

Mother stood near Verity, stroking her hair nervously,

completely floored by all this activity. 'Such a surprise . . .' she repeated, for want of anything else to say.

Verity's grandmother smiled at her, and patted her hostess's stomach with an air of possession. 'I came as soon as I heard.'

'Oh,' Verity's mother said, a little flustered. 'I, er . . .'

'Such wonderful news,' the old lady continued, her eyes still glassy, still cool. 'Such a proud time for Tom.'

'Marvellous,' Verity's mother agreed quickly to cover her confusion. 'So glad he was able to get word to you.'

Poppy slipped into view, holding a beautiful porcelain-faced doll with real hair and an exquisite outfit. 'Grandmother's brought some lovely presents,' she said.

Verity looked across the room to see box after box packed with delicacies, handwoven cloth, toys . . . She could make out a doll's house in one and a sewing basket in another. Poppy was now holding up a very fetching outfit, and handed another to her sister. 'This is for you,' she said excitedly.

Verity held the dress to her waist. It was lovely, but she could tell just by looking that she would be far too big for it.

The men had finished bringing Grandmother's property into the house. Informing her of this, they left with a large tip.

'Felicity, you have done well,' Grandmother exclaimed, swinging round to face her. 'Such beautiful little girls.' Stroking Poppy's head, she continued, 'This one so pretty and charming. And this one . . .' Leaning down, she pinched Verity's waist. 'So robust, so sturdy.' She laughed, looking around at her audience, who joined in.

Verity stood there feeling a little hurt.

'Goodness,' exclaimed Mother. 'I haven't even offered you a drink. Let me go and make some tea.' Poppy jumped up to help her, leaving Verity alone with their guest.

Moving gracefully around the furniture in the sitting room, Grandmother seated herself and patted the space next to her. Verity obeyed the unspoken instruction, realizing with a sinking heart that she was going to have to make polite conversation.

'Father hasn't mentioned you before,' she said eventually.

Her grandmother said nothing, choosing instead to peer curiously at Verity. Verity's heart pounded anxiously. That had come out badly.

'Will there . . . ? Is, er . . . my grandfather joining us later?' Verity continued, on the basis that if she'd never heard of the woman now sitting on the sofa, then perhaps any number of other relatives might be about to visit. Verity realized she knew she had a grandfather – even though she couldn't remember her parents ever discussing him. She seemed to have a vague impression he had been away from Wellow for a very long time. It was odd that she had never asked about him, she thought.

Still the old lady continued to take in her grand-daughter's appearance . . . Perhaps she was a little hard of hearing? *The weather.* She could talk about the weather.

'It's a shame you're here for the autumn,' she continued in a louder tone. 'The summer was very clement.' Verity found the silent scrutiny unbearable. Dredging her mind for something else to say, she added limply, 'Of course, today's squall must have made it very difficult for the *Storm*.'

Grandmother's eyes narrowed ever so slightly. 'Do you think so?' she asked, in a tone that made Verity long desperately to go back to uncomfortable silence.

Mother reappeared with Poppy. 'We could show you to your room while we wait for the tea,' she said to her guest, smoothing down her dress as she spoke.

'That would be lovely.' Grandmother had switched her demeanour in an instant.

Verity and Poppy hung back as Mother led their visitor up to the first floor and opened the door to the guest room. Looking over the street, it had a pleasant atmosphere: light and bright with a neat rose pattern on the wallpaper.

Grandmother walked straight over to the window and looked out at the view, then dismissively around the room. 'It's a little small,' she said. Before anyone could say anything, she swept out and headed up to the next floor. Entering Verity's room, once again she headed for the window and pulled aside the curtain. Taking out a handkerchief, she delicately polished away the smudge on the glass made by Verity's nose. 'This is much more suitable,' she said.

Verity stared, silently aghast. Was their strange new visitor really suggesting she have her room?

'After all,' her grandmother went on, 'when you are – like me – so near to the end of a long life, it's the simple things that bring you happiness. A nice view – a little space for the few possessions you have gathered . . .'

'But,' said Verity anxiously, 'this is my room.'

The old lady didn't appear to have heard her. 'Whereas a little girl who is just starting out in life – how many truly important things can she have, hm?'

Verity was outraged. 'I have my books—' she started.

'Books?' Grandmother looked around the room at the piles of reading matter everywhere. Suddenly Verity's chin was cupped in a thin, cold hand. The old sash window rattled as an icy wind blew into the room. Goose pimples rose on Verity's skin.

'Verity' – Grandmother's face was the very model of sympathetic concern – 'you must be careful not to fill your head with too much . . .' She paused, apparently searching for the right word. 'Information.' She spat the word out with distaste.

'Besides,' she continued, 'it is not attractive to be always with your head in a book. That is no way to draw admirers, hm?' Inclining her head slightly, she smiled coquettishly at Poppy, who giggled sunnily.

Verity gripped the wooden ball in her pinafore pocket. She didn't feel scared or hurt any more, just angry. 'I don't want the kind of admirers who like stupid girls,' she muttered crossly, watching everyone troop back out of her room – her *former* room.

'I hope you have not raised your children to cheek their elders and betters,' she heard her grandmother commenting as she made her way back down the stairs. Through the gap in the door she saw the old lady throw a look of pure venom in her direction.

Suddenly Verity felt scared again.

In the sitting room Poppy played a short piece from her primer on the piano, her long fair hair hanging smoothly down her back against a pretty dress that suited her slim figure so well.

'How delightful,' exclaimed Grandmother, clapping her hands together in a way that didn't actually make any noise. 'What an enchanting little girl you are, Poppy,' she added with a rather pointed look in Verity's direction that only she noticed.

'Well, this is all working out rather well,' said Mother happily as Poppy drew her by the hand to find another songbook.

Verity stared in disbelief. Could she really be the only one who noticed her grandmother's barbs? It was as if this intimidating old lady had simply waltzed in and woven a spell of enchantment over everyone in the house but her.

'I can't understand why you're being so obstructive, Verity,' Mother said as she helped to make the new bed. Moving around the room, she knelt down to pull Verity's nightgown straight. 'Honestly, I do wish you'd try to keep yourself a little neater. You could make anything look like a sack of potatoes tied in the middle. You have to be accommodating. Remember she's the guest.'

'Don't you think it's odd,' asked Verity, 'that Father didn't mention she would be visiting? And now he's not here . . .'

Mrs Gallant swallowed down her irritation at being left alone to deal with this situation by her ever-forgetful husband. 'It is a little unusual,' she agreed briskly. 'But Grandmother is the wife of your father's father, and we have a duty to welcome her.'

'It seems peculiar calling her Grandmother too,' said Verity. 'After all, she isn't really related to us, is she?'

'I do hope you're not suggesting that you address our guest by her first name,' said her mother briskly.

'Father has never mentioned Grandmother before,' Verity went on as she got into her new bed.

'Father doesn't like to discuss it,' said Mother, kissing her on the forehead.

'Of course.' Verity reflected that there were clearly any number of things Father didn't like to discuss.

Verity wasn't sure what time it was when she woke up. She sat upright, her heart beating jerkily.

She'd been dreaming. About the Keeper of the Wind. No. She'd been dreaming she *was* the Keeper of the Wind. And that everyone she met was charmed by her. It was wonderful. She was so popular and pretty, funny and charming. She had beautiful clothes, went to fascinating parties, and everyone wanted to be her friend. But after a while it . . . well, it was boring. No one ever seemed to disagree with her. No one dared.

Until eventually she started doing whatever she chose, to see if anyone would stop her. Until she found herself stealing anything she took a liking to. Until she killed at will. Until she took newborn children and drank their blood to make herself younger . . . That was when Verity had woken up.

She slipped out of bed. *It was just a dream*, she reminded herself. *It's just a book*. Standing at the window, she opened the curtains. The full moon was high in the clear night sky. Staring down at the street, Verity was astonished to see a tall boy with long chestnut hair and bright green eyes slowly walking under a lamppost on the opposite pavement.

As if sensing her stare, he looked up. His eyes locked with hers. Unaccountably embarrassed, her cheeks flushed pink and she hurriedly moved away from the window.

But Jeb Tempest – grandson of Isaac – was not making a detour past the Gallant house by accident. *So she's moved into the room with the sea view already. That was quick work*, he thought to himself. Above him in the clear night sky, a patch of dark grey cloud scowled down. In the gutter, little eddies of leaves swirled in the brisk wind.

# Chapter Five

When dawn broke the next day, it was as if the *Storm*'s arrival had cleansed Wellow, making it afresh. A mild autumn sun shone across the water, lending a sparkle to the gentle ripples. Many in the town would be making their way to the harbour. And Verity was to be among them, as it was the day of her mother's long-planned shopping trip, which meant a short ride on the ferry to the next large town of Niton.

Her head still raced with the events of the previous night. In the rose-patterned sanctuary of her new room, her mind played back once more the arrival of that great ship. In an instant she was up on the downs again, her head filled with the smell of sea water, her body drenched with rain. But each recollection was interrupted by an unwelcome memory of the other – less agreeable – arrival. Verity sighed.

Downstairs she heard Mother flitting about while Poppy got ready. Verity hid under the bedcovers with her red leather-bound book, unwilling yet to yield to the fuss of being pulled, primped and tweaked into her best outfit. She knew better than to hope for anything other than sensible clothes today. But at least they would also be looking at sailing kit for the school match, which would surely be more exciting.

Verity flicked absent-mindedly through the pages of her book, darting from one story to another. She frowned as she ran a finger along a line of text and remembered her nightmare.

*Those who are attractive and have charm* [she read], *push the liberties that their gifts afford them – behaving as badly as the world lets them. And She of the Wind was so very attractive and so very charming that she could be very bad indeed. And being so very bad, she became in many ways only the more charming and attractive.*

*But what begins as spoiled behaviour and is left unchecked must eventually turn to malice and cruelty. For the spoiled simply desire to have their own way; to be given power over others. Once you have that, where do you go next but to test that power? And She of the Wind went unchecked for a very long time.*

Mother would say that if it gave her bad dreams she should stop reading it. Verity frowned and gripped the cover a little tighter. She didn't want to. Besides, it was just a book.

'Verity.' Her mother's voice rang through the covers.

'Please hurry up.' She sounded cross. Verity pushed her prized possession down to the foot of the bed and got up.

'Won't this be nice?' said Mother as Verity sat down to breakfast. 'Our first outing with your grandmother.' Now recovered from the surprise, Mrs Gallant supposed there was nothing to do but adjust to the sudden arrival of her husband's stepmother. She had always been good at adapting to change without asking too many questions.

Their guest appeared silently and suddenly at the door. 'Up at last, little Verity,' she said, pinching Verity's cheek just a touch too hard. Verity unconsciously rubbed it with her sleeve.

Mr Gallant followed her into the kitchen, pouring himself a cup of coffee from the pot and saying nothing. As he sat down, his hand swatted at something which Verity could not see – it must have been a fly buzzing around his head. He looked dishevelled, as if he hadn't slept very well.

'Father, you're back,' said Verity, pleased to see him. 'Good morning.'

Mr Gallant looked up, as if only just noticing her presence. 'Certainly,' he agreed – the single word seemed to require a great effort. 'Certainly it's a good morning.'

Verity looked at him carefully. He was always a little distracted. But still, he seemed even more . . . distant. 'Mother wasn't sure where you were last night,' she said carefully. Questions were always frowned upon in the Gallant household, but she longed to know why Father had disappeared just as their mysterious guest arrived.

'I was out,' said Mr Gallant slowly.

Verity looked puzzled. It was almost as if he weren't quite aware who she was. 'I see,' she said, even though absolutely nothing was clear to her.

'Good, good . . .' muttered Mr Gallant, rubbing his legs and shaking his head.

Despite Verity's concerns about her father's behaviour, in truth, her main thought that morning was of seeing the *Storm* once more. By the time they got to the quay the ship had already drawn a sizeable crowd of visitors enjoying the weak autumn sunshine. An enterprising boat owner was even charging for short trips around the vessel itself. Less adventurous folk could pay to take part in a guided walk along the water's edge.

Lost in her own little world, Verity followed automatically behind Mother, Grandmother and Poppy as they headed for the ferry, completely unaware that she was surrounded by people who had a vested interest in her future and that of the *Storm*.

Families with infants milled about near the jetties, while older couples sat in companionable silence with their sandwiches and binoculars. Bigger children darted through the crowd with their friends. And on the lips of all were speculations and guesses as to why the great ship had returned to Wellow after so long.

A row of dinghies was moored in a line near the quay. In one particularly aged bucket sat Jeb Tempest and his grandfather. Gazing at the *Storm*, Isaac packed his pipe with a new wad of vanilla tobacco.

'Just as impressive today as she ever were,' he mused. 'The Mistress always did have exquisite taste.'

Jeb tutted in reply.

Gazing across the harbour, Verity started slightly at the sight of the strange boy who had been outside her house last night. Standing up in his rowing boat, he mockingly saluted in her direction. Verity was astounded – was it aimed at *her*?

Then she glanced up at Grandmother – and jumped in fright. The old lady was so angry she looked like a completely different person. Her previously elegant face was distorted with fury. Verity was terrified. She'd never seen anyone change so dramatically. So it was Grandmother the boy was signalling to . . . Now Verity was even more confused. Did that mean he *knew* her . . . ?

'*Pipe down.*' Isaac Tempest pulled Jeb firmly back into his seat on the dinghy. Jeb glowered but didn't argue. 'There's nothing to be gained from such bravado,' his grandfather said firmly.

'I'm not scared,' muttered Jeb defiantly.

'Well, you should be,' said Isaac. Changing the subject, he nudged his grandson to look in the direction of the quay. 'See there: Captain Abednego making his way to the Spyglass, if I'm not mistaken.'

Jeb followed Isaac's nod to find the dark giant. Abednego carried his powerful frame with an agile grace that seemed only to emphasize his strength. Ignoring the furtive glances and whispered comments, he expertly tied his boat to the town jetty and made his way across Wellow quay to the famous Spyglass Inn, pausing only to stare openly at the lone Preventative Officer who was happily making his way through the crowd.

Jasper Cutgrass had only just started working his way through the files of the Town Records Bureau, but he was certain that being in Wellow itself would bring him closer to the truth. For Jasper was a man obsessed. His sole preoccupation since he was a child had been the mythical technologies attributed to those smuggling villains, the Gentry. Wellow had so many records and documents he'd never seen before. He was positive the Gentry's paper trail would reveal what he sought.

Meanwhile he couldn't resist taking a few minutes out to see for himself the characters so familiar to him from the scandal sheets, articles and papers he had pored over during his long years of research.

There – closer still than his first glimpse last night – was Abednego. Jasper had seen drawings of the famed captain, read descriptions and imagined him for himself. But now he was just yards away, truly larger than life.

And Isaac Tempest – sitting in that boat with a young lad. The notorious Isaac Tempest: charmer, rogue, astute businessman . . . and former leading light of the Gentry. So it was true, he really *was* still alive.

For a second everything went black as a gigantically obese woman smacked head-on into his chest, winding him completely. 'Mind where yer going,' she snapped aggressively. A young man with a very unpleasant odour stepped around him.

Oblivious to the pain, Jasper hugged himself with excitement. That had to be two of the Usages. The unique combination of facial features was a clear giveaway. Jasper's face – so unreadable – betrayed nothing, but inside he was a maelstrom of emotion. Wellow was more than he could ever have hoped for. Soon, he knew, he would find out who had made the precious Gentry device that he kept in the bag at his side.

Villainous hurried to catch up as his mother continued to shove and push her way through the crowd.

'What the hell's a customs man doing in Wellow?' she spat. Through the crowd she sighted her quarry. Abednego was on the other side of the quay, heading from the Spyglass to the jetty. There could be no mistaking the dark Goliath.

As he followed his mother, the youngest Usage noticed that Abednego was lost in thought. Perhaps it was his imagination, but there seemed to be something in his bearing that spoke of loss. And fear.

Villainous said nothing to Mother Usage, of course. Anything that didn't concern her was meaningless to her.

Furiously she barged her way through the gawping strangers and their squawking children, seething with impatience. At last she came within snatching distance of her prey.

Mother Usage was a whale of a woman; a corpulent hulk of flesh so big your first thought was to wonder how much she ate in order to maintain that kind of weight; so large all you could do was stare in amazement. Not for too long though. Because a walking stick in the face is likely to hurt.

Extending a pudgy hand, she grabbed one of Abednego's immense arms, her pale, doughy fingers gripping the carved ebony of his muscle in a surprisingly vice-like hold. The noise level dimmed noticeably as, all around Mother Usage and Abednego, the crowd fell silent.

Abednego's reputation had preceded him for so long that there were few places in the world it hadn't reached, and Wellow certainly wasn't one of them. There were those who said that his air of serenity was the jaded response to a lifetime's violence. There were those who said he had seen things that would leave lesser men witless. There were those who said that he and his crew were the very devil and his demons. But there were none who said that he should be treated lightly.

Abednego stopped in his tracks and turned slowly to look down at whatever was impeding his progress.

'Excuse me, sir,' Mother Usage simpered in what she believed was a winning way.

Abednego continued to stare, his handsome face impassive and still.

'I did but notice you across the way,' she continued, 'and I said to my son, "Why, we must introduce ourselves" – didn't I, Villainous?'

Villainous nodded mutely, his face uplifted towards the legendary smuggler.

'I am the widow Mother Usage of the Usage family,' she continued, undaunted. 'The Usages – of the Gentry, sir,' she prompted in response to Abednego's silence.

As he stood there on the quay – like Gulliver being held by one very overweight Lilliputian – the solidity of Abednego's presence was at odds with his inability to drag his mind back to the here and now.

Finally he spoke – he must continue as usual, he reminded himself. 'I am not here on business.'

For many it would have been enough that Abednego could see her true purpose as if it were written on her face, but Mother was not to be put off that easily. Continuing in her best voice, she playfully pushed her other hand against Abednego's chest. He looked down at the place she had touched.

'Come now,' she persisted, determined to keep the conversation going at least. 'I was just saying hello.'

A hush of breaths being held. Abednego's expression still didn't change. 'There is nothing to be gained from a conversation with me.'

Mother's temper started to fray. 'I can always try other options,' she said, with an edge.

'You will find that unfruitful,' Abednego replied. The conversation was at an end. Loosening Mother's grip on his arm, he continued on his way, and this time there was no stopping him.

Around them rose up a hubbub of the 'did-you-see?' variety. Staring angrily after the disappearing Abednego, Mother Usage cursed and spat while Villainous moved anxiously from one foot to the other. 'He'll be sorry for that,' she said venomously.

Boarding the ferry after Poppy, Verity gazed with interest at the crowd gathered around the captain of the *Storm* and a woman so large she must have weighed even more than him.

'Come on, come on.' Verity steadied herself as she was nudged to one side by a portly man in very unflattering yellow trousers. 'We'll have just as good a view from here. Far cheaper, and you get a wonderful flavour of the local experience,' he said importantly, ushering others onto the boat. Brandishing a pamphlet, he loudly instructed his party on where to sit. 'Not there, Torquil. I find there's a better view from the starboard side.'

Shuffling politely around the central locker, the passengers arranged themselves on the benches in two tightly packed rows.

The ferryman stood on the gunwale with careless ease as

he cast off. It was a beautiful autumn morning. Verity took a deep breath and turned her face into the wind as the boat gathered speed. She gazed inland at the town – at the alleys and courtyards that could only be spotted from the sea. She was used to living near the sea and seeing boats, but being *in* one was a rare occurrence. Would the sailing match tomorrow be any more fun?

'Two hundred and twenty-five feet long, this fine craft was made from approximately six thousand oak trees – that's nearly forty hectares of woodland,' brayed Yellow Trousers, reading authoritatively from his pamphlet as they picked up speed.

Looking out to sea, Verity realized he was talking about the *Storm*. And to be fair, he was right: taking the ferry gave you a very good view of the vessel.

The ferryman did his bit by taking them a little out of his way to see the *Storm* from close to. She was certainly handsome.

'Her main mast is over three hundred feet tall and her rigging comprises a total of twenty-six miles of cordage,' Yellow Trousers continued, getting into his stride now. 'Requiring over forty crew members, she carries a hundred and sixty guns – purely for show now, of course – weighing just over twelve tons in total, and has an astonishing top speed of twenty knots. Note also the fine craftsmanship on the stern lantern – quite masterful. Other features of interest include the ship's bell, which is said to have been cast in Padua by the famous bellmaker Maria Pianissimo.'

Verity gazed up at the protruding cannon and pictured herself roaming the open seas in search of adventure.

'Carrying seven anchors, she can store up to six months worth of food . . .' continued Yellow Trousers in the background.

Drawing closer, they moved along the ship's vast hull towards the prow, until the figurehead came into view at last.

'. . . binnacle for the compasses . . . leather buckets of water or sand in case of fire . . . skylight for the dining room . . .'

Verity continued with her daydreaming, halfway around the world by now.

'Ladies and gentlemen,' Yellow Trousers trumpeted, 'do not neglect to admire the famed figurehead of this grand ship, the *Storm*.'

'The *Storm* is coming . . .' whispered Verity, thinking of her strange encounter with Abednego and wishing desperately she knew why he had given her the red leather-bound book. On the opposite side of the ferry, Grandmother's head snapped up and her pale blue eyes stared straight into Verity's. Fear coursed through Verity like a bolt of lightning. Petrified, she switched her gaze to the *Storm* herself.

The florid livery of the *Storm*'s name was right above her now. The ship's vast figurehead stared out at the open sea. Fierce and wild, with long black hair, she looked even more frightening when you saw that she only had one eye. Where the other had been was just a gaping socket.

'The right eye has been missing for a very long time,' Yellow Trousers was saying, 'rumoured to have been removed by a drunken crew member as a prank and then confiscated by the captain.'

Leaning over the rail, a swarthy crew member looked down on the ferry passengers. He was dressed flamboyantly in a white shirt, emerald waistcoat and vivid red scarf. His ears were pierced with gold. Catching sight of Verity, he winked. She blushed and looked away as he laughed at her discomfiture.

# Chapter Six

Verity and Poppy followed their mother and grandmother past the latticed windows of the townhouses in Niton's main street. Several hours had passed, and Mrs Gallant had finally reached the end of her shopping list. Verity was now well provided with white cotton vests, hard-wearing skirts and practical jumpers. Poppy was happily swinging a bag that contained a very pretty little cardigan that had not come in Verity's size.

'Just time for a pot of tea before we go home,' Mother announced with a happy sense of accomplishment. She'd forgotten how tiring it was being pregnant.

'What a good idea,' agreed Grandmother, patting her daughter-in-law sympathetically with a kid-gloved hand. 'I'm sure you could do with a rest.'

Mother smiled politely and shifted the large collection of bags she was carrying from one hand to the other in an effort to ease the strain.

Verity stared anxiously at her. 'Were you planning to look for sailing kit on the way back?' she asked hesitantly. Her mother looked blank.

'*Sailing* kit?' Grandmother laughed scornfully. '*You* are going sailing?'

'For the school match tomorrow,' Verity prompted. 'We talked about it the other day.'

'Oh. Of course.' Mrs Gallant was temporarily discomfited: it had completely slipped her mind. 'Well' – she put down the shopping – 'let's see now – what will you need?' Ticking off the items on her fingers as she went, she ran through a quick inventory. 'A pair of cotton trousers – you have plenty at home; a plain vest and top – again at home; a practical mac – you can borrow mine; and socks . . . There,' she finished triumphantly. 'We have all we require.'

Verity said nothing. She hadn't been expecting a completely new kit, but Mother's suggested mish-mash of items sounded like just the sort of thing her fellow pupils loved to laugh at.

'It's not as if you're going to take up sailing full time, is it?' Mrs Gallant smiled brightly.

'Quite right, Felicity,' Grandmother agreed, turning to smile nastily at Verity. 'I should find another hobby if I were you. Something that's a little easier to master.'

Verity bit her lip. 'I'm still going to need deck shoes,' she said quietly. Mother was obviously keen to avoid any further shopping, but she couldn't see how she would manage without them.

Poppy stepped in to defend her sister. 'That's right,' she said, beaming winningly at her mother and grandmother.

'Verity absolutely needs them. She'll damage the wood of the dinghy otherwise. Which wouldn't look good at all, would it, Verity?' Verity shook her head earnestly in thankful agreement.

Mrs Gallant sighed quietly. She looked across the street. Inspiration struck. 'Joliffe's,' she announced. 'Joliffe's will have something – and they're right here.'

Verity hesitated. She did love Mrs Joliffe's shoe shop. It was such a beautiful art deco building, with a curved walnut staircase and an intricately tiled entrance. But most of the stock seemed to be left over from the same era.

Mother sensed Verity's doubt and overrode it. 'There's nothing for it, Verity. Joliffe's will have to do.'

'Goodness me.' Mrs Joliffe smiled kindly as she took Verity's foot out of the measuring device. 'Up another size.'

'What a shame,' said Grandmother. 'Delicate feet are such an asset to a young girl, I have always found.' Verity wondered if it was also a blessing to be really good at making hurtful personal comments.

Mrs Joliffe returned with two rather faded pairs of deck shoes for Verity to try on. Even to Verity's untutored eye they looked old-fashioned.

'Do you have anything newer at all?' she asked hopefully.

Grandmother had been watching her silently for the last few minutes. Something appeared to be on her mind. 'Little Verity wants a pair of shoes that will help her look the part,' she said suddenly.

A small flame of hope lit up in Verity. 'That would be quite nice,' she admitted.

Casting her eye around the shop, the old lady gazed up the high shelves, where piles of boxes were stacked on top of each other. 'That pair,' she said, with astonishing eyesight for someone of her age. 'Aren't they in Verity's size?'

Mrs Joliffe looked at the dusty box indicated. 'Those styles would probably be a little out of date,' she said doubtfully.

'Nonsense,' said Grandmother. 'The picture looks quite charming to me.'

Verity was astonished – even she couldn't see the illustration from this distance.

'Well, there can't be any harm in trying them on,' said Mrs Gallant as Mrs Joliffe fetched them down.

Verity gazed in horror as they emerged from their box. They looked like something that might have been constructed by someone who had never seen shoes before and had only read a description of a moccasin in a hurry. In fact, they looked more like a pair of leather Cornish pasties than an item of footwear.

'They're not very flattering,' said Verity quietly as she tried them on. Just looking at them made her stomach shrink with fear at the shrieks of laughter they would provoke.

Mrs Joliffe started to take them off and pack them away. 'Not what a young thing like you wants, are they?' She smiled reassuringly at Verity.

'But what is wrong?' demanded Grandmother, putting a hand on the box.

'I think I might prefer one of the other styles,' said Verity with a careful smile.

'They seem perfect to me,' snapped Grandmother. 'I have to admit I find it quite hurtful . . .' she continued with a little quaver in her voice. 'My first day as a guest and already my advice is unwanted.'

Verity stared in disbelief. Why was Grandmother so determined that she should have these hideous shoes?

'Not unwanted,' said Mrs Gallant hurriedly. 'No, I was just about to say that they'll be really quite practical. Won't they, Verity?'

Verity looked at her with alarm. 'Mother, I'm not sure I want them,' she said at last.

'I don't think they suit Verity,' Poppy agreed supportively.

'Nonsense,' said Mrs Gallant, who had seen the determined glint in her mother-in-law's eye and was anxious to avoid a scene. 'They'll be fine.'

Turning to Mrs Joliffe, she smiled and handed over the objects of dispute. 'We'll take them,' she said.

That afternoon Verity made her usual trip to the library, books in hand. In truth she'd been pleased to get away. Grandmother had been there less than a day, but already Verity felt her presence in the house like a physical weight.

'*Verity*,' a lone voice shouted as she reached the top of

the undercliff path again. She looked up with a grin to see the unmistakable figure of Henry – wrapped in a woolly hat, scarf and gloves – waving in her direction.

'How was your morning?' he asked.

Verity's heart sank at the very thought of it. 'Awful,' she said. Then, remembering that Henry didn't know, added, 'My grandmother arrived unexpectedly last night.' She realized that the latter wasn't any explanation of the former, but in a way it was.

'You don't get on well then?' asked Henry. 'Can't please everyone in your family,' he added philosophically. 'Bitter experience has taught me that.'

'I've never met her before,' said Verity, not quite able to believe the strange train of events herself. 'Mother says she's the wife of father's father, but they've never mentioned her. She just appeared on our doorstep. I don't think Mother has met her before either.'

Henry looked surprised. 'That *is* unusual – even by the standards of elderly relatives. What's she like?'

Verity considered this point. 'I'm not too sure yet. She seems a bit . . .' She paused, trying to think of the right word. 'She sort of demanded my bedroom,' she said eventually.

'I hate that,' Henry sympathized. 'Every time anyone comes to stay I'm always first to be booted out of my bed and put on the rubbish camp-bed downstairs and it's—' But before he could continue with a theme that was clearly very dear to his heart, Verity remembered the conversation that had been cut short at Alice's house.

'When I was making tea,' she interrupted, 'you asked Alice about someone called Rafe Gallant: my grandfather, you said. But Alice changed the subject.'

Henry looked at her. 'Well, yes . . .' he said slowly. 'He would have been your grandmother's husband. Your father's father; and leader of the Gentry.'

Verity gawped silently for a couple of seconds, processing what Henry had just said.

'Crikey.' He grinned, obviously surprised. 'Your family *really* don't like to talk about it much, do they?'

Verity knew about the Gentry of course. Who didn't? They had been as much a part of Wellow as the cliffs, the harbour or the sea. They had made Wellow. Almost literally. But they'd always been referred to in the past tense. As something that once was, but had finished. Not as a part of her family so close it was within living memory.

'My grandfather was the leader of the Gentry . . .' said Verity slowly. She was astonished. How could her new friend know more about her family than she did?

'I'd always heard his wife was dead though,' Henry continued conversationally, as if such revelations were an everyday occurrence.

Verity thought of her parents' lifelong dislike of questions. In her mind she recalled a flurry of fleeting whispers; of comments that hadn't made any sense and conversations that had been brought to a halt when she entered the room. 'I mean . . . it's not a surprise that I *have* a grandfather. I knew that . . . somehow. I just don't know anything about him. My parents have never spoken about him *at all.*'

Henry shook his head in sympathy at the unfathomable ways of parents.

'*Why* haven't they ever said anything? Why didn't I ask more?'

'I expect your dad just wants to pretend it never happened,' commented Henry consolingly. 'When my parents won't discuss something, it's as if the words don't exist. I can't tell you how many times I've tried to bring up the subject of motorbikes, and it's as if they can't hear a word I'm saying.' He rolled his eyes. 'It's as if I'm not even talking . . .

'A lot of people feel pretty ashamed about the Gentry now,' he went on sympathetically, remembering what he was supposed to be talking about.

Verity didn't understand. 'But why?'

'Because the Gentry didn't stop at smuggling, did they? There was a craft, a skill to it. But some wanted more money and an easier way of getting it, so they began wrecking.'

'Wrecking?'

'Luring ships onto the rocks – to smash them to pieces – then helping yourself to whatever is washed ashore. And ignoring all the people who are dying – or killing them if they get in the way,' said Henry.

Verity was stunned. It sounded horrific. 'You think my father did that?' she asked anxiously.

'No, he's too young, for a start. No, I just meant that Wellow tends to be divided between people who see the time of the Gentry as the town's finest hour and those who consider it a pretty shameful episode.'

Verity stood there quietly. Henry realized he'd gone too far, as usual. 'Would you like to come back for a cup of cocoa?' he asked.

Verity paused for a second. Her mother would prefer it if she went straight home – straight home to sit quietly on her own in the front room and read.

'It's a bit of a squash, and quite noisy, but Mum's a great cook,' continued Henry anxiously, to fill the silence. 'Or do you have to get back for your grandmother?'

That settled it.

Verity smiled. 'Cocoa would be lovely.'

Verity followed Henry through the kitchen door as he took off his hat, ruffling his hair to get rid of the static. His mother was at the oven, her ample frame protected from the hazards of baking with a blue apron.

'Hello, cherub.' Mrs Twogood beamed in greeting, turning round to plant a kiss on his cheek.

'Mu-um,' Henry protested, wiping his cheek furiously for fear of telltale flour residue.

'Brought a visitor, have you?' she asked cheerfully.

Henry stared in reproof at his mother's shameless pretence of not knowing who Verity was. 'Mum, Verity; Verity, Mum,' he muttered.

Mrs Twogood smiled warmly at Verity, then took both hands in hers. 'Just as I thought, half frozen. A nice hot drink and some biscuits – that's what you need.'

Verity smiled instinctively.

''S there any milk?' asked Henry, inspecting the larder.

'Some fresh from Aunty Jean,' said Mrs Twogood as she put a kettle on to boil.

Verity leaned against the dresser. The pressure of her weight caused a small piece of paper that had been tucked away under a shelf to fall down onto the counter. She picked it up. Pinned to it was a sprig of dried rosemary, and written on it a peculiar verse:

'*Protect us, oh lords, from the Mistress of the Storm*,' she read aloud. '*She who roams this land and would take what is not hers*. How unusual,' she said. 'What is it?'

Henry looked at it in shock. 'It's a Gentry blessing,' he said, taking it from her to examine. 'For gullible idiots. Don't know what it's doing here.'

Mrs Twogood moved briskly over to snatch the blessing from her son's hand.

'For nitwits . . . and my mum,' said Henry, realizing who must be responsible for the hidden slip of paper. 'Does Dad know that's in the house?'

'Can't do any harm,' said Mrs Twogood defensively, tucking it back into place.

'Can't do any good either,' said Henry.

'What's a Gentry blessing?' asked Verity, intrigued.

'The Gentry spread rumours and stories to scare people

and keep them in their houses. They had a real gift for it. Made out they had supernatural powers; that they could control the weather, control the sea . . . protect people. That sort of thing.'

'Really?' asked Verity. Henry clearly didn't approve, but she was charmed.

'It was just a load of mumbo jumbo to control the credulous,' he said dismissively.

'The Mistress of the Storm?' Verity ran a finger along the words of the blessing. Somehow the name rang a bell.

'One of their most famous scare-tactics: she was supposedly a witch who protected the *Storm*. Now she's more of a fairy tale.'

'How exciting,' said Verity, thrilled at the sound of it.

'Complete rubbish,' said Henry authoritatively.

'So, were the Twogoods part of the Gentry?'

Henry nodded. 'Until they got into murdering and stealing, yes.'

'That's enough now,' interrupted Mrs Twogood, handing Henry a plate of biscuits. 'Your dad'll be back any minute.'

Henry grabbed a rectangular wooden box inlaid with different coloured squares from the kitchen table. 'Do you play backgammon?' he asked Verity.

Verity rolled the dice.

'Another double,' groaned Henry in disbelief. 'Are you sure you don't know how to cheat at throwing them?'

'Beginner's luck.' Verity grinned, moving two more of her counters off the board.

'You can have too much of that, you know,' said Henry, trying – unsuccessfully – to get back into the game by landing on a point Verity hadn't covered off.

'Do you know where my grandfather is now?' asked Verity, keen to get back to their former topic.

Henry shook his head. 'No idea,' he said, passing the dice to her. 'I just know he left Wellow a long time ago.'

'Did he go because of . . . because of the wrecking?' Verity continued, a little anxiously.

Henry pulled a face. 'I'm not sure. I know it was about the same time.'

'Biscuits,' exclaimed a disembodied head, peering round the door of the Twogoods' sitting room. A second appeared just inches below it. Both displayed shocks of straw-coloured hair.

'My brothers Percy and Will,' explained Henry resignedly.

Percy – the eldest of the three – strode into the room and extended a hand towards Verity, while simultaneously snatching a biscuit from Henry's plate. 'Miss Gallant. Very pleased to make your acquaintance. You seem to have appalling taste in new friends but we shan't hold that against you.'

Verity grinned in silent bemusement as Percy expertly fended off his outraged younger brother and proceeded to eat the stolen contraband.

'How long's your grandmother going to be staying?' Henry asked, more to change the subject than anything else.

Verity felt her happiness deflate a little. 'She hasn't said.' Just thinking about her elderly relative made her feel flat. 'I don't think she's very keen on me.' Saying it out loud made her feel even more unpopular than usual.

Henry gazed up as if pondering one of life's great mysteries. 'Sometimes people take a sudden and inexplicable dislike to me,' he said. 'Which baffles me – because I'm fantastic.'

His two brothers hooted with derision.

'Fantastically annoying, don't you mean?' said Percy, pummelling Henry to the floor in response.

'I wouldn't worry about it too much,' said Will. 'Lots of old people have peculiar views on all sorts of things. Hoarding buttons, going to the shops in your slippers . . .'

Verity smiled at him, appreciating the sentiment. She leaned against the sagging sofa with the threadbare arms. It didn't match the other chairs in the room, but she didn't notice. She didn't take in the brass fire ornaments, which had been polished so many times they'd lost a significant amount of detail, nor the wool rug that had come off worse in a tussle with some moths. All she could see was that it was happy and it was noisy. Would her own home be more like this once the baby arrived?

'Perhaps Mother will have a boy . . .' she wondered out loud.

'Is she expecting?' asked Percy.

Verity nodded.

'Better hope it's not,' he advised. 'I can tell you first-hand that there are few things more irritating in life than a younger brother.'

Will noticed the backgammon board. 'You've missed a trick with those spare counters over there.'

'Verity doesn't need any *more* help,' yelped Henry indignantly. 'She's only been playing two minutes.'

'Well, in no time she'll be wiping the floor with you, won't she?' Will started to show Verity what he meant.

It was the end of the day at last. Verity's mind was still churning with curiosity and excitement about the mysterious and inexplicable events of recent days. She was looking forward to losing herself in her new book. Safely tucked in bed, her wooden ball clasped in her hand, she turned to a section titled 'Control and Punishment':

*And she used her power to box him about the head till he was driven near mad with the torment of it. 'Release me,' he begged. But she would not. The sight of his suffering served only to make her more satisfied at her own cleverness. 'Let that teach you to deny me,' she told him. And she had peace in her cruel and covetous heart, as much as a cruel and covetous heart can ever have peace.*

Sitting with her knees up, the reading lamp casting out

a warm glow, Verity felt cocooned from the world. Funny how the sailing match tomorrow no longer seemed so daunting. She knew it was silly, but holding the ball seemed to make her feel better, as if it were lucky.

Downstairs, her mother opened the door of her husband's study. By the time he'd returned home last night she'd been asleep. So – given their tacit agreement not to quarrel in front of the children – she'd had all day to rehearse this conversation.

'Your stepmother has taken Verity's room,' she began briskly.

Mr Gallant was sitting facing away from his desk, looking out of the window. He didn't reply.

Not unused to this state of affairs, Mrs Gallant continued with her speech, gazing with irritation at the cluttered shelves that were so difficult for Sophia, the maid, to clean. 'I really do think, Tom, that if you are going to invite guests to the house, the least you could do is warn me of it. And possibly make sure you are here to welcome them too,' she added with more sarcasm than was usual.

Still her husband said nothing. Mrs Gallant huffed with frustration. This was intolerable. 'Are you just going to sit there and say nothing?' she asked crossly.

He remained silent. Mrs Gallant drew herself up to her full height. 'Fine,' she said coldly, closing the study door with an abrupt bang.

\*　\*　\*

On the other side of Wellow, Villainous Usage opened the front door of the fisherman's cottage that he and Mother shared, letting in a fierce gust of cold in the process. His stoaty face scrunched up as he squinted into the gloom of the front room.

'Muvver,' he bellowed (quite unnecessarily given that the entire property consisted of two downstairs rooms and two up).

She was in the kitchen, treating the range to a monologue. 'Who's he to talk to me like that?' she demanded, surveying it with ill-concealed contempt.

Villainous stood at the doorway and extracted the carcass of a rabbit from inside his coat. 'Gutted it just now, I did,' he explained with enthusiasm. 'Fair stank.'

'Who's he to deny me my family's trade?' she continued, grabbing the proffered gift without a word of thanks. 'If the *Storm* isn't here to do business, then what's her purpose?'

Villainous stared anxiously and said nothing. No words sufficed when Mother got like this.

'Well, there's more 'n one way to skin a rabbit,' she snarled, holding up the bloody specimen in illustration of her point. 'The *Lady Georgia* heads this way in November, packed with gold, and I must have that cargo. If he won't provide the service I need, I'll go round him.'

## Chapter Seven

Sunday morning dawned with a crisp, fresh autumn breeze. Verity needed to be at the sailing club for nine o'clock so she was already gathering together Mother's suggested outfit, trying to ignore a quiet sense of misgiving.

She hadn't packed any cotton trousers when evicted from her room, so she went upstairs to get some. Standing at the door, she breathed in the familiar scent for a second or two. A ray of late autumn sun shone through the window. A few motes of dust floated peacefully through the air. It was so calm up here, but already it looked completely different somehow.

Verity went over to the window. On the sill lay a pair of delicate gilt and enamel binoculars. Without thinking she picked them up and looked out across the rooftops. The binoculars were superbly crafted: they made everything seem so close. Verity felt like a bird swooping above the town and heading out over the sea. The *Storm* came into her line of sight, still anchored in the bay.

Adjusting the binoculars with their mother-of-pearl

wheel, Verity eagerly focused on her. First the rows of mullioned windows and the elaborate decoration of the taffrail at the stern. Then the galleries and intricate ship's lanterns. Then the vast lattice of spars and sheets, shrouds and ratlines that held and controlled the sails.

Suddenly the faintest of noises . . . Verity hadn't heard anyone coming up the stairs, but she knew she was being watched. Turning round, she saw her grandmother standing in the doorway. Verity felt a cold shadow pass across her. The old lady was clearly very angry. As Verity looked into her eyes, a blast of fury hit her as if she had been slapped.

She hugged both arms around herself for comfort. For some idiotic reason she wished she had the strange wooden ball with her, but it was still tucked under her bedcovers with the book. Grandmother looked completely different – just as she had when the strange boy bowed to her yesterday, or perhaps more so. Her face was warped. There were no traces of the usual imperious good looks: her eyes were sunken and hollow; her parched skin showed every angle of bone.

Grandmother advanced angrily. Her anger pinned Verity back against the window like a gale. Snatching the binoculars from Verity's hand, she leaned in very close. 'Do you make a habit of prying in other people's rooms?' she hissed.

Verity's stomach shrank instinctively into a tight ball of fear. Grandmother's reaction to her presence was as petrifying as it was extraordinary. This had been her room, after all. 'I was looking for some clothes—' she tried to explain.

Grandmother's face flickered with animosity. 'You were snooping,' she insisted.

'No,' said Verity earnestly. 'I came in to look for some trousers to sail in, but then I went to take a look at the view – because I do love it so – and . . . picked up your binoculars. They're very pretty,' she added quickly in an attempt to change the subject and somehow diffuse the situation.

It seemed to work. Grandmother looked out of the window for a second, and when she faced Verity again, appeared more like her usual self. Verity had to wonder whether she'd imagined the terrifying transformation.

'She's a beautiful ship,' she said tentatively. 'Did you travel on her with my grandfather?'

'You would love to know more, wouldn't you?' said the old lady venomously.

Verity shrank away. Now she knew it hadn't been a flight of fancy.

'These things are nothing to do with you,' her grandmother went on. Then, as if the subject were at an end, 'Your clothes are not here.'

Verity moved over to the bed and knelt on the floor to pull out the box underneath it. 'No, you wouldn't have noticed them,' she started, 'because they're under the bed. I don't wear them very often, you see.' She waved a hand under the bed, feeling for the case. 'That's odd . . .' She tipped her head down to the floor to see. There was nothing there.

A thought occurred to her. She turned slowly to look around the room. No wonder she'd felt it looked different – there wasn't a trace of her left in it.

'My things . . .' she said, confused. 'My books . . .' She went out onto the landing to see if there were any boxes. Nothing. She returned to her room. 'My books,' she repeated. 'All my things – they're gone.'

Grandmother's face was perfectly still and yet somehow exultant. She said nothing. Verity went over to a drawer and pulled it out. Empty. She turned round to look at the old lady.

Verity couldn't have cared less about the clothes, but her books were irreplaceable. She had spent her whole life searching them out in charity shops and church fairs. Her books told of people who lived in strange lands full of adventure and mystery – of children who sailed and fought. They were her refuge.

'Where are all my things?' she asked in disbelief.

The corners of Grandmother's mouth turned up just enough to form a perfectly malicious smile. 'They are not here,' she said. 'I threw them out.'

'Verity dear, your grandmother is very old,' Mother said, helping her on with a pair of her own trousers, which were consequently too large. 'Sometimes when people get older they do things without quite understanding.'

Verity was in no doubt that Grandmother had known exactly what she was doing, but she realized there was nothing to be gained from saying so. What really puzzled her was how she had removed all her possessions so completely.

Verity knew that the subtleties of this would be lost on her mother at the best of times, but it just wasn't that easy to pack up dozens and dozens of books and carry them down two flights of stairs. It was as if all her possessions had simply been spirited away.

'We'll buy you some new books,' said Mrs Gallant in response to Verity's silence.

Her daughter stared helplessly. 'You won't be able to find them,' she said limply. 'They were all out of print.'

'Well, exactly, Verity,' said Mother, clearly tiring of this particular topic. 'They were all old. So much nicer to have new ones, don't you think?'

Verity wondered if there was any point trying to explain what they meant to her. 'Father seems to have been acting a little strangely,' she commented, deciding that there wasn't.

Mrs Gallant sniffed crossly. 'Indeed,' she agreed tartly. Then, remembering who she was talking to, 'I expect it's just the worry of another little mouth to feed. We both have any number of things to think about at the moment.'

'Yes, of course,' said Verity quietly. 'I'm sure you both have a lot on your minds. I shouldn't be bothering you.'

'Exactly,' said Mother, kissing her on the forehead as she left the room. 'I'm so glad you understand.'

With her mother gone, Verity stared despairingly in the mirror at her hotch-potch outfit. Even she could see that the combination did nothing to lessen her height or stoutness. The dreaded deck shoes added the finishing touch.

Poppy's head appeared round the door. Verity looked at her bleakly.

'It's not too bad,' said her sister reassuringly, darting forward to pull at the trousers a little. Verity stared at her pointedly. 'I'm sure everyone will be far too busy sailing to worry about clothes,' Poppy insisted brightly.

Verity sighed. She looked dreadful, and even Poppy couldn't deny it.

'Did you know that our grandfather was a man called Rafe Gallant?' she asked, thinking that she might as well talk about something more interesting.

Poppy nodded. 'The leader of the Gentry, you mean?' she asked, rolling up Verity's sleeves.

Verity was astonished. 'Yes. But how did you know that?'

'People talk, don't they?' Poppy shrugged as she tied and then re-tied the leather laces on Verity's shoes in a futile attempt to change their appearance.

Verity thought to herself that, yes, they probably did. It was just that they didn't talk to her. 'Mother and Father have never mentioned it,' she said. 'Don't you think that's a little odd?'

'It's best not to ask,' said Poppy. 'Hardly anyone's parents like to talk about the Gentry. They get cross.'

'I always thought smuggling sounded quite exciting.' Verity didn't mention the fact that she'd scarcely been able to stop thinking about the Gentry since she'd discovered that her own, distinctly dull, family were once world-famous adventurers.

Poppy considered the point. 'I suppose so,' she said. 'They're quite like all those books you read, aren't they?'

Now it was Verity's turn to shrug. 'A little,' she admitted.

'Just a bit?' Poppy asked teasingly.

Verity smiled. 'Maybe quite a lot.'

Verity's father was hidden away in his study again, which wasn't particularly unusual. She opened the door to say goodbye, secretly hoping for some words of support. He was standing at the window but she'd never seen him looking so scruffy. He'd taken off his tie and undone his collar as if he felt particularly hot.

Smiling, Verity explained her interruption: 'I'm off to my first sailing match, so I thought I'd' – her sentence trailed off as Father ignored what she was saying and instead concentrated on trying to push up the sash – 'come and say goodbye.'

'Good, good . . .' Father said distantly, shaking his head as if trying to avoid a fly. He waved a hand sharply past his eyebrow.

Verity stared at him, a little disquieted. 'It must be nice for you to have Grandmother here,' she said conversationally.

Father paused in his task for a second, his head tilted to one side as if trying to understand her.

'I was wondering if you might be able to tell me a little more about your father, my grandfather,' Verity persevered. 'He sounds like a very interesting relative.'

Mr Gallant was gazing around the study now, but something in this last comment appeared to register. 'Very interesting,' he repeated. Then he laughed, eventually trailing off. 'Oh yes. Very interesting.'

Verity gave up and closed the door behind her as she left.

'Curiosity is a particularly unbecoming trait,' said Grandmother, appearing noiselessly in the hall. She smiled with a sinister sweetness. 'I dislike idle questions. You will avoid them if you know what's best for you.'

Verity stared at her silently in shock.

'What an original ensemble,' her grandmother continued, drawing a line under the previous topic. 'I'm sure it will provoke any number of comments. Do you have any friends?' Verity said nothing. Grandmother raised an eyebrow. Leaning in, she whispered in Verity's ear: Verity felt her skin prickle with goosebumps. Was a window open? she wondered.

'Perhaps the little fat boy will be there to keep you company. I suppose he will have to do if none of the girls like you.'

Verity felt as if she'd been slapped. How did Grandmother know? Was it that obvious?

The hall of Wellow sailing club was packed to the gills with assorted family members and friends. Next week was half-term and everyone seemed to be in a holiday mood. With a cold dread Verity walked through the door and realized that she was going to be the only person there with no supporters.

She stood near the entrance, thinking unhappily about what Grandmother had said and wondering why she didn't fit in. What was it about her that made her so unlikeable? She remembered the strange wooden ball, hidden upstairs in her bedroom. Verity knew it was stupid, but she really wished she'd brought it with her: she could have used some good luck.

'*Verity*,' a familiar voice shouted through the throng. 'Excuse me, excuse me. Boy with arms, and mouth, full.'

To Verity's astonishment Henry appeared from behind a disgruntled would-be spectator, holding a plate piled high with buffet food. 'The sausage rolls are always really good here,' he said, pointing to booty he'd already started work on. 'Though not up to Mum's standard, obviously. Want one?'

Verity shook her head. She was far too nervous. 'What are you doing here?' she asked.

Henry shrugged. 'Thought it might be fun – thought you might like some support,' he said.

Verity smiled gratefully at her new friend, not knowing quite what to say. 'I wonder if my grandfather ever came here?' she wondered, looking around.

'I think he built it—' Henry was suddenly interrupted by Percy and Will.

'I didn't realize the match would offer such rarefied company,' exclaimed Percy, jumping up and down in mock excitement. 'I can see the Blakes from here – would have put my best underwear on if I'd known.'

'I feel quite at home myself,' said Will, nodding in what he considered to be an imitation of someone engaging in sophisticated banter. 'Always fancied a bit of hobbing and nobbing.'

Percy helped himself to a devilled egg from Henry's plate.

'Get your own,' his younger brother complained.

'I'm doing you a favour,' Percy insisted. 'Morning, Verity,' he added. 'Ready to show us how it's done?'

Verity laughed. He must be joking. She looked across the room for the rest of her team-mates. There was Miranda Blake, competing for Whale Chine. She waved delicately at Verity, then made a comment to her friends – who all looked at her and burst out laughing. Verity's insides turned over.

'That girl is a piece of work,' said Will.

Verity frowned. Standing next to Miranda Blake was someone who looked familiar. A tall slender figure in deceptively simple clothes. She was deep in conversation with a pinch-faced lady and a whiskery gentleman and had her back to Verity. Could it really be . . . ? Verity stared again in astonishment. It *was*.

'That's my grandmother,' she exclaimed, grabbing Henry's arm. 'Talking to the couple over there. How did she get here so quickly? And why didn't she mention that she was coming?'

'They're the Blakes.' Henry injected a healthy amount of disdain into the one short sentence.

'Mrs Blake looks very pleased to be talking to your grandmother, I must say,' said Percy.

The conversation appeared to have ended. Now, at a word from Miranda, Grandmother swung round. Spying Verity, she headed over and looked questioningly at her granddaughter, who introduced the three boys nervously. She took in Henry, Percy and Will with one dismissive stare.

'I'm surprised to see you here,' Verity added nervously.

'What company you keep, Verity,' said the old lady, ignoring the comment and the Twogood brothers. 'I am going now.' And without further comment she left the hall.

Verity felt her face burn with shame and anger.

'Well, she seems really nice,' said Percy, opening his eyes wide and pulling a face.

'Looks like you're not the only person she doesn't like,' said Henry.

'I'm so sorry,' said Verity, embarrassed.

'Don't worry about it,' said Will. 'We have tons of barking relatives.'

Verity sighed. 'She certainly is very strange.' She turned

to Henry. 'I know this probably sounds really weird . . . but this morning she got so angry it was almost as if her entire face changed.'

'Yeah, Mum looks pretty terrifying when she decides we're playing up,' said Henry.

Verity shook her head. 'No, *really*. She looked completely different. I know it sounds odd, but she did.'

Henry didn't believe in mystery or the supernatural. It wasn't part of the Twogood outlook. Normally he would have quashed any such speculation with a guffaw, but he could tell Verity was on edge, so he just smiled sympathetically.

There was a loud call for all girls to assemble in their teams.

'You'd better go,' he said kindly. 'I'll see you later.' He gave his wide, honest smile and Verity couldn't help grinning in return.

## Chapter Eight

Things weren't going so badly, Verity thought to herself as she went down the wooden stairs that led from the side of the boat club to the slipway. Maybe she didn't need the strange wooden ball for luck after all. A flurry of activity was already underway. Competitors from both schools were pulling their dinghies down to the water on metal trolleys, sails furled.

At school matches like this it was traditional for the visiting school to borrow boats from the host team – which meant that the Whale Chine girls were using a selection of dinghies owned by Priory Bay and its pupils.

'I can see why none of your parents bother buying any-thing decent for you lot,' sniped Miranda Blake as she expertly tightened the sheets on an admittedly rather battered vessel, 'but I don't understand why *we* have to be lumbered with your leaky tubs.'

Looking up, she spotted the latest arrival. 'Here at last, Gallant?' Studying Verity's outfit, she paused to execute an exaggerated double take. 'Are you wearing your mother's clothes?' she enquired.

Verity blushed hotly. Then Miranda spotted the shoes. She shrieked with delight, grabbing her team-mate's arm. 'Look at Gallant's deck shoes,' she trilled at the top of her voice. 'Quite the latest thing.'

All the Whale Chine girls cackled with laughter – at which the Priory Bay team members looked up from their tasks.

'Talk about letting the side down,' said one crossly. 'How are you going to get about the boat in those old-fashioned clodhoppers?'

'Gallant the Galumph and her Cornish pasty shoes,' Miranda giggled. 'As if you didn't weigh enough already.'

'There you are, Gallant,' boomed Mrs Watson, oblivious to any pre-match altercations. 'You're with Makepiece.'

Judy Makepiece was a small girl with curly dark hair and big brown eyes. Verity smiled nervously; the girl glared balefully in reply.

The assembled spectators started to make their way out onto the wooden balcony that looked out over Wellow harbour and the ocean beyond. At the westernmost corner an old man leaned against the rail. His clothes smelled faintly of vanilla smoke; occasionally he would lift his pipe or raise an eyebrow in greeting. His young companion absent-mindedly kicked one of the posts while he looked anxiously out to sea.

A small sandy-haired boy jostled past with two companions who were clearly his brothers, immersed in excited conversation: '. . . bound to wipe the smirk off Blake's face . . . Verity must have been racing for years.'

The old man smiled wryly.

'She's really never sailed before?' Jeb Tempest asked his grandfather quietly, unable to keep the disbelief out of his voice.

'Not once,' said Isaac calmly.

Jeb shook his head.


Verity gazed up at the club building as she and Judy manoeuvred their craft down the slipway into the water. She frowned. There was the strange boy again.

'*Hello*. Are you going to pay attention?' her team-mate shouted angrily. Verity stared blankly in reply. 'I *said*, it's a south-westerly today so we're going head to wind.' Judy rolled her eyes and leaped nimbly into the dinghy. 'Just get in the water and hold the boat,' she said crossly. 'I'll sort out the sails.'

Verity jumped gamely off the slipway and into the shallows where the dinghy was bobbing. She gasped. It was absolutely freezing. She tried grabbing hold of the pointy end of the boat. It was very slippery.

'There,' Judy snapped, slapping the side of the boat. '*That's* the gunwale.'

Verity stood in the water, teeth chattering, while her team-mate unfurled the red sail and briskly hitched various ropes to some straight metal bolts.

Most of the other dinghies were moving off now, so theirs was no longer hemmed in. As the sails began to catch the wind, the boat started moving.

'Get in, you idiot,' Judy shouted angrily.

Verity tried to pull herself over the edge. It was really difficult. How did the other girls manage to hop aboard so easily?

Miranda Blake, sitting neatly at her helm, screamed with laughter. 'What style, what grace,' she taunted. 'You're agility personified. Look, everyone. Look at Gallant trying to *haul* herself into the boat.'

Verity steeled herself to make one last-ditch attempt to get herself into the dinghy. Suddenly she felt her dreadful deck shoes sinking deep into the sticky seabed. Her feet started to come out on their own. *No, no, no.* Mother would be beside herself if she lost them after just one outing. And she'd be convinced Verity had done it on purpose.

A gunshot went off from outside the club.

'Hurry *up*,' Judy bellowed. 'That's the ten-minute gun. Honestly, I'd have been better off with a sack of potatoes.'

There was nothing for it. The shoes would have to go. Verity pulled herself in at last, barefoot.

'Reach away to the beach, girls,' shouted Mrs Watson to them as their boat started to move off. 'You'll be fine.'

Verity wished she could share her teacher's confidence.

'How could a Gallant living in Wellow get to her age and still not know how to sail?' Jeb asked.

'Because Tom chose to protect his daughters from everything it meant to be Gentry,' said his grandfather. 'Something Rafe was never there to do for him. Too busy.'

'Travelling the world,' sighed Jeb enviously.

Isaac smiled ruefully. 'Running an empire,' he acknowledged. 'Losing sight of what matters.'

'You're sheeted in too hard,' Verity's team-mate shouted as they started to move off.

Verity flinched: she had no idea what that meant. Judy gestured angrily at the small sail to the front of the boat. It was almost completely flat.

'I need you to loosen that rope there,' she huffed. 'To let more wind into it.'

They were heading for the natural beach, marked by a row of fishermen's huts on the opposite side of Wellow harbour. Verity vaguely remembered something about this from the tactics session. Weren't they going to be racing around a triangle marked out by something called a channel mark, a sandbank buoy and a mark set down by the club?

'We're tacking round to get to the starting line, which is between those two boats over there, *remember*?' Judy snapped sarcastically, clearly resenting having to explain anything at all. 'Ready about,' she continued, and then, practically in the same breath, 'Lee ho.'

Verity sat where she was, hoping that the meaning of one or both of those phrases would become clear.

'Ooph.' The piece of wood attached to the bottom of the

sail hit her squarely in the chest as another gunshot went off. Verity started to feel just the tiniest bit fed up. This was the complete opposite of fun.

'What are you *doing*?' shouted Judy, incensed. 'Jump to the other side of the boat. Uncleat the jib sheet – that *rope*, *there* – and re-cleat it here. Lord of the Sky, we're already on the five-minute gun. Why did you agree to come when you don't know the first thing about sailing?'

Verity had no idea. And she was prepared to admit – although not to her moody team-mate – that it had been a pretty stupid move. There was clearly so much more to sailing than she had ever imagined. Why had Mrs Watson thought she could do it?

They were heading towards the starting line now, where the other dinghies were all gathered, jostling for position. Some appeared to be going up and down in small zigzags; others were almost circling in their anxiety to be as close as possible to the starting line when the final gun went off.

'We'd better tack here,' shouted Judy sulkily. 'Lord only knows what mayhem you'd cause if we got too close to the rest of them.'

As they turned the boat round, Verity managed to hop across – un-cleating and re-cleating the jib sheet – with a little more agility this time. A third gunshot went off in the background. Verity looked around, slightly puzzled. Had the race started?

'Oh *yes*,' crowed Judy. 'What a scoop. We're in front.'

Behind her, Verity could hear Miranda Blake fouling the

air with a string of heartfelt expletives. She giggled. Looking across at her team-mate, she grinned, and to her astonishment Judy smiled back.

'Look at that – we've managed to rattle Blake,' she said happily.

On the club's balcony the crowd were paying attention now that the race had begun.

'First across the starting line,' said Percy to Will and Henry in admiration. 'She really must be good.'

Nearby, Mrs Blake glared with distaste at the three boys. 'What does Miranda think she's playing at?' she hissed to her husband.

In the corner, Jeb watched Verity and her team-mate prepare to tack. 'She don't seem to be doing too bad,' he said hesitantly.

Isaac Tempest smiled. 'Give her time to get a feel for it,' he said. 'She'll come into her own.'

'Does she need to?' asked Jeb, still unsure what was to be required of the solemn little girl on the water.

'She's going to need the confidence and spirit it can bring,' his grandfather replied.

Verity and Judy tacked round the first marker laid down by the club. In spite of the fact that she was soaked from the waist down, Verity realized she was enjoying herself. Maybe it was the clean sea air or the sharp cool breeze, but she felt alive. In a small dinghy like this you were so close to the sea and its movement. She felt as if this was where she belonged.

They were approaching the second marker: a large orange triangle attached to a floating barrel. 'We've got to do a controlled gybe round this one, then a run to the next point,' shouted Judy with a hint of anxiety in her voice. 'It's going to be more violent than a tack because we're moving to put the wind directly behind us.'

Verity nodded, even though she hadn't understood any of that. They were racing along now. As they approached the channel marker, Judy pushed the tiller to swing the boat round it in a sixty-degree turn. The wind caught the little red sail and snapped the boom across the boat in a violent judder, but they were ready for it. Verity managed to adjust the jib sheet quite nimbly as they swapped across to the other side. Having no shoes on made her feel in tune with the boat. Her movements were certainly quicker and lighter.

'Try not to worry,' shouted Judy as she sat back down on the other side of the tiller. 'Gybing feels quite hairy, but it's all right most of the time.'

Verity grinned. 'I'm fine,' she shouted back happily. And she was.

Jeb and Isaac stared out to sea as Verity and Judy gybed neatly round the channel marker.

Isaac nodded to himself. 'Not bad,' he said quietly. 'Not bad at all.'

'How did the Usages worm their way into the Gentry in the first place?' Jeb asked.

'Didn't have to worm their way in. They were part and parcel of us.'

'But they're not real Gentry.'

'Yes they are,' said Isaac evenly. 'That's the nub of it, you see. At the heart, there's as much greed and selfishness in the Gentry as there is honour and valour. And until we admit that, we'll never overcome—' He broke off. 'What has to be overcome,' he finished.

Jeb followed his grandfather's gaze. He was staring thoughtfully at a patrician old lady, who was watching the match from a passageway beside the club.

Further along the balcony Henry grabbed his brother Will's arm. 'That's Verity's grandmother over there,' he said, frowning. 'By the post office jetty. I thought she was leaving . . . She really is the most peculiar woman.' She was watching the match intently.

'Maybe she's interested in how Verity does, after all?' said Will.

'Mm,' said Henry uncertainly. If so, she didn't look very happy to see that Verity's dinghy was winning. In fact she seemed furious. Anger distorted her fine features and her hands twitched as if she longed to take some form of action. Finally, almost unconsciously, she snapped her fingers in frustration.

\* \* \*

Judy looked up at the little flag at the top of the mast. It was pointing away from the main sail. Her face fell.

'The wind's changed,' she shouted, looking anxiously at the water. They were tearing along now, with a strong breeze behind them. 'We're running on the lee.'

Verity grinned happily, not understanding the words or registering her team-mate's anxiety.

'The mainsail's on the wrong side of the bow for the wind direction,' Judy snapped angrily, all former bonhomie lost in an instant. 'We could gybe again at any time.'

Verity's brow furrowed with concern. 'Well, let's gybe then,' she said simply.

'*Oh, let's gybe then,*' mimicked her team-mate furiously. 'Yes, let's just do that.'

'Look at Moody Makepiece.' Miranda Blake's spiteful little voice gusted towards them across the water. 'She's going to blub like she did last time she capsized. She wet her knickers too, you know.'

'We'll be fine,' soothed Verity. Instinctively she placed her hand on top of her team-mate's at the tiller, hoping to calm and reassure the obviously scared girl. But in the same moment a gust of wind seized the dinghy's sail. Judy cried out with fear.

The sail jerked across the boat, and with no conscious thought Verity dived over, sticking her bare feet under the straps and using them to attach herself to the boat. Instinctively she threw all her weight out of the dinghy, her body thrust out across the water to counteract the force of

the sail. Then, as it righted itself, she moved back just as swiftly to the centre of the hull.

Jeb Tempest had noticed Verity's grandmother smirk and raise an eyebrow; now he whooped with glee. 'Did you see that?' he shouted jubilantly. 'Not a second's thought – just sat her weight out and kept it upright. Fearless.' Turning round to his grandfather, he grinned.

Isaac was a little more circumspect but he still smiled. 'And she had the instinct to jump back to the middle,' he agreed. 'Looks just like her,' he added proudly.

He and his grandson gazed at the daring young girl with the flowing brown hair and pink cheeks. With a triumphant smile Jeb turned to stare pointedly at Verity's grandmother. The old woman looked furious.

'Crikey,' said Percy to his younger brother. 'Your girl's got some spirit.'

'She's not my girl,' said Henry automatically, gazing in astonishment at Verity's dinghy. 'Charming,' he added as Mrs Blake elbowed her way furiously past him.

Verity looked around and saw that they were still in one piece. And in the lead. She beamed with happiness. This was brilliant fun. But as Judy Makepiece opened her eyes and realized they had not capsized, her relief turned to embarrassed anger.

'What the hell do you think you were doing, showing

off like that?' she shouted at Verity. 'I should have known you'd think you were something special.'

Verity was baffled and confused. 'I'm sorry,' she shouted back. 'It just seemed like the right thing to do. I thought it helped.'

Still shaking, her team-mate recovered a little. She knew she wasn't being fair. They were going to win, and it was all down to Verity; but there was no way Judy was going to admit that. 'Let's just get round this final marker and call it a day,' she snapped.

Verity stood once more in the freezing water, holding the dinghy by the gunwale while Judy furled the sails and cleaned the ropes. She paused occasionally to glare at Verity. 'Never raced with someone so unprofessional . . . Should have known you'd pull a stunt like that.'

Verity could feel the sticky sandy mud oozing between her toes. She had no idea what she'd done. Just as she thought things couldn't get any worse, Miranda Blake's dinghy came speeding towards them with an incensed occupant.

'Beginner's luck, Gallant,' she snarled across the water. 'That and the fact that your lousy team-mates saddled me with a leaky tub.'

'Shut up, Blake,' shouted a familiar voice further up the slipway.

'The Twogoods,' Miranda sneered, investing those two words with a world of disdain.

Henry and his brothers gave her a hard stare as they came down to congratulate Verity on her win.

Jumping nimbly from her boat onto the dry slipway, Miranda stared challengingly at her as she shivered in the water. 'What a delightful couple you make, Verity,' she said, tilting her head to one side. 'You have so much in common: second-hand clothes, archaic sailing gear . . . robust physiques.'

'Pack it in, pygmy-girl,' shouted Percy.

But Miranda was on a roll now and she wasn't giving up. 'Goody Twogood and Gallant the Galumph.' She smiled brightly at Verity. 'Goody and the Galumph.' She laughed spitefully and Judy Makepiece joined in.

'Goody and the Galumph,' Verity heard someone giggle. 'That's quite good.'

*Gallant the Galumph.* Was that what everyone was going to call her? Verity was devastated. She was cold, she was wet and she'd had enough of being teased and bullied for one day. Pulling herself up onto the slipway – and studiously avoiding anyone's gaze – she hurried away from the dinghy before her welling tears overflowed. She could hear people shouting, but she didn't care. She just kept pushing blindly through the crowd, heading for the exit and escape.

On her own at last, Verity gave in to the unhappy hurt of being laughed at in front of so many people. Grandmother's words rang in her ears: *Do you have any friends? I suppose the little fat boy will have to do if none of the girls like you.* She was useless. Nobody liked her – not even when she was in the winning boat.

At the corner she heard Henry shouting. Verity was angry now. And Henry was there. 'Just leave me alone,' she shouted back. Henry's honest, open face looked confused and hurt but she didn't care.

'But you—' he started.

'I'm what?' Verity snapped, tears streaming. 'The only person in Wellow who can't sail? Incredibly unpopular? Dressed like an old woman?'

'No, you were—'

'I'm one half of *Goody and the Galumph*,' Verity interrupted. 'Even by my standards, that has to be a new all-time low.'

'Oh,' said Henry as she stormed off down the road, still crying bitterly.

## Chapter Nine

The next morning Verity woke up feeling terrible. Why had she been so mean to Henry? The only person at school who'd ever been nice to her and she'd been horrible in return. She wondered what Alice would make of her behaviour. Hating herself, she headed downstairs for breakfast.

Father was already at the table reading his paper, peculiarly dressed in a thick jumper and scarf which he wore over his dressing gown. His breakfast lay untouched.

Clutching at straws, Verity wondered whether perhaps Henry might be used to tempers, having six brothers. 'Do boys mind hurtful comments as much as girls?' she asked.

Mr Gallant moved his paper to one side and stared distractedly at her. He was sweating profusely. 'Only if they care about the person who made them,' he replied. Patting her hand reassuringly, he added, 'So you should be fine.'

Verity watched silently as he concentrated on buttering a piece of toast. He had always been off in a dream world, but there was something very different about him now.

Why did only she notice it? She'd tried mentioning it to Mother and Poppy, but according to them it was simply another example of her overactive imagination.

Verity was sure there was more to it than that. She shrank slightly at the thought of having even fewer people on her side.

Verity sat on the bed in her new room. Even reading the book couldn't take her mind off things: she was no closer to figuring out why Abednego had given it to her, and every story she read was so horrible it made her feel worse.

*There was once a woman who was a real witch, and her soul was as black as charred wood. The witch had a servant girl who was both beautiful and good, and she hated her with all the blood in her heart.*

*Now, the servant had a sweetheart, and when the witch saw him she desired him very much. 'Stay with me,' said the witch, 'and I will give you as much gold and silver as you can carry, for I am wealthy.' But the sweetheart was as noble and honourable as the servant girl was beautiful and good, so he refused.*

*The two lovers agreed that night to hurry away on the sweetheart's boat. But the witch learned of their flight and called up a mighty wind, which dashed the little boat upon the rocks. The witch waited on the shore for the pair, whom she had commanded to be washed up. And when they crawled out of the sea, she killed first the sweetheart in front of the servant girl. Then she took the servant girl home, where she threw her about the ground until she was dead.*

*Tales of murder and torture have increased in frequency over the last two hundred years* [the notes read]. *Her appetite for cruelty appears to grow with each century. References to blackened souls are also numerous. An oblique allusion to outward appearance?*

Verity wiped a tear from the side of her nose. The half-term holiday stretched out like a vast expanse. Perhaps Father was right: maybe Henry didn't actually like her that much anyway – and if he had before, he'd certainly have been put off her now.

She reached under the bed for the strange wooden ball, turning it over and over in her hand, listening to the familiar click and rattle. Holding it up to the light, she frowned. Perhaps if it made a noise, it was meant to open? Pressing her fingertips on either side, she strained to pull it apart. Sure enough, a gap showed. Excitedly she applied more pressure.

The wooden casing clicked open with a snap. Inside was a white marble ball. Verity gazed at it curiously. It didn't look as if it would come out. She spun the marble round in the wooden casing, then shrieked. The ball fell to the ground. Gazing at her from the other side was an extremely realistic eye.

Picking it up, Verity noticed that the room seemed

infinitely still. She thought of her trip around the *Storm* on the ferry.

The eye of the *Storm*'s figurehead – it had to be, she thought, turning it around in wonder. Abednego had given it to her, after all. And the eye was famously missing – that had been plain to see. But why would he give it to her?

Turning it over, she realized that if her parents knew, they'd insist she hand it back. Verity felt a pang of concern at the mere thought. It was her talisman. She had better keep it hidden.

Hurriedly she snapped the wooden ball shut and stuffed it into her coat pocket. A thought occurred to her. She should go to Henry's house to apologize. It wasn't a very attractive prospect: his mother and brothers must be really cross with her too. But she knew she would feel terrible until she'd done it.

Verity knocked anxiously on the front door of the Twogoods' house. Even though Henry had explained they rarely used it, it seemed a little presumptuous to walk round to the back. A few doors up, a dog barked, but this house was very quiet. They must all be out.

Verity turned to walk back down the path. As she reached the gate, she heard muffled cursing. Someone was trying to open the front door despite the heavy mass of coats, hats and scarves that hung from it.

Turning round, Verity saw a man of medium height and solid build. He was handsome in a sturdy and dependable way. In his vest and trousers, with salt and pepper hair askew, he looked like someone who had recently been asleep and was not particularly pleased now to be awake. Verity swallowed anxiously: this must be Henry's father.

Walking back up the path, she smiled nervously to break the ice, gripping the strange wooden ball in her pocket. 'I'm so sorry to disturb you,' she said, 'but I was looking for Henry.'

Mr Twogood stared at Verity for a second. ''E's not here. Gone fishing with his brothers,' he said. 'Told 'em to take 'im so I could get some sleep,' he added pointedly.

Verity had spent the entire walk to Henry's house rehearsing her apology. It hadn't occurred to her that he might not be in when she got there. She stared limply at Mr Twogood, overwhelmed with disappointment.

Henry's father decided to put an end to this fascinating discourse. 'I'll tell 'im you called,' he said, and shut the door.

Verity stared at it, then headed for the gate – only to hear the sound of coats, hats and scarves being shoved against the wall for a second time. She waited for Mr Twogood's head to appear once more.

'Gallant girl, was it?' he asked. Verity nodded mutely. Mr Twogood appeared to be thinking. 'Hmph,' he said, and shut the door again.

Verity walked home slowly and sadly. Henry had clearly already told his family about her behaviour. Not that she could blame him. They probably all hated her now.

The first few days of Verity's half-term dragged by. Father was still acting strangely while Mother was constantly tired from the pregnancy – and more than a little irritable as a consequence. Poppy had been invited to an even larger number of parties and events than usual, which left Verity on her own to fend off the worst of Grandmother's jibes.

There had been no reply from Henry. Verity wasn't sure if it was because she was hoping to hear from him but there seemed to be a cruelly higher number of callers that week. Each time the doorbell rang her hopes rose. But it was never for her. Henry must be really angry. She could have kicked herself for being so horrible to him.

'No sign of the little fat boy?' asked Grandmother, appearing silently and suddenly in the room where Verity was reading. How did she always manage to do that? 'He's probably laughing about you with his brothers,' she mused, picking up Mother's favourite porcelain figurine.

It was only what Verity believed herself, but it was horrible to hear it said out loud.

'I expect you thought you were quite the daring little seafarer out there,' Grandmother continued, holding the twee figure up to the light and examining it with distaste.

Verity's heart sank. It was true. She really *had* believed she could be good at sailing.

The old lady glanced in her direction. 'It's your silent insolence that I find particularly trying,' she said curtly. Still Verity couldn't find any words that would ease the situation.

Astonishingly the little ornament suddenly leaped from Grandmother's fingers and dashed itself on the hearth. It smashed noisily on the marble. Verity stared in amazement and horror.

'Really, Verity,' scolded Grandmother in a loud, clear voice. 'Isn't that one of your mother's particular favourites?'

Mrs Gallant hurried into the room. 'What's all the commotion—? *Oh*.' She knelt down to examine the shattered pieces.

'I did warn Verity to be careful. But of course she rarely listens to her elders and betters,' soothed Grandmother.

Verity stared at her in outrage. 'That's a complete lie—' she started.

'Verity, *really*.' Mother was holding the broken shards with evident sadness. 'How dare you cheek your grandmother. To your room *now*.'

Verity opened her mouth to object once more and then shut it again. As she traipsed unhappily up the stairs, she reflected that thanks to her own stupid temper she didn't even have Henry to confide in about her hateful relative.

She couldn't blame him for not wanting to speak to her, but life without him seemed even lonelier than before. As much as she hated to admit it, Grandmother was right. Her one chance at having a friend, and she'd blown it. And to make things worse, it left her with no one to ask about either her grandfather or the Gentry. Why had Alice chosen now, of all times, to disappear off on a trip? Verity sighed. She missed her terribly.

'Miss Cameron, the librarian, stopped me in town this morning,' said Poppy, sticking her head round Verity's bedroom door. Her sister was sitting on the bed dejectedly. 'About a book. She asked if you could come in this week.'

Verity stared at her. A cold feeling hit her stomach. Had Miss Cameron realized she was in possession of the red leather-bound book? She wondered how much trouble she would be in. Was she technically in receipt of stolen goods?

'Something you ordered? Quite a mystery actually . . .' Poppy continued. 'She asked me to be discreet when reminding you about it. Said it was *a slightly delicate matter.*' She recited the last four words in a remarkably accurate imitation of Miss Cameron's dulcet tones, then grinned. 'I had no idea the world of librarianship could be so intriguing.'

Now Verity was confused. Poppy handed her a small brown envelope. She opened it gingerly. Inside was a reservation card. She stared at it in astonishment.

Title:      *Rafe Gallant and the Gentry of Wellow: A detailed history*
Author(s): Dill, Pinkerton & Lane
Ref. no.:   375/6449
Hold for:   3 days from the above date

The library. Of course. Why hadn't she thought of that before?

'Everything all right?' Poppy asked her sister gently.

'Yes,' said Verity. Then beamed. 'Everything is fine.'

She practically ran to the library after lunch. Pushing through the red double doors, she looked around eagerly. Miss Cameron was sitting placidly at the entrance desk.

'Ah, Verity,' she murmured. 'Here for that reservation?'

'Yes please,' said Verity, trying to hide her excitement.

Miss Cameron reached into a cupboard near her feet and extracted a slim green volume. 'Reference only, I'm afraid. So if you could just read it here in the main hall, that would be extremely helpful.'

Verity took it, and Miss Cameron went back to her cataloguing. Verity stood watching her; she looked up again.

'Is there anything else?'

'Not really . . .' said Verity hesitantly. 'It's just that I don't . . . I don't recall ordering a book of this title.'

Miss Cameron smiled politely. 'How extraordinary.' She held out a hand. 'Shall I put it back for you?'

'No,' said Verity quickly, clutching the book to her chest. 'I mean,' she corrected herself, 'that won't be necessary. Thank you.'

Going to the library each day to read the slim green book – and the many others that Miss Cameron subsequently excavated for her – did at least give Verity the opportunity to get away from Grandmother's increasingly spiteful barrage of comments.

Compared to the battleground her home had become she found the library safe, inviting even. Miss Cameron was always pleasant and helpful in her quiet, reserved way. There was something very comforting about her reliable efficiency. And now that Verity was able to spend her time finding out more about her mysterious ancestor, nothing could have kept her away.

She didn't know whether it was personal bias, but it seemed to her that the early history of the Gentry was fairly dull. To begin with they were just a group of men who spent a lot of time and effort bringing tubs of brandy or sugar across the Channel and then hiding them in apple stores or cellars. It was as the band of smugglers developed that things got exciting. In particular, once Rafe Gallant took over as leader – a topic the slim green book covered well:

*Rafe Gallant inherited leadership of the Gentry from his father, James* [Verity read]. *He is acknowledged to have been the sole architect of the meteoric rise of the Gentry from low-level smuggling outlaws to vastly successful international businessmen of fame and repute. His influence was also the primary factor in the metamorphosis of Wellow from remote village to flourishing port and acknowledged centre of architectural excellence.*

Verity eagerly absorbed everything she could find on her dashing grandfather.

*Rafe's efforts began with a focus on the smuggling infra-structure of Wellow. This was improved first through the introduction of a complex series of tunnels and escape routes, the engineering of which was at the time particularly advanced.*

*He invested heavily in the development of maritime systems that improved the process of smuggling as a whole, and devised many tools and techniques which were later adopted in both the commercial and governmental sectors.*

She was enchanted. Rafe's life sounded absolutely thrilling. How she would have loved to meet him – to be a part of the Gentry herself.

*A keen and skilled sailor from an early age, Rafe was famously said to have the fearlessness of the devil and the precision of an angel. He prized good seamanship above all and was the sole founder of Wellow's former School of Sailing, now sadly defunct. Rafe was also a generous sponsor of public amenities, such as the harbour master's office, the Town Records Bureau and Wellow's fine library.*

No wonder everyone had assumed she could sail, Verity thought to herself sadly. It must seem extraordinary that someone as clumsy as her could be the granddaughter of such a sportsman. She obviously hadn't inherited any of his talent. Perhaps the new baby might do instead?

*Rafe's reputation as a man of charm with a taste for high living proved difficult to shake. In the end it was this image that overshadowed the true portrait of a cultured business-man and great sportsman of keen intellect. Fatherhood came easily to Rafe, but the thing he nurtured with most affection was the enterprise of the Gentry. He left behind him many children, including three from his first marriage and two, Ruby and Tom, from his second to Rose, a much-loved wife who died in childbirth.*

Verity stared at the book and felt a pang of loneliness. Ruby and Tom. Tom, her father. It felt so strange to see his name there; to be learning about his life from history books because he chose not to share it with her himself.

*It was during Rafe's leadership that the mythical Mistress of the Storm came to prominence as a key part of Gentry lore. The Mistress was said to be a fearsome witch who could control the weather. Used by the Gentry as a scare-tactic to keep opponents in check, they claimed that she sailed with the famous smuggling ship, the* Storm.

Verity frowned. A witch who could control the weather. She knew she'd heard that name before: *the Mistress of the Storm*. She reached down to her bag on the floor and pulled out the red leather-bound book. It fell open at a page.

*From that day forward her fate was sealed* [she read]. *For it is a crime against the universe to steal a child from those who love it, and each time she did so, another little part of her soul became tarnished and black. From that day forward the downfall of the Mistress was sure and certain.*

*The Mistress* . . . Verity flicked rapidly back to another page, then another . . . *She of the Wind is Mistress of the Storm* . . . *She goes by many names, and Mistress is one of them. For she demands obedience from every living thing.*

Verity turned the book over excitedly in her hands. Of course. How could she have missed this before? The heroine was the Gentry's Mistress of the Storm. But her excitement quickly turned to frustration – she was still no closer to understanding why Abednego had given it to her.

Verity meandered through the streets and paths of Wellow, in no hurry to return home before she absolutely had to. Finally she found herself at the park. She gazed down the stone steps that led to Alice's road. It was silly, she knew, but she felt as if just walking past her home would be a comfort.

She opened Alice's gate and went up the path. It felt uncharacteristically still, as if the property knew that its bustling owner was absent. The garden had been stripped back by Norton, the handyman, in preparation for winter. It was now only bare earth and exposed bushes. There was no consolation to be had here.

Turning back to head home, she realized that Miranda Blake was standing on the pavement, observing her with amusement.

'Gallant,' she lisped, sauntering confidently up Alice's path. 'Loitering here won't bring her back, you know.'

How did Miranda know about her friendship with Alice? Verity was determined not to give her the satisfaction of appearing to care. Then she frowned. Strolling on the other side of the road was the strange long-haired boy. And he was staring at them.

Overwhelmed by curiosity, Verity couldn't stop herself. 'Do you know who he is?' she asked.

Miranda looked at her superciliously. 'Jeb Tempest?'

'Tempest . . .' said Verity, thinking what an unusual surname it was.

'The Tempests of Tempest Bay, next to Soul Bay,' said Miranda impatiently, then raised an eyebrow. 'Oh dear, has he got your attention?'

Verity was taken aback. 'Oh. No, that's not what I meant. I was just curious because . . .' She realized that explaining her interest was just going to make it worse. 'Well,' she continued, 'not for any particular reason at all really.'

'No, of course not,' said Miranda, permitting herself a little smirk.

'So are your family ruling the roost yet?' asked Verity, remembering Miranda's strange comments from the tactics session.

Her diminutive enemy stared archly at her. 'Soon,' she replied.

'I don't suppose your family were *tremendously* wealthy,' said Verity airily, to see if this would get more out of her. It worked.

'We wanted for nothing,' said the little girl sharply. 'Mother says there would have been an endless supply of beautiful dresses and jewels for her. Blake parties may not have gone on for weeks like the ones at the Manor, but they were the epitome of luxury.'

Verity wondered why Miranda made such particular reference to Wellow's landmark house? Verity had always assumed it was deserted. Certainly she'd never seen anyone entering or leaving.

'And of course we commanded respect then. *Real* respect,' Miranda continued, deadheading a lone flower with vicious efficiency.

Miranda turned to leave. It occurred to Verity that she was going somewhere special. She was decked out in a burgundy velvet dress, with matching coat and shiny black patent shoes.

'Visiting someone nice?' she asked.

'Visiting someone lucrative,' Miranda replied scathingly. She paused to stare disdainfully at Verity. 'The Gallants were a proud family once,' she said. 'Not the kind of people who would have associated with Twogoods or Tempests.'

## Chapter Ten

It was Saturday morning at last: the half-term break was nearly over. Another caller rang at the door. Grandmother bustled into the hall, motioning Mrs Gallant to sit down. 'Don't trouble yourself, dear.'

Verity tried to remind herself that however unpleasant Grandmother was to her, she certainly seemed keen to help Mother.

This time Verity didn't even bother asking if it was for her. It never was. Putting on her coat, she prepared to leave for the library. But as she turned the corner of the street, she heard a shout of '*Verity*,' and was unceremoniously accosted by a breathless Henry. He'd obviously been running.

She swivelled round, astonished and delighted.

'If you're still angry, you could at least explain why,' he said urgently. 'And if you *are* still angry, I don't understand why you called for me . . . ?'

Verity was thrilled. 'I'm not. I thought you were—'

'So why did you pretend you weren't in all week?' he demanded.

Verity was confused. 'I didn't,' she said. 'I've been to the library a lot . . . trying to avoid Grandmother.'

'Well, I called just now and she said you weren't in . . . but you must have been, because here you are,' said Henry.

'She said *what*?' Verity couldn't believe it. Grandmother had walked right past her.

'Yeah,' said Henry. 'Then she *smirked*,' he added indignantly.

Instantly Verity knew he was telling the truth. She nodded glumly. 'She does that.'

'So she knew you were in and just kept telling me to go away?' Henry was outraged. 'She's horrible.'

Verity nodded again. Then she remembered what she needed to say. 'Henry, I'm so sorry I shouted at you after the sailing match. It was inexcusable. And I didn't even mean it: I was just upset because everyone was laughing at me.'

Henry looked at her like she was an idiot. 'I know,' he said. Verity was taken aback. 'I've got six brothers,' he reminded her. 'I have some experience of arguments. And I know how vile Miranda Blake can be. Then, with your grandmother making life tough for you too . . . I know why you were upset.'

Verity looked at him. 'I won't do it again,' she promised.

'Too right you won't,' said Henry cheerfully. 'I'm sure a week without my company has helped you to see the error of your ways.'

Verity grinned.

He looked at her intently. 'It's not your fault, you know. Sometimes people – grandmothers – aren't very nice.'

Verity looked dismayed. 'I've really tried to get on with her and it doesn't work. It's just . . .'

'What?'

She shrugged. 'Even my own grandmother doesn't like me,' she said quietly.

'*I* like you,' Henry told her.

'I really missed you this week,' said Verity, smiling.

'Me too,' said Henry enthusiastically. 'Percy and Will helped me look around town to see if we could spot you, but no luck. We had all sorts of plans. Still,' he added philosophically, 'we know now.'

Verity nodded. 'I won't let her do it again.'

'So what you doing today?'

'Nothing much.'

'I've got the dinghy,' said Henry. 'Would you like to go sailing?'

Verity's stomach turned over. 'I think I've messed up enough on boats for the moment,' she said.

Henry frowned. 'You'd really never crewed before the race?'

'Never.'

He shook his head in astonishment. 'Your parents are a funny lot,' he said. 'Don't talk about your family. Never taught you to sail.'

Verity looked a little sad.

Henry realized he was doing his usual trick. 'Well, it

must be true,' he said, changing tack. 'It must be in your blood, because you were a natural.'

'But Judy Makepiece was really angry with me,' Verity countered.

'Moody Makepiece is terrified of capsizing.' Henry grinned. 'School legend has it she wet her knickers last time she went overboard. She must nearly have had another accident when you gybed the boat like that.'

'Really?' Verity giggled in spite of herself. 'I thought Miranda was just being mean.'

'Yeah, but if you hadn't, you'd probably have capsized anyway, and lost the race to boot.'

'Oh,' said Verity.

'How did you know what to do?' Henry asked.

'I didn't. It just sort of happened . . . it felt right.'

'Hm,' he said, quietly impressed. 'Well. Let's see if the famous Gallant instinct rears its head again today.'

Verity smiled.

'The library . . .' muttered Henry as they continued down the road together. 'No wonder we couldn't find you.'

Verity and Henry headed towards the shingle beach on the western side of Wellow harbour. It was the one she'd aimed for during the race. It looked very different when you approached by foot, Verity thought, remembering how tiny the fishermen's huts had seemed from the water.

'One of Dad's friends lets us keep our dinghy behind his hut,' Henry explained as they followed a narrow footpath between the wooden shacks. As they emerged beside one that was built into the cliff, Verity caught a gust of fresh sea air and smiled nervously. This was bringing back mixed memories of the sailing match.

Stopping beside one of the huts, Henry pulled at a particularly smelly piece of tarpaulin to reveal a small wooden dinghy, mast lowered. He looked down at Verity's feet and nipped into the hut. Verity could hear him scrabbling about, throwing things to one side. After a couple of minutes he emerged, bearing a pair of deck shoes. They were old and faded, but looked just like the ones all the other girls had.

'They're a bit shabby,' he said, 'but that's often considered to be a good thing in sailing. Sort of makes you look like you've been doing it for a while.' He grinned. 'And they're lighter than your other ones.'

Verity couldn't help but laugh. 'I think there are marble statues that weigh less than those shoes.'

'How did your parents find such an old-fashioned pair?'

Verity pulled a face. 'My grandmother spotted them in Joliffe's.'

Henry shook his head. 'She really doesn't like you, does she?'

For once, Verity found it quite funny. 'No,' she giggled, 'I don't think she does . . .

'I suppose it must be quite expensive to moor at the harbour instead of here,' she said sympathetically as Henry started putting up the mast then rummaging around in the hold for a smaller sail, which he attached at the front.

Henry looked at her quizzically. 'You can't lease a mooring in Wellow: they're handed down from generation to generation. We just don't have one.' Apparently ready now, he began pushing the dinghy down the steep shingle beach to the shore.

'But it sounds like the Twogoods have been in Wellow a long time?'

'Yeah, that's right,' said Henry, taking off his shoes and socks and rolling up his trousers. 'Our mooring was taken away from us.'

'Taken away? Why?'

'When we left the Gentry,' he said, looking at her as if she were being a bit stupid.

'They took your mooring away?'

'They took everything.'

Henry bustled into action. 'OK. If you jump in, I can push off. We're facing head to wind at the moment. So we need to pull the nose round a bit.'

'Right,' said Verity. Had he been listening when she explained she'd never sailed before the match?

Apparently he had. He slapped the front of the dinghy authoritatively. 'This is the nose,' he said. 'Or bow, if you prefer.' He pointed up to the largest sail. 'This is the mainsail . . . and that's the jib,' he continued, pointing to the small sail at the front.

Verity nodded. It was sounding familiar. She must have absorbed more than she thought.

'This is the mast. And the horizontal bar attached to it is the boom – the thing that hit you in the chest . . . I thought you weren't paying attention.' Henry grinned. 'Didn't realize you had no idea it would be heading your way.'

Verity smiled. She could laugh about it now.

Henry passed her a rope. 'This,' he said, 'is called a jib sheet – all the ropes that control the sails in relation to the wind are sheets in fact – and your job is to unfasten it and re-fasten it in these things here called cleats, just like you did in the match. We have to tack to get out of the bay because the wind is blowing in to the shore. Then it's a nice easy journey up the coast and back again.'

Verity nodded. She could tack. She'd done that in the match.

'Hop in,' said Henry, 'and we'll get going.'

'You're really getting the hang of this.' Henry sounded slightly surprised. The breeze was good and they were going at a brisk pace, but Verity was fine.

'It's brilliant fun,' she replied as they both leaned out of the boat to stop her heeling. She couldn't believe how at home she felt again. It hadn't been a one-off. The air was fresh and sharp, the green waves glistened and the sky was a vivid shade of blue. She breathed in deeply and smiled.

'There's Soul Bay,' said Henry, pointing back to land.

'Miranda Blake mentioned that the other day,' said Verity. 'She said it's near Tempest Bay.'

Henry nodded. 'Tempest is the next one round: a bit far for us to go today. Soul Bay was the Gentry's favourite place for outrunning the Preventative Men,' he added, nodding to the shore with his head.

'Really?' Verity's ears pricked up instantly.

'Yeah. There's just one route through the ledge to the shore, and only they knew it. So they'd head here if they were being chased and the Preventative Men wouldn't be able to follow.'

'Why not?' asked Verity, betraying her lack of sailing knowledge.

'Because most of the water is too shallow and rocky to sail over,' explained Henry. 'Any boat would be ripped to shreds. Apparently the Preventative Men would be stuck out here just watching the Gentry unloading their goods. Nothing they could do.'

Verity was intrigued. 'Why not wait on the shore for them?'

'Private land,' said Henry. 'Had to ask permission – and by the time they got there it was too late. Plus they never really got the hang of the tunnels.'

'I found out more about Rafe Gallant,' Verity told him. Somehow it didn't feel quite right to say Grandfather. 'In the library,' she added, feeling quite proactive.

'Did you?' Henry grinned. 'That's a particularly Verity way of going about things.'

She ignored him. 'One of the books said he has a daughter . . . I have an aunt I've never met.'

Henry looked at her and chewed his lip. 'Was her name Ruby?' he asked.

Verity looked up eagerly. 'Yes. Do you know her?'

Henry looked uncomfortable. 'She died in a sailing accident when she was twelve. It's quite famous. I'm surprised it wasn't mentioned too. Your father was just a baby at the time. I think it hit your grandfather quite badly.'

Verity was silent. Poor Father. She wondered if he could remember losing her.

'Best if we anchor off here,' said Henry, changing the subject as he let some wind out of the sails and drew the dinghy to a halt. 'It's not worth going in: this is a lee shore.'

Verity looked at him questioningly.

'The wind blows in to the land,' he explained, 'so it's difficult to get back out again. That's what made the wreckers so successful: once a ship had been lured onto the rocks she had no way of returning to safe sea.'

'Does this boat have a name?' Verity asked as Henry lowered the little folding anchor.

He smiled. 'Yeah, *Poor Honesty*.'

'That's pretty,' said Verity.

'Mm,' he agreed. 'It was a dig at the Gentry. After we left, they put the squeeze on us financially. Maybe they thought we'd back down. But my grandda wouldn't budge: "Better poor honesty than rich deceit," he said. So when we lost the family boat, that's what he named our dinghy.'

'Did your dad tell you that I called round?' asked Verity, taking the proffered sandwich.

'Yeah, of course.' Henry rearranged the cheese and salad in his for optimum distribution. 'Did you think he wouldn't?'

'He didn't seem very pleased about it, no,' she admitted.

'Well, he'd been on nights. There's a lot of work on since the *Storm* arrived. You woke him up,' said Henry.

Verity nodded thoughtfully. 'It wasn't because I'm a Gallant then?' she asked, taking a stab in the dark. Bull's-eye. Henry looked embarrassed.

'The Twogoods had a pretty hard time from some of the Gentry when they left,' he explained, 'so he's not very keen on thoroughbred Gentry families.'

Verity smiled. 'That's quite funny, isn't it? Being disapproved of as Gentry, when I don't actually know anything about them?'

'Dad's just a bit too much of a Twogood, that's all,' said Henry. 'They take history very seriously.'

'Henry,' said Verity, staring out to sea, 'there's something peculiar going on, I just know it.'

He frowned at her.

'The *Storm* has returned to Wellow, and her captain gave me that red book. Grandmother – whom my parents had never talked about before – arrived at the same time. And my parents deliberately kept it a secret that my grandfather, *my father's own father*, was Rafe Gallant, leader of the Gentry.' Verity looked at him searchingly.

'Don't you think it's just coincidence?' he sighed quietly. Why did people always invest the Gentry with mysterious properties? Couldn't they see it was just superstition and hocus-pocus?

Verity watched him with frustration. She could tell this wasn't getting through. 'There are other things as well; little things. There's a boy – Jeb Tempest – and I'm sure he's following me. He seems to know Grandmother too. Alice has disappeared. And Father is acting really *strangely*.'

'There's nothing mysterious going on,' Henry reassured her. 'I don't know why your parents don't like to talk about Rafe Gallant, or the Gentry. Maybe they think it's best left in the past. And Alice told us she was going away for a bit. The Gentry were just a group of smugglers who no longer trade. The *Storm* is just a ship . . . and you met her captain. That's all.'

In the Twogood world view there was a rational explanation for everything: that was their particular religion.

'Why did he give me the book? You know, it talks a lot about the Mistress of the Storm?'

'Well, there you are then,' Henry said patiently. 'It was a book of mythology about his ship. Perfectly natural for him to take an interest in it.'

'But why give it to *me*?' Verity repeated.

Henry paused for a second to think. 'You *asked* him for the book. Remember? You told him he wasn't supposed to take books from the library without signing for them. Maybe he thought you were the library police.'

Verity was disappointed. He was being obstinately

sceptical. 'The strange boy?' she asked. 'How does he know Grandmother?'

'*Seems* to know her,' Henry corrected. 'And anyway, you don't know the Tempests: they're a peculiar lot. Apart from Isaac.'

'Grandmother arriving on the same night as the *Storm*?' Verity demanded.

'OK, so it's a coincidence,' conceded Henry, 'but that's all it can be.'

'There's something really quite frightening about her,' Verity persisted. 'When she loses her temper, she looks completely different, like a skeleton almost. It's terrifying. And you can feel her anger. I don't understand how she could possibly have been married to Rafe Gallant.'

'Verity,' said Henry, not unsympathetically, 'your grandmother is just a nasty old woman who likes picking on people. And your dad is probably worried about having an extra mouth to feed. It's entirely understandable to want a special explanation, but there's nothing weird going on.'

'No, Grandmother *is* odd – I don't care what you think. There's something strange about her. She's not normal.' Verity thrust her hand into her pocket, wondering if she should show Henry the strange wooden ball.

'You don't like her, that's all,' he insisted bossily.

Verity gave up. 'No, I don't,' she conceded. 'But she *is* peculiar.'

Back at Wellow, the pair dragged the dinghy up the beach.

Verity looked across the horizon to the famous silhouette of the Spyglass Inn.

'Rafe Gallant commissioned the tunnels, didn't he?' she asked Henry.

'Not as many as some people make out. But yes, there were tunnels leading from Soul Bay to other parts of Wellow.'

'Didn't that make it awkward to move stuff around?'

Henry shrugged. 'Not as awkward as being caught. And anyway, there wasn't much difference: it's not like you could have driven a cart down to the beach. Everything had to be carried up by hand. You might as well do that in a tunnel. They used them to meet up too,' he added. 'To begin with at least. Then, eventually, the Gentry were so powerful they did whatever they liked out in the open.'

'Have you ever seen one – a tunnel, I mean?' asked Verity.

'A few times, yeah,' admitted Henry. 'With my brothers. We've broken in to have a look; admire the Twogood craftsmanship.'

'Twogood?'

Henry smiled. 'Yeah. Rafe Gallant commissioned the tunnels, but they were Twogood-built, every single one.'

'So the Twogoods were the Gentry's tunnel-builders?'

'We were their *engineers*,' said Henry a little indignantly.

Verity looked puzzled.

'We invented all the things they're famous for. It was Twogood thinking that kept the Gentry ahead of the game.

To begin with we worked out how to build the tunnels, but then we started inventing all sorts of things: newer and faster ways to navigate and sail; better communications . . . better weather prediction.'

Verity was silent, taking it all in.

'We just like finding out how things fit together: it's kind of a family obsession,' Henry told her. 'And once you know how something works, you can improve it. Some of our inventions are still the best you can find,' he added proudly. 'Hardly any of them were acknowledged as ours, because we were Gentry. We did tons of work on compasses, barometers, telescopes . . . lots of modern devices.'

Verity frowned. On the far side of the shore she could see the strange boy. 'Jeb Tempest,' she said excitedly.

Henry rolled his eyes disapprovingly. Ignoring him, she ran along the beach towards the boy.

'Verity, where are you going?' Henry called after her.

'Excuse me, excuse me,' she shouted at Jeb. He stopped and looked in her direction. 'How do you know my grand-mother?' she asked.

He stared at her for a second, then quickly turned to head towards the town.

'He completely ignored me,' said Verity, turning back to Henry in exasperation.

He had finally managed to catch up with her. 'I told you the Tempests are peculiar,' he said. 'Come on. Let's go home.'

Jeb continued striding towards the Spyglass Inn, cursing himself. He hadn't expected the Gallant girl to come running up to him – all windblown hair and pink cheeks – asking questions about her grandmother like that. Especially with the Twogood nipper standing there looking so snotty. It had completely thrown him.

On the other side of Wellow, Villainous Usage was also discomposed. He sat quietly in the corner of the room as Mother took a fourth bun from the paper bag she was holding and bit into it angrily. This last week he'd found that keeping quiet was the safest option.

Villainous couldn't make head nor tail of it. He knew from Mother – and any number of Spyglass regulars – that the glory days of wrecking, led by his father, had yielded easy money. Now the *Storm* was back in Wellow there should have been no obstacle. And yet every usual avenue of opportunity they tried had been unexpectedly or mysteriously cut off. The great ship was there, right there to be seen, anchored at sea. The *Lady Georgia* was due any day: an entire packet ship which they knew for sure carried an extraordinary cargo of gold bullion. And still no way of driving her onto the rocks.

Mother's mood was not improved at present by the unexpected visitor standing in front of her. Jasper Cutgrass continued with his unfruitful enquiries. He paused for a few seconds before speaking. Jasper *always* paused for a few seconds before speaking. It was one of the characteristics that divided opinion on him so fiercely.

'It does seem surprising to me,' he said, 'that the *Storm* should be in Wellow and yet a family of the Usages' heritage is unable to board.'

'To both of us, sir,' Mother snapped angrily. Could he have phrased a question that would aggravate her more?

Jasper sighed and went over to the tiny dirty window, gazing out. Villainous stared mutely at their peculiar guest as he gingerly swapped the strap of his custom-made canvas bag from one shoulder to the other. Villainous was good at watching people. He got a lot of time for it in the company of Mother, who discouraged unsolicited conversation. Jasper adjusted the bag to sit more snugly against his hip, moving it carefully – as if his life depended on it.

'The, er, *device* your husband commissioned . . .' he began, getting back to the real reason for his visit.

This was too much for Mother. What little patience she had dissolved. 'If we had it still, do you think I'd be sat here talking to you when there's cargo I could be claiming?' she spat.

Jasper decided to put this comment down to the famous Gentry sense of humour. 'Ha,' he laughed cautiously. 'Well, quite.'

Mother hauled herself out of her chair and lumbered over to look her unwelcome guest squarely in the eye. 'Whatever you're looking for,' she snarled, flecks of angry spittle flying as she spoke, 'you en't gettin' any 'elp from me. So I suggest you 'op it.'

Jasper's eyes widened. Her breath alone was quite terrifying. Questioning the Usages had been a long shot, he knew, but even he could sense it was time to leave now.

# Book Two
# WINTER

## Chapter Eleven

We all need to feel we belong somewhere, so it was not particularly surprising that as Verity became less comfortable in her own home, she grew fonder of Henry's. And since it seemed clear that Verity's grandmother had been trying to keep them apart, both Verity and Henry were all the more inclined to stick together like glue.

The *Storm* remained anchored at sea: a dark and brooding presence lodged just outside the remote little town. The circumstances of her return were nothing like the tales of her halcyon days. It was if she were waiting.

Verity couldn't shake the feeling that there was something unusual about recent events. But Henry was not likely to abandon a lifetime of believing that there is a logical explanation for any phenomenon. Instead he focused on taking her mind off things. Which was easier at some times than at others.

'Verity, no one goes sailing in the winter. It's too cold,' he grumbled as they pushed *Poor Honesty* down the shingle beach.

'It's a lovely day,' she said.

Henry sighed and decided it was easier to keep pushing the dinghy. They'd had this debate many times now and he never won. Though he had to admit that the weather *was* lovely. The air was crisp and cold. The sky was icy blue and the sun was shining low and dazzling.

'Well, I'm not casting off.' It was an admission of defeat.

'That's fine,' said Verity, cheerfully taking off her socks and shoes. 'Hop in.'

Watching her hold the rudder in place, then jump deftly into the boat, Henry thought how quickly she'd taken to sailing. She really was a natural. It never seemed to matter how choppy the sea got, or how fast the wind blew, Verity just enjoyed the thrill all the more. And her technique was good too. Whenever you explained something to her, she listened very intently and then did precisely what you'd told her to.

Out here on the open sea, she seemed so different to the solemn little girl who turned up at Priory Bay each day. Henry decided not to ask her how life was at home. He knew what the answer would be. 'Still no sign of Alice?' he said instead.

Verity pulled a face that indicated not. There had been neither sight nor sound of her since she had dropped them both off at the club for the tactics session, and rather mysteriously mentioned that she would be 'going away'.

'I wonder where she is,' mused Henry.

Verity said nothing. Obviously Alice was free to come and go as she pleased, but Verity couldn't help feeling a little abandoned by the friend who had been a part of her life for as long as she could remember.

Henry nudged her, nodding towards the horizon. 'Here's trouble,' he said. 'That's the Blakes' dinghy.'

Verity's heart sank as she recognized the diminutive figure of Miranda heading straight for them.

'An entire channel to sail through,' said Henry, 'and we bump into her.'

Henry started to steer away from the other dinghy, but Miranda was too fast for him. Anticipating his move, she sliced in front of *Poor Honesty*. He swore and went head to wind.

'Gallant,' Miranda cooed across the water. 'Spending time with your little friend?' Verity said nothing. 'What a practical outfit,' the venomous girl added with a smirk. 'Another classic combination . . .'

Verity glanced down at Henry's loaned deck shoes, Mother's trousers and a moth-eaten jumper she'd rescued from the jumble. Inside she shrank with shame.

'Back off, Blake,' barked Henry angrily.

Miranda watched them for a second. 'How sweet,' she lisped as she manoeuvred her boat away. 'Always there to defend you, isn't he?'

'Poisonous shrimp,' said Henry contemptuously as Miranda's smirking face receded into the distance.

Verity smiled, but in her heart of hearts she knew Miranda was right. As her mother was always saying, she looked like a sack of potatoes tied in the middle. A really sensible, quite lumpy sack.

'You should know better, Henry,' Mrs Twogood scolded as she vigorously towel-dried Verity's hair.

Verity stood in the middle of the room, enjoying the fragrant warmth of the wood-burner after the icy cold of outside. Sitting in an armchair, only Henry could see her mischievous grin as she was buffeted about by his mother's determination to remove every last drop of moisture.

'Encouraging young Verity to catch her death on that blessed boat.'

'It was quite a nice day,' said Henry mildly as he bit into another slice of hot buttered toast.

'That's not the point,' said Mrs Twogood, picking up a brush with which to drag Verity's hair into submission. 'Nice young girls like Verity aren't as hardy as you boys. You need to think on that.'

Verity winced as the bristles made their way through her unruly locks.

'There you go, my love. Finished at last.' Mrs Twogood smiled. 'How about another pot of tea?' Not waiting for the answer, she disappeared into the kitchen.

'Hair-brushing hurt, did it?' asked Henry.

'A bit,' admitted Verity.

'Good,' he said, taking the last slice of toast.

'Backgammon?' she suggested.

They played by the Twogoods' sitting-room fire. Around them and over their heads raged a heated battle about Percy's cricket bat, with regard to current whereabouts (unknown), last previous sightings (in Will's possession) and Will's ability to comprehend the concept of ownership (brought into doubt by Percy).

Henry took his last piece off the board. 'Three all,' he crowed victoriously.

Verity frowned. 'Why do you think Wellow in particular was home to the Gentry?' she asked, returning to her favourite topic of conversation.

Henry pulled a face. Verity's obsession with the Gentry and her grandfather was relentless.

'Isolated places have always been ideal for smuggling,' he said matter-of-factly. 'Once the government imposes high taxes, you're guaranteed to find someone who's prepared to smuggle goods.'

'I found a section on Gentry shanties today,' said Verity, setting out the counters for a new game. (She didn't have to ask – she knew Henry would want a re-match.) 'They're quite gruesome – listen to this one. She fished a book out of her school bag and read out the scribbled notes:

*'So she cracked on his ribcage, clackety-clack,*
*And she broke it in two, snappety-snap,*

*She fetched out his heart when she tore him apart,*
*So he won't be coming back, Mrs Jones,*
*No he won't be coming back.'*

She laughed. 'Isn't that horrible?'

Henry rolled his eyes, shaking a dice to start. 'It's a song,' he said, refusing to rise to the bait. 'They made up mumbo jumbo like that to frighten people. They used violence and intimidation to get their own way, and now you're perpetuating it.'

Percy looked up from his current task of attempting to stuff a struggling Will head-first down the side of an arm-chair. 'Are you *still* going on about the blasted Gentry?' he asked Verity in mock indignation. 'Good lord, girl, if our father could hear you. They were a bunch of wrong 'uns – that's all you need to know.'

Verity giggled. She knew Henry and his dad disapproved of the Gentry, but to her they were thrilling: outrunning customs men on the high seas, travelling the world making deals, making up tall tales to keep people in line . . . it was captivating.

Returning home as late as she dared that afternoon, Verity closed the front door nervously, gripping the strange wooden ball for comfort. Since Grandmother had arrived she could never tell what kind of atmosphere she'd have to face, and she dreaded it. Usually it was best to slip unnoticed to her room, and read.

Poppy came bounding down the stairs. 'There you are,' she said, beaming. 'You'll never guess . . .'

Verity wondered what could have happened. A small flicker of hope lit in her stomach. Perhaps her grandmother had decided to leave?

'Little Verity . . .' Grandmother appeared silently in the hallway, a look of thinly concealed anger dancing across her features. 'It appears you have a mysterious benefactor.'

Verity had no idea what she was talking about. The old lady leaned over and, with a single finger, closed her granddaughter's jaw.

'Do come and look.' Grabbing her sister's hand and pulling her up the stairs, Poppy opened the door of Verity's room to reveal a gigantic brown leather trunk dominating the bed. 'It just arrived,' she breathed. 'Isn't it exciting?'

Verity stared at it. A label glued to the side announced that the contents were for Miss Verity Gallant's personal attention only.

'We're all dying of curiosity. I for one am desperate to know what's inside,' chattered Poppy. 'Quite lucky you came back now,' she added more quietly. 'I think Grandmother was about to investigate herself.' Poppy giggled at her little joke.

Verity smiled wryly and reflected that her sister was probably closer to the truth than she realized.

'Open it then,' urged Poppy, scarcely able to contain herself.

Verity moved forward to undo the brass clasp. The

heavy lid swung open with a thud, restrained only by its inner straps. She pulled off the top layer of tissue. The two girls gasped. Piled into the copious trunk were layer upon layer of clothes, interlaced with tissue and other boxes, presumably containing smaller items.

Balancing on top of it all was a delicate pair of black patent shoes with a tiny embroidered flower on each outside heel. Verity picked them up in wonder. Inside one was a card.

'*With love from Alice*,' she read aloud. She smiled happily. Wherever she was, her old friend hadn't forgotten her after all.

'They're *beautiful*,' squealed Poppy excitedly. 'Try them on.'

Verity placed the shoes carefully on the floor. They fitted exactly. Unable to stop herself, she beamed with joy. 'They're perfect.'

'Look underneath,' said Poppy, jumping up and down and giggling with anticipation.

Verity lifted out a gorgeous party dress in scarlet silk and held it against her waist. She could tell it was just the right size.

'It's divine. Here – step into it like *this*.' Poppy bustled around, expertly guiding Verity into the stunning red creation, then leading her along to Mother's bedroom mirror.

Verity stood in front of it, biting her bottom lip as her sister fussed and tweaked. Then she grinned. The dress was magical. And incredibly flattering.

'You look lovely,' Poppy clapped her hands happily and gave her a kiss.

Verity turned to glance anxiously at her. 'Some of the clothes must be for you too . . .'

'Don't worry about that,' called Poppy as she ran back into Verity's bedroom. 'Here,' she said, carefully pulling off a layer of tissue to reveal a velvet-trimmed coat, then a kitten-soft cream scarf with matching gloves. 'Try these next.'

Verity was touched by Poppy's unremittingly generous nature. She put her hand into the trunk to retrieve the next layer and gasped with delight. This was best of all: a neatly folded pair of navy blue cotton trousers and an oilskin smock. 'For sailing . . .' she whispered. 'Oh, Alice, how did you know?' She looked at Poppy, somewhat embarrassed.

'It's all right,' said Poppy soothingly. 'I know why she did it. You always seem to come off worse when we go on shopping trips – those dreadful sailing shoes, for example.'

'They were pretty hideous,' agreed Verity, able to smile about them now as she lifted out a charming floral dress that was just the right length. Her sister was playing with a second scarf and glove set, this time in pink.

'You should have those,' Verity insisted. 'They're much more your colour anyway.'

'I couldn't,' said Poppy, putting them down.

Verity handed them to her. 'I'd really like it if you did.'

Poppy couldn't resist any longer. 'Well, they are very pretty . . .' Jumping off the bed, she gave Verity a hug of thanks, then ran out of the room to show Mother.

Verity reached into the trunk to remove the last vestiges of tissue paper. There at the bottom was a note. She opened it.

*Dearest Verity,*

*I'm so sorry that this trip has taken longer than expected. I miss our weekly chats more than I can say. But I have every confidence that Henry is looking after you very well. Of course the one benefit of travel is that you come across any number of boutiques. I hope you approve of my choices. All were selected because I thought they would suit you particularly well.*

*You are in my thoughts, and I hope that from time to time you think of me also.*

*With love and regards from your friend,*
*Alice*

Verity smiled warmly. Dear Alice. How she missed her.

'You needn't think it'll be easier at school because of a few clothes,' said Grandmother, appearing silently at her bedroom door. 'It's you they don't like.'

Striding angrily to the window, she swept past with a force that literally knocked Verity off her feet, then smirked as she picked herself up from the floor. 'Do watch where you're going, child,' she said. 'You might cause a mishap with such clumsiness.'

\*   \*   \*

Mrs Gallant sat at the dining table, polishing the silver cutlery set reserved for visitors and special occasions. Each knife, fork and spoon was carefully wiped and buffed, before being slotted back in its allotted niche within the canteen. She sighed. She had forgotten how uncomfortable it was being pregnant. And how inelegant.

Meanwhile her husband was of scant comfort. She frowned irritably. Since the moment they announced the news he'd been really quite useless. As her mother-in-law was constantly reminding her, she needed as much help around the house as she could get. Surely he could see that? She could only assume that his latest manuscript must be particularly consuming.

Mrs Gallant wondered how much longer their unexpected guest would be staying? Somehow the topic never came up in conversation, and it was impossible to get any constructive information from her husband.

As if summoned by her thoughts, the old lady appeared silently in the room. Mrs Gallant quelled her natural impulse to jump.

'I find your condition very often unsettles the nerves, dear,' commented her mother-in-law. Taking a knife and the polishing rag out of her hands, she began to rub industriously.

Mrs Gallant stifled a feeling of irritation. She found tasks like this quite soothing.

'There will be no opportunity for such things when the baby arrives,' commented her guest. 'Such an exciting time for you.'

'Oh . . . er, yes . . .'

'I too cannot wait,' said the old lady thoughtfully, lost in her task for a moment. 'Truly, I cannot wait. Such a shame Verity cannot bring herself to share in your pleasure,' she continued lightly, herself once more. 'I suppose it is not in her nature.'

Mrs Gallant blinked, a little taken aback. 'Verity has always been very reserved,' she explained. 'I'm sure she'll be more enthusiastic when the baby is here.'

'I'm sure,' agreed Grandmother soothingly.

Meanwhile Jasper Cutgrass could not afford to make even one stumbling or ungainly move. He turned off Wellow's rope walk and made his way carefully through the puddle-filled yard of Lapp and Muster, taking care not to disturb the contents of the custom-made square bag on his shoulder.

In front of him rose a row of immense wooden boat sheds lining the water's edge. Approaching one, he pushed open a small cut-out door. Jasper stepped over the ledge and into a cathedral-like space filled with light and wood-dust. He stood there for a few seconds, breathing in the heady scent of hemp, spruce and pitch: the raw materials of boatbuilding.

Spread out on benches lay various sections of mast, some hundreds of feet long, waiting to be split or glued. Jasper walked past a huge pile of rope coils and a line of labelled sacks, then down one of the long narrow gangways between the workbenches. He asked first one man, then another. Eventually he was pointed in the direction of the sail-making loft above.

A solid man with salt and pepper hair was spreading out a large piece of cloth for cutting. His honest, intelligent face frowned with the effort of concentration.

'Dan Twogood?' asked Jasper. 'Mr Daniel Twogood?'

The man didn't look up but he stopped what he was doing. 'Revenue man,' he said.

It wasn't the most welcoming introduction Jasper had ever heard (although it was by no means the worst either), but as a succinct statement of fact it couldn't be faulted.

'Mr Twogood,' said Jasper, 'I'm here to ask you about a device I believe was originally invented by your family.'

Daniel Twogood looked at the custom-made canvas bag hanging from Jasper's shoulder. He noted his unseasonably brown skin. 'Lots of things bin invented by the Twogoods,' he said roughly.

'Indeed,' said Jasper. 'I see from documentation in the library that many useful modern instruments can in fact be attributed to the Twogoods' ingenuity – but few were quite as brilliant or clever as this.'

He opened the bag and lifted out a glass globe within which two separate liquids floated, like water and oil. It sat in a custom-made gimble. Like a maritime compass, the gimble held the ball so it was constantly upright, constantly unshaken.

Mr Twogood stiffened. 'Where did you get it?' he asked eventually.

'We excavated it from a casket on the Atlantic sea bed,' said Jasper.

Mr Twogood's face darkened. '*We?*'

'My former colleague and I,' Jasper elaborated.

'You found it by accident?'

'No. I deducted that its existence – although improbable – was certainly possible. Then we tracked down its various likely locations. Luckily we were right first time.'

'Lucky indeed,' said Mr Twogood bitterly. 'Well,' he continued, 'strikes me that two men clever enough to find it don't need my help. So unless you've a warrant to enforce your questions, I suggest you leave.'

'I know how to control it,' said Jasper quickly as he turned away.

Mr Twogood swung slowly back. 'No one knows how to control it,' he said darkly.

'It works on the principle of centrifugal force.' Jasper sensed he had a very small window of opportunity here. 'The fire and ice are held in the two immiscible liquids, which stay perfectly balanced, so that it is in fact spinning relative to its outer surface.

'The human body acts as a counterweight,' he continued, 'so by holding the ball at arm's length you lessen the effect. But the faster you move it, the more violent the meteorological disturbance. That's how my colleague died, I assume . . .'

Mr Twogood nodded. *Former colleague*, of course. 'Shake it, did he?' he asked.

'I imagine so,' said Jasper.

'Find much of him afterwards?'

'Not a lot.'

'And it was worth it, was it? Losing a life to gain the knowledge?'

Jasper bit his lip and said nothing.

'I expect you felt mighty pleased with yourself when you worked it all out,' Dan Twogood commented. 'Holding it gives you quite a feeling of power, I'm told.'

Jasper couldn't help it. 'I was pretty excited, yes,' he said. 'The first person in decades to hold a Storm Bringer, when everyone thought they were just a myth. It was exhilarating.'

'So why are you telling me this?'

'Your family made the original. It must be the prototype,' said Jasper enthusiastically. 'Together we could make more.'

Mr Twogood banged a hard wooden block down on the workbench in fury. 'Make *more*?' he shouted.

Jasper misunderstood him. 'My inquiries indicate you are at least as capable as your father, Mr Twogood. I have every faith you would be able to replicate the craftwork. There are so many applications it could be put to,' he added animatedly. 'All kinds of purposes.'

'You interfering pillock,' cursed Mr Twogood furiously. 'Have you any idea what you've brought on us?'

Jasper took a step backwards.

'I expect it all seemed absolutely fascinatin' when you

was sat in your library reading up on it,' growled Dan Twogood. 'But now you've got it there in your bag, how long do you think you'll keep it safe?'

'I'm a Preventative Man,' said Jasper primly. 'I have the law on my side.'

'Oh, the law . . . Good for you.' Mr Twogood walked up to Jasper and stared him straight in the eye.

Jasper swallowed nervously.

'There are those in Wellow – never mind the rest of the world – who would use that thing to get whatever they want, no matter how many they kill as a consequence,' said Mr Twogood carefully. 'I hope you can live with that.'

## Chapter Twelve

Verity couldn't wait to go to school and wear her new clothes. The shoes sparkled in her mind for the rest of the weekend. On Monday morning she felt like a princess as she walked through the park in her velvet-trimmed coat. The cream scarf and gloves were so soft she kept furtively stroking them against her cheek and smiling.

'Been on a shopping trip at last?' asked one girl at the school gates.

'Not bad,' said another approvingly. 'For a beginner.'

Verity skipped up to Henry, whom she'd spotted trudging in through the western gate. He looked a bit bed-shaped.

'Morning,' she trilled.

'You're perky,' he grumbled.

Verity beamed sunnily. 'I have a feeling it's going to be a good week.'

'Hmph,' said Henry blearily. 'Well, new clothes will do that for you.'

\*　　\*　　\*

At first break their form teacher bore down purposefully on Verity and Henry.

'Gallant,' Mrs Attrill started. 'Just the person.'

Verity looked at her warily.

'Got a new pupil here: Martha Platt. Needs looking after.'

Verity and Henry craned round her. A small girl with precisely bobbed hair, a round freckled face and even rounder gold-rimmed glasses peered owlishly at them.

'Never easy starting a new school mid-term,' said Mrs Attrill loudly, as if this would somehow make her charge feel better.

It was pretty clear from the look on Henry's face that he wasn't thrilled at the prospect of chaperoning this new pupil. The owlish girl blinked.

Verity knew all too well what it felt like to not fit in. 'Of course we'll look after her,' she said to the teacher.

Henry's face leaped into a new arrangement intended to convey extreme alarm and disapproval. He might as well have shrieked, *What are you doing?* at the top of his voice while flapping his arms wildly.

Verity ignored him. 'I'm Verity,' she said to the new girl. 'And this is Henry.'

Half an hour later Verity was already regretting her decision. She was regretting it bitterly. The new girl was now sitting between her and Henry, talking loudly and at speed. Her arms were folded and she was leaning back, looking as if this was the last place on earth she wanted to be. Occasionally she tucked a sleek lock of hair behind her right ear.

Already they knew that Martha had moved to Wellow against her wishes . . . that her parents were doctors . . . that the Platts were 'terrifically intelligent' . . . that they took Martha with them wherever they were studying, often as a research assistant . . . that she had quickly formed a very low opinion of Wellow and its amenities . . . and that great things were expected of her academically. On this topic she was currently holding forth.

'All our family read at Cambridge – wouldn't dream of going to Oxford. I'll read physics or chemistry. The arts are so plebeian these days.'

Verity scowled silently, unable to get a word in edge-ways. How could someone look so sweet and then be so insufferable? 'She's full of herself,' she said to Henry as they scurried across the park, having dodged Martha at last bell. 'Why does she need anyone to keep an eye on her?'

'She's just talking like that to try and buoy herself up,' he replied, not quite sure why he was defending her.

'She's so disapproving too,' Verity added. 'Nothing's right for her here.'

'Mm,' said Henry. 'Another person to look down on us.' He smiled ruefully.

Verity looked at him. 'I didn't realize there'd be people *outside* Wellow who wouldn't like us.'

Henry smiled at her optimism.

'Well, that's quite good then, isn't it?' she replied.

He pulled a face. 'Yeah, it's great.'

Verity elaborated: 'I mean, if people are always going to think we don't fit in, then we shouldn't worry about it, should we?'

Henry was staring at her with a barely suppressed grin. 'It wasn't weighing heavily on my mind,' he said. 'So Miranda Blake thinks I'm a commoner . . . and a few of the girls at school don't like some of your clothes. Who cares?' He shrugged. 'I'd be more worried if they *did* like us.'

Verity giggled. Henry was right. The only opinions that mattered were those of the people she cared about. Above them, the brooding winter sky swirled as the clouds were pushed and shoved by the wind, so dark they looked as if they were scowling down on the happy little girl and her friend.

Christmas was approaching rapidly now. At Priory Bay all the pupils exchanged cards like sweets and discussed plans excitedly. Henry was particularly animated because it looked like his long-term campaign to inherit a bike belonging to an older brother might at last come to fruition. Meanwhile Verity was dreading time off school because it inevitably meant more at home.

They resigned themselves to being stuck with Martha Platt during lessons but developed a sophisticated system of signals and excuses to ensure they rarely saw her during breaks or lunch times. And that they never, ever got stuck with her at close of day.

Occasionally Verity caught a glimpse of Martha standing on her own in the distance, looking lonely. But then she reminded herself of the pompous bore lurking underneath.

Finally the last day of term arrived, and with it the Priory Bay Christmas Spectacular. This event was always held in partnership with Whale Chine, in what was billed as a seasonal display of goodwill but was in fact a biennial exercise in outdoing the other school's efforts.

This year it was Priory Bay's turn to host, and the entire school thrummed with excitement at the prospect of showing those Whale Chiners how to throw a party. There would be stalls – with tombolas and mince pies and gingerbread and hot spiced drinks – and a Father Christmas, and carols and an end-of-year revue . . . it was all anyone could talk about.

Verity followed uncomfortably in her new red silk dress as Grandmother swept into the main hall, not appearing to notice the small children who were wrong-footed by her suddenly and imperiously flinging open the entrance doors.

Beside her, Poppy gasped. Every wall was covered in wreaths of holly. Mistletoe hung from the chandelier. In the crook of the grand staircase stood a gigantic tree, adorned with candles, golden glass baubles and garlands of tinsel. Lights shone prettily from every available window space or niche.

'It's just beautiful,' she breathed happily, grabbing Verity's arm. 'Isn't it?'

Verity nodded quietly. She watched as her mother carefully negotiated the room, mindful of her bump. Father had elected to stay at home in his study. What would it be like next year when the baby was here? Would Grandmother still be with them? Was this their new family now? To be honest, the festivity of the revue made her feel all the more sad that she was dreading Christmas at home so much.

'Is it not good enough for you?' demanded Grandmother snidely, poking her in the ribs.

Verity bit her tongue, unwilling to make a scene in public and spoil Poppy's day out.

'Oh, Grandmother, you are silly,' giggled her sister as she beamed in greeting at friend after friend.

Verity stifled a momentary flash of irritation. Why did Poppy and her mother never notice the spite in the old lady's comments?

'My holiday homework,' Poppy exclaimed, tapping her head in remembrance. 'I should collect it now, before I forget again.'

'Verity will go for you,' said Grandmother, giving Verity an unseen shove that made her stumble. She frowned, and the old lady glared in response. 'Have you something better to do?' she asked sharply.

'Could you, Verity?' asked Mother. 'It would be such a help.'

'She'll only waste time talking to the little fat boy otherwise,' Verity heard Grandmother saying as she walked off. 'Such a shame she can't find any proper friends.'

The room was filled with excited babble, children darting confidently from group to group, comfortable in their surroundings. There was Henry, queuing for raffle tickets.

'Where's your family?' he asked, sucking a humbug.

'By the tombola,' said Verity. 'Grandmother sent me on an errand for Poppy.'

Henry pulled a face in sympathy.

'No, it's better this way,' she pointed out. 'The less time I spend in her company, the better.'

'Just what everyone looks for in a house guest. No sign of her leaving then?' he asked.

'None at all. And I wouldn't dare ask. She's really quite frightening. Sometimes she moves so fast it's as if she can be in two places at once.' Verity caught Henry looking at her with misgiving. 'But of *course* I realize she's just an ordinary old lady and nothing peculiar is going on,' she added sarcastically.

'Poppy's got one of the lead parts, hasn't she?' said Henry, changing the subject.

Verity nodded. 'She's been looking forward to the revue for months – which reminds me' – she recalled the task at hand – 'I should go and collect her books.'

She slipped into the quiet of Poppy's form room, pleased to have escaped the throng for a second. She made her way over to her sister's desk and retrieved the forgotten homework, lingering to have an inquisitive flick through . . . Verity froze in mid page-turn. She had just heard the unmistakable sound of someone sniffing underneath the desk. She peered around to see who was there. Crouched on the floor was Martha Platt, her face puffy and red, a few telltale tears running down her cheeks.

Verity felt awful. 'Martha . . .' she said softly.

The bookish girl clambered out of her hiding place and sniffed again, her hair noticeably less perfect than usual.

'What's the matter?' asked Verity kindly.

'I thought I'd come because it was a party,' said Martha unhappily, 'and it would be fun' – her voice broke a little – 'but it's still lonely when nobody wants to talk to you.'

Verity didn't know what to say. She was a terrible person. Here was this girl, in a similar situation to herself, and she'd just ignored her.

'I know I come across badly,' blurted out Martha, wiping her face with a shirt sleeve. 'I think it's nerves . . . or something. I'm not as stuck-up when you get to know me.'

Verity smiled. 'I haven't been to many parties,' she said kindly, 'but Henry tells me they're often not as good as you think they're going to be . . . something about fun not being fun when it's organized.' She reached in her pocket for a clean hankie and handed it to Martha. 'We shouldn't have avoided you,' she told her.

'It's all right,' sniffed Martha. 'I don't make it easy for people to like me.'

'Why don't we go to the loo and wash your face?' Verity suggested.

By the time Martha looked a little less blotchy, the

end-of-year revue was in full swing on the temporarily erected stage in the Hunter Hall. Verity craned to look across the seats, hunting for her family, but there were no spaces anywhere near them.

As the two girls stood together at the back watching the show, Verity's attention started to wander. Gazing across the crowd, she realized that the Blake family were all seated a few rows in front of her. Miranda was completely dwarfed by George and Oscar – both pink of cheek and blank of eye, with unruly floppy hair. Their smaller blond brother was tucked away on the other side of the Blake parents. How confident they all looked, mused Verity. As if the world were theirs for the taking.

Looking round, Miranda Blake caught sight of her and said something to her mother, who smiled superciliously. 'Not at all surprised . . .' Miranda stage-whispered. 'If she were my relative I wouldn't want to be seen with her either.'

Verity gripped the wooden ball – her constant companion – in her pocket. *It would be more of a worry if she did like you*, she reminded herself, and stared blankly at Miranda, determined not to give her the satisfaction of looking hurt. Then she raised her hand, mimicking the patronizing wave Miranda had used at the sailing club. The shrewish little girl looked furious. Verity felt a small glow of triumph.

'You don't seem to have spent a lot of time with your family,' observed Martha cautiously as they shuffled out at the end.

'No, but actually it's been quite a relief,' Verity admitted. Realizing how that must sound, she started trying to explain herself.

'It's all right,' interrupted Martha. 'I think I understand . . . It can be pretty lonely living with my parents,' she elaborated. 'I mean – I suppose it's good that they treat me more like an adult, but sometimes I think they forget I'm there.'

Verity smiled sympathetically.

'And just recently,' said Martha sadly, 'they haven't been getting on very well. Sitting at the dining table through one of their "debates" can be pretty depressing.'

Verity didn't know what to say. No wonder Martha could be awkward at times.

'Thanks for being so nice to me,' the new girl said as they reached the main hall.

Verity blushed, embarrassed to think that her thoughtless behaviour had contributed to Martha's unhappiness. 'Happy Christmas,' she said, and gave Martha a hug that was also an apology. The little girl felt so small and vulnerable, even wrapped up in her thick winter coat. Her woollen scarf tickled Verity's face.

Martha smiled and hugged her back. 'See you in two weeks' time,' she said.


It was Christmas Eve at last. The air was fresh and sharp, the sky so clear that each star, each swirl of firmament could be seen. The night was velvety silent, as, in each and every home, children went quietly to bed, anxious for this one last chance to show how good they could be.

All save Miranda Blake – who was instead proving her worth by sitting in the cabin suite of the *Storm* with her parents. She looked again in satisfaction at her new ivory silk dress with puffball sleeves and accompanying mulberry velvet cape. She twirled her ankles to get a better view of the matching slippers that adorned her feet. This, she felt, was entirely as things should be.

'Don't you think they're pretty?' she asked her mother, tugging at her skirts for attention.

Mrs Blake glanced down at her only daughter with barely concealed irritation. 'Not now, Miranda. Father and I are talking.' She turned back to her husband and continued *sotto voce*, 'And the furnishings . . . everything to the very highest specification, Rupert.' Her eyes darted greedily around the wood-panelled dining room, fitted with stunningly crafted lockers, decorated with the most sumptuous materials and lit now by weighted bronze lamps.

'There's always been money around the *Storm*,' her husband replied in a baritone rumble deepened by the liberal and regular application of port and cigars.

A thought occurred to Mrs Blake, and she turned to her daughter again, smoothing her dress and pinching her cheeks to bring a colour to them. Miranda smiled at the attention, trying to catch her mother's eye.

Mrs Blake ignored her. 'Don't mess this up, Miranda,' she said briskly. 'We're relying on you.'

Miranda stared at her reflectively, thinking of the dozens of visits she'd already made to the *Storm* as part of this charm offensive. 'Of course not,' she replied efficiently. 'You can rely on me.'

Abednego came silently into the room. Today he wore a soft white shirt and an emerald jacket. The gold jewellery in his ears and on his wrists and neck shone brightly against his ebony skin. 'The Mistress is ready for you now,' he said.

Miranda's parents headed for the doors that led to the heart of the cabin suite, Mrs Blake struggling to hide her anticipation.

Abednego's handsome almond-shaped eyes glinted with tears as he watched her push her only girl child eagerly in front of her. *A minnow to catch a shark*, he thought to himself sadly as he closed the doors regretfully behind them.

For Villainous Usage, Christmas Eve was a less stately affair. He sat quietly on his own, eating a bowl of broth and thanking his lucky stars Mother was out. The last few weeks had been a time of bitter frustration for her, and consequently of uncomfortable anxiety for all in her vicinity.

The window of the front room shook as the door swung open violently. Villainous shrank back in his chair. But the black mood that had dogged Mother over the last six weeks seemed to have lifted.

'There's a *second* packet ship,' she announced jubilantly, with a slight slur that made it obvious she'd discovered this news in the Spyglass. 'The *Lady Georgia* is to be followed by the *Helmingham*.' She pinched Villainous' pustule-ridden cheek. 'Tardy Paul has said we can borrow his rowing boat.'

Villainous waited to find out why.

'We must go directly to the *Storm*.' Mother swung an arm out in the general direction of the harbour. 'If I can just talk to Abednego a while longer, I'm sure he'll remember how profitable the old days were, and see sense. We can't miss this one. It's meant for us.'

Villainous' ferret-thin face went a little pale. 'Approach the *Storm* uninvited?' he said. 'Are you sure, Muvver?' His mind crowded with rumours he'd heard of the sometimes fatal manner in which the *Storm* dealt with unannounced guests.

Mother swayed towards him. Her eyes were having difficulty focusing but the menace could still be clearly felt. 'We must go there now, son. And you will row me.'

Villainous reflected that a death later on the *Storm* might be less inglorious than one in the cottage at the hands of Mother. 'I'll get my coat,' he said.

But Mother was not to need her passage to the *Storm*, for there on the harbour, as Villainous helped her down the narrow street, was Abednego himself, assisting Miranda Blake and her parents out of a tender. It was dark now, and the inky black water lapped gently against the quay.

Mother Usage hissed with righteous indignation. She pulled herself up to her full rotund height and bustled along as fast as her weight would allow in the direction of her quarry.

'So it's like that, is it?' she demanded of the *Storm*'s captain. 'Only got need for such as the Blakes?'

'*Really*,' Mrs Blake whispered disdainfully. Not too loudly, because even she knew that Mother Usage was not someone to cross.

'There was a time when our plans were acceptable,' Mother carried on full throttle. 'What's changed that you can turn us away so high and mighty? Just one storm,' she demanded angrily, so lost in her ill temper that she gave no thought to the captain's reputation. 'Just one to bring us a little good fortune.' She squared up to him, her short round body contrasting with his tall lithe figure. 'Surely we are owed that?'

A spark of fury flashed in Abednego's eyes. He seized Mother Usage and gripped her tightly by both arms. 'You have your son,' he said with a chilling passion.

Mother Usage felt her courage draining – from the pit of her stomach and down her legs – as if it were a physical fluid.

'You have your son, and you are safe,' he repeated softly.

Mother gaped at him, a soft squeak of fear her only sound.

'That is fortune enough,' Abednego concluded.

# Chapter Thirteen

Christmas Day dawned crisp and cold. There was no snow, but the sky was a swirl of icy white, with the peculiar glow that told you it must be one of the shortest days of the year.

At midday Abednego, captain of the *Storm*, sat at the head of a heavily laden table and watched his crew – the closest thing he had to a family – celebrating.

The meat platter groaned with roast goose, duck, beef, pork and pheasants, edged by little partridges. Buttered chestnuts vied with sage and bread stuffing, baked figs and jellied fruit sauces, while large bowls of vegetables steamed quietly (mostly ignored – save for the roasted, fried and mashed potatoes). The eating and drinking would go on all day.

The men were only just beginning to tuck into the plentiful supply of port and rum, but already spirits were high and toasts were being made.

'To the Mistress,' came wafting across the air amidst cheers and jeers. A handful of those with instruments had started to play, and Abednego heard snatches of song:

*'She'll cover you in diamonds, she'll crown you with gold, she'll drown you in pearls but you'll pay with your soul . . .'*

His mind wandered back to the celebrations of his childhood . . . some happy times among the memories. He recalled the day when his older sister had received her beloved peg doll – the shiny, worn figurine that now spent every day in his pocket.

His uncle had been drinking since the morning – sitting out in the street with the other neighbourhood men and a cask of wine, playing cards, talking nonsense and having stand-up arguments with the local harlots.

Abednego had adored his sister, Abigail. Since their parents died she had been both mother and father to him, always happy to hand over food from her own meagre portion to assuage his rumbling stomach. Always there to dart in front of their uncle when he tried to beat Abednego.

He had saved all year to buy that peg doll, scraping aside a fragment of coin here, another there, until he had what he needed; until his uncle demanded the hard-won money for more drink. But Abednego stood firm and refused.

His uncle gave him such a hiding he couldn't sit down for a week. But he wouldn't say where the money was. And when his uncle grew bored of hitting and cursing, Abednego crept off secretly to the shack of the lady who sold the peg dolls, and carefully selected the prettiest one for his sister.

Abigail was enchanted by her new toy. She was the envy of her friends. Her smile shone so brightly when she held the little wooden mannequin . . . Abednego could still see it now. It had been worth every cut and weal.

Underneath the table he pulled out the doll and stroked one of the scraps of faded material, so worn now it was as soft as velvet. To continue his life as a sham . . . or to lose it with honour? This was the question that had churned around his head since that fateful day in Wellow library.

For Verity, Christmas was simply yet another day of snipes and barbs, of difficult conversations and oppressive moods that brooded over the house like a cloud. But for the moment at least, she was hidden upstairs brushing her hair and enjoying a minute's peace from Grandmother.

Giving up on the task of making herself neater, she nearly jumped out of her skin to find her elderly relative waiting on the landing. Suddenly Verity felt herself pinned against the wall. Even through her alarm, a little voice in her head wondered how someone of Grandmother's age could be so strong. But looking down, she realized that the old lady was a foot away from her. She was being held up by something she couldn't see or hear. Her clothes and hair were pressed back as if she were walking through a gale. Her throat constricted with fear, her mouth held shut. *This can't be happening, it can't be happening,* she repeated to herself in reassurance.

'Did you like your presents, Verity, my dear?' asked Grandmother, in a voice that was obviously intended to carry downstairs.

Verity looked at her. The old lady's appearance was terrifying: her skin as dark as ancient wood; her face so sunken that all her features had practically disappeared – no eyebrows, no cheeks; just the shape of a covered skull, with scraps of long dry hair in patches on her scalp.

In a bid to keep her head, Verity focused her attention on the pretty brooch Grandmother was wearing. It had an enamel centre with a picture of a dark-haired woman against a starlit backdrop, surrounded by a delicate gold frame set with pearls. Verity stared at it, desperately trying to concentrate on something that was real and solid. But still she felt cold fear trickling through her. *This can't be happening.*

'It's terribly rude to ignore your elders, Verity,' said Grandmother.

Suddenly Verity heard footsteps coming up the stairs. Unable to twist her head, she strained her eyes to the right and realized it was Father. Relief flooded over her. Now at last someone would see Grandmother in her true colours.

He stopped opposite Verity, but did nothing. Verity stared imploringly at him, still unable to speak. In reply he gazed at her as if she were a curiosity. He reached out to pat her cheek, then inspected his hand in wonder.

'You are quite a bad-mannered little girl, aren't you?' continued the old lady.

Verity mustered every ounce of will to force out a reply. 'Yes, Grandmother,' she answered politely, then felt herself slide to the floor, the mysterious force releasing her.

Her grandmother gazed at her contemptuously, then bent down and pressed her face very close to Verity's. She looked furious, as if she would very much like to hurt her but couldn't. 'Soon . . .' she whispered, almost as if it were a promise to herself.

Verity's father went to his room, shutting the door firmly behind him. Outside, the wind rattled the hallway window.

On Boxing Day morning Verity closed the front door behind her. Hardly daring to breathe, she walked quietly down the path, terrified that at any moment she might be called back in. Then, at the corner, she ran: ran as fast as her legs would carry her to get away from the brooding place that her once dull but benign home had turned into.

'Happy Christmas,' said Henry cheerfully, wrapped in a newly voluminous scarf and hat, both presents from his mother.

Verity said nothing.

Henry pulled a face. 'As tough as you expected?'

'Slightly worse actually.'

'Aren't you going to tell me about it?'

Verity shook her head. 'You wouldn't believe me,' she said emphatically.

Henry stared at her thoughtfully. *Things must be pretty bad*, he reflected.

Priory Bay was closed for the next fortnight but Verity

was desperate not to spend that time at home. And it didn't seem fair to force herself upon Mrs Twogood again.

'Six bored brothers and my dad,' said Henry, rolling his eyes. 'When I'm not being used as a punchbag, I'm having my ear clipped for back-chat.'

The air was bitterly cold, with a sea wind that cut you like a knife. Verity would happily have sat outside to freeze, but by midday she had to concede that her toes were painfully numb and her cheeks stung like fury. Even the usually hardy Henry was starting to look despondent as they sat together in a little wooden shelter on the seafront. The wrought-iron bench was so cold you could feel it seeping through your clothes from the second you perched on it.

They said nothing for at least five minutes, staring out at the churning grey sea instead. Henry had managed to cover up his face with the new scarf so that all you could see was his grey-blue eyes. They looked dejected. Verity felt really guilty. She knew he was just keeping her company.

'Why don't you go home? I'll just hang around a little bit longer,' she lied.

'' M OK,' said Henry, trying to sound like he was. 'Why don't we start walking again?' he suggested.

Getting up from the seat, which was definitely making her feel worse, Verity looked despairingly back up at Wellow and rolled the strange wooden ball around in her pocket for comfort. She'd still not mentioned it to Henry. Sometimes that made her feel guilty, but she couldn't bear the idea of him dismissing the effect it had on her – or, worse, insisting that she return it. She carried it everywhere with her now.

She wondered what the Gentry would have done when expelled by their enemies. She was pretty certain Rafe Gallant wouldn't have settled for wandering around miserably in the cold. Then Verity spotted a familiar building. Of course: sanctuary.

'The library,' she exclaimed. 'The library might be open. We could go there.'

Henry looked at her as if she'd just suggested they take a walk into a lions' cage. 'No, it's all right,' he said quickly.

Verity pulled a disbelieving face at Henry's biblio-phobia. 'You don't have to read just because you're there,' she said. 'It's Christmas. If it's open, there definitely won't be anyone else in it.' Spotting his hesitation, she pressed her point home. 'It'll be warmer than out here. Why don't we just give it a try?'

Verity pushed on the familiar red double doors, then beamed ecstatically as the right-hand one opened.

Henry shuffled in after her with the air of one who has grave misgivings. 'I'd like it to be known that I'm going along with this against my better instincts,' he grumbled.

'I think that's obvious,' replied Verity. They stood together by the entrance desk.

'Well, the heating's on,' conceded Henry.

Miss Cameron was standing on a set of library steps in

the corner of the main room, dusting a top shelf. She looked round calmly at the sound of visitors. Nothing ever discomposed Miss Cameron. 'Ah, Verity,' she said, with no outward show of surprise. 'You'll find your friend in the reading room.'

Verity and Henry looked at each other in astonishment. Who could she mean?

'Martha.'

Verity and Henry stood by the entrance to the reading room, absorbing the fact that the other person seeking refuge was their fellow outsider. Martha was sitting in a threadbare green wingback chair with her legs tucked under her. Two more upholstered chairs that had seen better days were arranged around a worn and faded rug near the fireplace. A small blaze was cracking and popping quietly, letting out a comforting glow and the fragrant scent of wood smoke. Verity was astonished: Miss Cameron never lit a fire in this room.

She had never paid much attention to the library's reading room before, but now it looked like the most welcoming place she'd ever seen. The dark burgundy walls and wooden panels gave it a warmth that contrasted with the bitter weather outside. The portraits of Wellow residents past smiled kindly down on the three children.

'What are you two doing here?' Martha asked in surprise. Then, checking herself, added, 'Sorry. That came out wrong. I just thought you'd both be at home. Like everyone else.'

Verity stood by the fire, enjoying the heat. 'Christmas didn't go well at our house,' she admitted.

Martha pulled a sympathetic face.

'You too?' Verity asked.

The other girl shrugged unhappily. 'I decided to go for a walk after Mother started throwing crockery at Father because he didn't agree with her theory on erythrocytes and reticulocytes.'

Henry was pulling off his hat and unwrapping his scarf. 'This is all right,' he said approvingly. 'There's a fire . . . and chairs.' Striding around, examining the facilities, he grew more jubilant by the minute. 'And a backgammon board too,' he added excitedly.

Verity sat down in one of the chairs, her feet tingling and itching as feeling was gradually restored. Henry and Martha moved furniture around to accommodate a table next to the armchairs. Henry went over to the window and climbed up to stand on the windowsill.

'Brilliant view from up here,' he said. 'You can see the *Storm* as clear as anything.'

Martha pulled a chair over and stood on it. 'She's quite amazing, isn't she? And isn't it strange that she's returned after all these years?'

Henry shrugged, unwilling to admit the wonder of anything related to smuggling.

'Henry doesn't approve of the Gentry,' said Verity drily.

Martha looked at him in astonishment. 'But don't you think they sound terribly thrilling?'

He threw Verity a dirty look. 'There's nothing exciting about being murdered or robbed,' he said firmly.

'You mean the wreckers?' said Martha. 'But the Gentry weren't all scavengers. I believe they made quite a distinction between the two things.'

'How do you know so much about it?'

Martha looked surprised. 'Well, obviously when I found out we were moving to Wellow I made an effort to read up on its history.'

'Obviously,' Henry grumbled.

'Naturally I won't know as much about it as you two,' Martha conceded, which made Verity laugh.

Henry huffed disapprovingly as she launched into a detailed explanation of recent events, including the strange acquisition of the red leather-bound book, her grandmother's arrival and her father's increasingly odd behaviour.

'How *fascinating*,' said Martha. 'I wonder why your father never mentioned that he's Rafe Gallant's son?'

'And how could Rafe possibly have been married to the woman who claims to be my grandmother?' Verity was thrilled to have found someone who didn't think the whole thing was just one big coincidence.

'It all started when you found the captain of the *Storm* here, in this library?' asked Martha.

'Yes,' said Verity, perking up. 'Peculiar, isn't it? Why would he give me the book?'

Henry scoffed loudly. He was over by the fire again now,

setting up the backgammon board. 'The only strange thing is that you spend so much time concocting a web of intrigue from a series of totally unrelated events.'

Verity felt a flash of irritation. 'It's easy for you to criticize,' she said crossly. 'You're not the one having to live with a terrifying relative who turned up out of the blue . . . Your father isn't acting really oddly either.'

Martha put a comforting hand on her arm. 'Why don't we have a cup of tea?' she said. 'Miss Cameron gave me a kettle and a hook for the fire and I took some cake while Mother was smashing the bowls.'

Tucked away in the library's reading room – hidden from the eyes of Wellow – Verity, Henry and Martha spent the next fortnight happily playing backgammon, chatting and reading.

Perhaps in a spirit of seasonal goodwill, Miss Cameron relaxed her usually careful approach to the spending of library funds. Each day a fire was lit before they arrived, with a basket of chopped logs set in the hearth to keep it going. Nor did she appear concerned about the usually stringent rules on talking in the library.

Following the additional introduction of a toasting fork, their new kingdom was complete. Henry brought in supplies from his mother:

'She's packed bread, butter, milk, jam, cheese, eggs, pickle, preserves, ham, liver paste and tomatoes,' he listed, revealing their booty. 'Do you think that's going to be enough?' His brow furrowed at the thought of so little food to last a full day.

'I think it will just about do,' said Verity with a grin.

It was like having their own sitting room – a home away from home. Each afternoon they pulled the thick red curtains shut when it got dark, and it felt like the safest place in the world; nothing could possibly hurt them in this oasis of calm and warmth. Gradually Martha became more comfortable with her new friends: less likely to gabble and more likely to think before she spoke – until the three of them were completely at ease in each other's company.

In addition to backgammon, Henry introduced Verity and Martha to a Turkish game called Okey, played with chips of different colours and numbers. Both girls picked it up quickly and they spent hours playing, eating toasted crumpets and drinking tea.

Martha sighed and leaned her head back against the wingback chair. 'It's so peaceful here,' she said appreciatively. 'So much nicer than being at home.'

'Mmm.' Verity nodded happily. The Gallant home – for the moment at least – felt a million miles away.

'*The eye of the storm*,' Henry said, looking appreciatively around at their hideaway. 'Much better than the chaos at our house, I can tell you.'

Verity and Martha look at him, puzzled.

'It means the calm at the centre of the gale,' he explained. 'A Gentry phrase.'

Verity smiled. 'It does feel like that,' she agreed. She

could cheerfully have stayed there for the rest of her life.

'Have you read the book?' asked Martha one morning. Verity looked up. 'The book – the one Abednego gave you on the beach.'

Henry sighed. 'Oh, she's read it all right. About a million times.'

'It's an interesting book,' Verity retorted.

'I could have a look through it,' said Martha. 'I might be able to spot something – a clue to why Abednego gave it to you. My parents have been using me as an unpaid assistant since I could read.' She tried unsuccessfully to keep the bitter tone out of her voice. 'I may as well put my skills to some use for my friends now that I have some . . . That's, um, I mean—'

Henry leaned over and shoved her affectionately on the shoulder. 'Well, of course you're a friend,' he said. 'You don't think I'd fritter away my holidays playing back-gammon with any old riff-raff?'

'Definitely,' agreed Verity earnestly.

Martha beamed, her freckled face radiant with happiness. 'Well, um, that's . . .' She tucked a strand of hair behind her right ear and looked slightly flustered.

'Why not now?' said Verity, moving over to her bag and carefully removing the book.

'Don't tell me you carry that thing around with you?' Henry said incredulously.

Verity glowered. 'I just don't trust Grandmother not to

snoop in my room. She threw away all my other books. Carrying it with me is a . . . sensible precaution.'

Martha reached out to take the red book. Verity passed it over, suppressing her irrational worries about letting it out of her possession.

Martha stared at it in astonishment. 'Is this a joke?' she asked.

Verity and Henry frowned at her, puzzled.

She smiled in wonder. 'You don't know what this is, do you?'

Verity felt a little irritated. 'I think Abednego was reading it because it talks a lot about the Mistress of the Storm,' she replied.

'I think Abednego was reading it because it's not often you come across a book that famously doesn't exist,' contradicted Martha drily.

'What do you mean?'

'This is *On the Origin of Stories*. By Hodge, Heyworth & Helerley.'

Verity nodded. It said that on the cover.

'For a literary scholar,' said Martha, 'finding this would be a bit like . . . tracking down the Golden Fleece. My parents would just die if they knew you had a copy of it in your school bag.' She giggled.

Verity looked slightly alarmed.

'Don't worry. There's no way I'd tell them. They'd probably chain me to a desk and make me research it for the next twenty years,' Martha added slightly sourly. 'The authors of this book had a theory about folklore and fairy tales,' she explained. 'They believed that some stories – which were told in many different countries around the world – came from one original source. Their claim was that these – Original Stories, they called them – were history, not fiction, and that they appeared to be repeated over and over again. Even more bizarrely, they believed there were places around the world where a story could be read aloud, and then become true.'

'That's what it says in the Prologue,' Verity agreed excitedly.

'Oh, for crying out loud,' grumbled Henry. 'Not *both* of you.'

'Shut up, Henry,' said Martha without rancour. 'So they travelled the world, cataloguing incidences of different stories, and apparently looking for these "magical" locations. Unsurprisingly, nobody paid any attention to them.'

'Oh, really,' said Henry sarcastically.

'When they returned,' Martha continued, 'they couldn't find a publisher who would take on the book, so eventually they printed a hundred copies themselves. And then . . . they disappeared. Which has made them a source of literary intrigue ever since. Most people don't believe they ever existed,' she added.

'Disappeared?' asked Verity. 'The authors disappeared?'

'The authors *and* the books. All three authors. And all one hundred copies.'

Verity looked at the book with renewed interest. 'And all the time, one was sitting in Wellow library,' she said.

'Which just goes to prove that you really are the only person who comes here,' commented Henry. He turned to Martha. 'It must be a hoax. Someone made it and left it here as a joke.'

Martha turned the volume over in her hands, inspecting it. She pulled a face. 'It could be,' she conceded. 'I'm no expert. But this yellowing appears to be genuine ageing. If it's a fake, it's an old one.' She examined the spine and frowned, holding the book up above her head. 'I think there's a section missing,' she said.

Verity's heart skipped a beat. 'Really?' she asked, gazing at the book anxiously.

Martha nodded. 'See this gap in the binding?' she said. 'It looks as if there should have been an additional chapter there: some kind of introduction perhaps?'

'But why?' Verity was angry now that anyone could damage her precious book.

'You'd be astonished at the amount of vandalism that occurs in libraries,' said Martha.

'Positive dens of iniquity,' said Henry sagely. 'This is why I stay away from them.'

'What are the stories about?' Martha asked. 'Perhaps the thief wanted one in particular.'

'A girl who can control the wind,' said Verity. 'She and her three sisters were created to harness the elements, but it's really all about her. Sometimes she's called the

Mistress – as in the Mistress of the Storm. I thought that's why Abednego came for the book – that he might have been reading about her.'

Martha was flicking through the book with interest. 'The Keepers,' she said, nodding.

'That's right. Have you heard of them?'

'They're a myth that crops up in many different countries,' said Martha. 'Let me fetch a reference book . . .' She trotted out to the main room.

'Here they are,' she continued, returning a few minutes later, 'in this collection of mariner's folk tales from around the world.'

Verity took the proffered book. There were illustrations and pictures in the centre section. She leafed through them: strange creatures carved in whale bone, models made of driftwood and walrus tusk, etchings of mythical ships and scenes. On the final page was a woodcut illustration of a terrifying-looking creature towering over a group of cowering sailors. The swirling lines around them conveyed a formidable wind.

'There she is,' said Martha. 'That's the Keeper of the Wind.'

Henry looked over the two girls' shoulders. 'Looks like your grandmother.' He grinned, then took a bite of his apple.

Verity stared at the picture. The banshee's face was twisted and distorted but she looked . . . just like Grandmother did when she lost her temper. Verity had a very peculiar feeling in her stomach – as if everything in it were draining out. *As if she were scared*. Her heart was beating rapidly.

'I was joking,' said Henry. 'She doesn't look *that* bad.'

'Not normally, no, but when she's angry, her face changes and that's *exactly* what she looks like.'

'It's just a woodcut, Verity,' Martha reassured her.

Suddenly they heard the soft click of the door closing. The three children turned round. It was Miss Cameron. Had they been making too much noise? they wondered.

'I think it's time we talked,' she said calmly.

## Chapter Fourteen

'*Time we talked?*' repeated Verity, wondering if the librarian felt they had outstayed their welcome in the reading room.

'About your grandmother,' said Miss Cameron, smoothing down the front of her skirt.

Verity's blood ran cold. Was Miss Cameron a friend of the old lady's? Perhaps she'd heard them being rude about her? 'Do you know my grandmother?' she asked carefully.

'About the fact that your grandmother is indeed the subject of your book,' Miss Cameron continued, as if they were discussing library lending policies.

Verity, Henry and Martha stared at her in shock.

'All these years of silence and books – it can't be good for you,' said Henry.

'I'm perfectly sane, thank you, Henry Twogood,' replied Miss Cameron crisply. 'I'm afraid, Verity' – she returned immediately to her main concern – 'that there are things you need to know. And the first of these is that your grandmother – your grandfather's estranged wife, that is – is in fact the Mistress of the Storm. Or the Keeper of the Wind, as she was previously known.'

'The Mistress of the Storm is a Gentry fairy tale,' said Henry, as if talking to a simpleton.

'She is much older than that,' corrected Miss Cameron. 'They merely took her legend and retold it in their own way.'

'No,' said Verity vehemently. 'She *can't* be the character in my book. The Keeper of the Wind was beautiful and charming, and popular.'

'She was. But over time she became many other things too.'

Verity sat there silently, staring at the librarian. Her sensible plaid skirt and neatly styled hair seemed to emphasize the unreality of the situation all the more.

'The authors believed the stories were true,' said Martha thoughtfully. 'If the Mistress did exist – and the Gentry knew that – how artful of them to pretend they'd invented her.'

Henry frowned at Martha. 'Not you too,' he said crossly.

'Henry,' said Martha patiently, tapping the red book, 'this is a mythical object.'

'So?' he demanded.

'So perhaps we should consider other possibilities that might previously have seemed far-fetched,' she pointed out calmly.

Miss Cameron turned to Verity. 'She is enchanting, isn't she? Absolutely captivating. Often, when I read the book, I find myself dreaming of her for days afterwards.' She smiled ruefully. 'Occasionally I dream I *am* her . . .'

Verity's heart skipped a beat in recognition. The nightmares were terrible. But sometimes . . . sometimes she woke wishing she could go straight back to her dream. She studied the librarian carefully. There was no trace of anything other than the eminently sensible and reliable woman with whom she had probably spent more time than her own family. She thought of the intimidating guest who had taken over her home; of her mysterious ability to appear silently without warning; of the way she could knock Verity over or pin her up against the wall without even touching her; and of her terrifying appearance when angry.

In that moment Verity knew that she believed Miss Cameron. No. She knew that Miss Cameron was telling the truth. It was time, she realized, to stop listening to people who told her that the strange events and coincidences of recent months could be explained by something other than this. Because they couldn't.

'Why would you wait until now to tell me this?' she asked.

Miss Cameron raised an eyebrow. 'Would you have believed me before?'

Verity laughed – a nervous reaction. Of course not. She could scarcely believe she was having this conversation now.

'You knew so little about your family history,' said Miss Cameron. 'You needed to at least begin to work things out for yourself.'

'You *did* order the book on the Gentry for me,' Verity exclaimed. 'It wasn't a mistake.'

Miss Cameron smiled quietly in agreement.

'But how do you know all this?'

'I am the librarian of Wellow.' And as if that explained everything, Miss Cameron picked up Verity's book from the table in front of her.

'*So He of the Sky said, "I will give each element a Keeper,"*' she read aloud.

Verity recognized the words instantly – could repeat them along with her unprompted:

'"*. . . to control them and protect my people." And he read out a story of their beginning: of four sisters whose duty it was to control the elements. It was a joyous event, and as he spoke, the words fell from the sky. Each place where they landed around the world became a sacred one of special powers, so that when a story was read aloud there, it would become true.*'

Henry snorted. 'That's just a load of religious guff,' he insisted.

Miss Cameron smiled mysteriously. 'The authors' theory was correct, Martha,' she continued. 'The Original Stories were all significant. Each of them was created by your grandmother, Verity. She and her three sisters knew the secret places around the world where a story could be told, and then become reality. But the Mistress – being as she is – couldn't resist taking advantage of this knowledge and telling stories from which she would benefit. Favourite amongst these were tales that centred around the acquisition of possessions . . . or other things. And her stories were destined to become true over and over again.'

'Like the smart aleck who gets granted three wishes . . . and asks for three more?' said Martha.

'Precisely,' agreed Miss Cameron. 'The authors noticed these stories and made it their work to piece them together by travelling the world and collating different recurring tales – gathering evidence for their theory, if you like. It was difficult, of course: your grandmother had been careful to cover her trail most of the time. But they were a very clever trio. When she found out, she was furious that her abuse of power had been exposed. It was she who destroyed the authors and all but two of the copies. Yours she defaced by removing the Introduction, in which they set out their purpose.'

'I knew a section was missing,' said Martha triumphantly.

'Is that why Abednego gave me the book?' asked Verity. 'So I'd realize who my grandmother really was?'

'I don't know,' admitted Miss Cameron. 'Abednego has always been fiercely loyal to his Mistress. But at any rate, he did. And that was a thoroughly good thing, because without it, you would have struggled to accept the truth.'

Verity thought for a minute about the character from her book: a woman so powerful she could create storms simply because she wished to. In her mind she was back at the window of her former bedroom, on the night the *Storm* arrived in Wellow . . . the rain beating down on the glass so heavily you could scarcely see single drops . . . the wind furiously buffeting the wooden sash frame. Grandmother had created that.

'Does she know about you?' she worried. 'Will she be suspicious that you might have told me?'

'Only your grandmother knows what she plans to do in Wellow,' said Miss Cameron. 'Her confidence is such that she won't be able to believe you are any threat to her. But you must make sure she does not change her opinion. You must not provoke her anger, Verity – that is crucial.'

Verity felt a small chill of fear. Miss Cameron was a master of understatement. If she said a thing was important, it could well mean your life would depend on it.

The librarian looked out of the reading-room window. It was dark. Looking in turn at the three children – one anxious, one indignant and one intrigued – she appeared to make a decision.

'I think that's quite enough to take in for one day,' she announced. 'Can I suggest you go home now? We can gather here tomorrow afternoon – if you are all free?'

The question was hardly necessary. Come hell or high water there was no way either Verity, Martha or even Henry would have missed the opportunity to find out more.

# Chapter Fifteen

*You must not provoke her anger, Verity – that is crucial.*

Secretly, Verity had always thought it would be exciting to discover that she was at the heart of an adventure, just like one of the heroines of her books. But the reality was a lot less exhilarating and quite a bit scarier. Miss Cameron's words kept ringing through her head. Her mind whirled with the new information she'd had to take in.

As she made her way home, she was painfully conscious that, despite the shocking revelations of the day, her behaviour had to be exactly the same as before. Closing the front door behind her, she racked her brain to remember the Verity of this morning. That person seemed aeons away now.

Mr Gallant was in the sitting room staring intently at the ceiling, as if he could see something she couldn't. Verity stood in the doorway gazing sadly at him. What had happened to him? She now knew it must have something to do with her grandmother. It couldn't be a coincidence. There had been no coincidences since she'd arrived.

Mr Gallant looked at her and grinned beatifically. His face was flushed, his hair dishevelled. 'Is something wrong?' he asked.

'No, Father,' said Verity quietly.

'Well, don't stare, child,' he said, shaking his head as if something were whisking past him. 'It's very rude to stare.' He giggled. 'Bad things happen to rude people.'

This man in front of her was not Father, Verity thought. Suddenly she turned and saw Grandmother approaching. A chill breeze floated down the hall with her. Fear gripped Verity's stomach. Their guest had everyone under her control. Miss Cameron was right: she must not provoke the old lady's anger. Who knew what the price would be if she did?

Mother was heavily pregnant and having difficulty moving around. The fabled bloom of maternity seemed to have eluded her. She looked tired and uncomfortable. Verity and Poppy helped to carry in the vegetables for dinner. Grandmother brought in Mother's prized cornflower-detail gravy boat, with a lot of fuss.

The meal started in silence, punctuated only by the uncomfortable scraping of cutlery on china and the barbs thrown in Verity's direction by her grandmother. She had come to dread dinner times.

'Little Verity has spent a lot of time enjoying herself this holiday,' said Grandmother. 'So pleasant for her,' she added with an acid smile, 'but surely a more dutiful daughter would have volunteered to help her mother?'

Verity silently spooned carrots onto her plate and stared at the jade patterned wallpaper.

'It is not too late though,' the old lady continued, running an elegant hand through her immaculate hair, as if the idea had just occurred to her, 'for her to help with the chores.'

Verity looked at her appraisingly. Why was this suddenly being brought up?

Grandmother casually twirled her string of pearls around a finger. 'After all, with Verity's looks she is unlikely to marry. She should learn to make herself useful if she is going to be a burden.'

'I might choose to work,' Verity muttered, glaring at the impostor she was so powerless against. She knew it would only make her enemy more spiteful, but for a second she didn't care.

Grandmother shot her a look of pure fury, making her skin prickle. 'A little time at home might help improve her manners,' she said. 'Perhaps it is the company she's keeping these days . . .'

The penny dropped. Her friends: Grandmother was trying to keep her away from her friends. Mother seemed flustered. Verity realized the tense atmosphere was making her uneasy.

'Of course I'd like to help,' she said, to diffuse the situation. 'But it will need to be outside of school hours – otherwise I'd be truanting, wouldn't I?'

'Always ready with an answer, little Verity,' muttered the old lady.

'That would be lovely, wouldn't it?' said Mother, trying to keep the peace.

Grandmother's mouth pursed in a moue of disapproval, which instantly robbed her patrician face of its beauty. 'I suppose it will suffice,' she said.

Verity stared at the starched linen tablecloth, chosen so carefully by her mother many years previously. She knew all too well from the stories in her book that she shouldn't be riling Grandmother. She knew it put her and her family in danger, but she couldn't help it. The old lady brought out a rebellious streak in Verity that she found hard to quell.

The next day was Verity, Henry and Martha's first back at school after the Christmas break. Never had six hours passed with such agonizing sloth.

As soon as the end-of-school bell rang, the three children sprinted from Priory Bay to the library.

'I can't stay long,' said Verity anxiously, 'otherwise Grandmother will kick up a stink.'

'So why is she in Wellow now?' asked Henry, cutting generous slices of moist plum cake from the slab donated by his mother. Verity poured the tea.

'Your grandmother believes an Original Story is unfolding which will bring about her demise,' said Miss Cameron in her usual soft voice. 'And she wishes to stop it.'

She paused to smile kindly at Verity. 'I realize this must be an awful lot to take in, so I've invited someone else to tell you a little more . . .'

Verity heard the faint slam of the red double doors, followed by a series of purposeful steps.

'Just in time,' said Miss Cameron.

The door of the reading room opened. It was the strange boy.

'Verity, Henry, Martha,' said Miss Cameron, 'I'd like you to meet Jebediah Tempest. Or Jeb, as he prefers to be known.'

Jeb Tempest stood uncomfortably in front of them, looking hot and a little flushed.

Henry made no effort to disguise his lack of enthusiasm at this new arrival. 'What's *he* doing here?' he exclaimed, managing to convey a healthy dollop of disapproval in that one question.

Jeb shot him a look of equal animosity. 'Least I'm no Twogood turncoat,' he growled.

'The Tempest family have a long and honourable history in Wellow,' said Miss Cameron. 'I'm sure you know that, Henry.'

'Honourable if you're Gentry,' Henry muttered.

Martha peered in shock at the new arrival. Jeb was staring at the floor self-consciously, hands shoved deep into the pockets of his faded and torn trousers.

Verity's mind was a whirl of vindication. 'You *see*,' she said, swivelling excitedly round to Henry, 'I *told* you I kept seeing him,' just in case he hadn't got the point.

'Hmph,' said Henry.

'*Were* you following me?' she asked Jeb directly.

He nodded awkwardly, his shyness rendering him stiff and graceless. He stared silently at the elder Gallant girl. He noticed the way her long brown hair flowed over her shoulders as she chatted confidently to her friends.

'Jeb is here to tell you a little more about your grandfather,' said Miss Cameron. 'I should begin with Ruby, if I were you,' she suggested to Jeb before she left the room, quietly shutting the door behind her.

'With Ruby?' asked Verity. 'My father's sister?'

Jeb nodded, pulling a Jacobean chair towards him and sitting on it.

'Didn't she die at sea?'

'She drowned. In her dinghy. Your grandmother killed her.'

Verity was horrified at Jeb's matter-of-fact statement. 'She—? But how? Why?'

Martha removed the cup and saucer that were dangling precariously from Verity's hand and put them on a nearby table.

'Rafe were a clever man,' said Jeb. 'But at the beginning of their marriage he had no idea of the Mistress's malice, or her greed. She hid it, and he was fooled by her.' He drew in a long breath and exhaled. Talking to an audience was harder than he'd expected.

Verity smiled reassuringly in encouragement.

'While Rafe travelled the world, she and Barbarous Usage brewed up a plot,' he continued.

'Barbarous what?' interrupted Martha.

'Usage,' said Henry. 'The leader of the Usage family – and the wreckers,' he added contemptuously.

''S right.' Jeb nodded. 'Barbarous recruited the laziest, the most corrupt of us. And as every likely ship passed these shores, the Mistress brought about a storm to sink her. Our traitors salvaged the cargo . . . and gave the Mistress her share. Thousands died. It's why these shores have such a fearsome reputation.'

Verity stared at him wordlessly.

'When Rafe found out about their collusion, the scales fell from his eyes,' said Jeb. 'He cast the Usages out from the Gentry and vowed to have nothing more to do with his wife – your grandmother, the Mistress.'

Henry whistled.

'It were a long time coming,' Jeb went on. 'The Mistress concealed her true self because she wanted Rafe, but it were always going to show eventually. Rafe was a good man. He hated cruelty, dishonesty and greed.

'At first the Mistress were astonished . . . I don't suppose she really believed he wouldn't forgive her. But Rafe refused – until eventually her shock turned to fury, and her anger to a desire for revenge. She waited until the next time Ruby went to sea–' He stopped for a moment, as if gathering his thoughts.

'Rafe had told Ruby not to go out in her boat,' he continued, 'but she were a right wilful thing by all accounts. The Mistress whipped up a storm – a storm so terrible Rafe would know for sure it had been meant as punishment for him. And Ruby drowned.

'It broke his heart,' said Jeb simply. 'He left Wellow that night and never returned. And it shattered the Gentry.'

'But why has the Mistress returned to Wellow now?' asked Verity.

'When Rafe found Ruby dead – and the Mistress had killed her – he vowed to avenge her death,' said Jeb. 'So he made a pledge.'

'A pledge?' repeated Martha.

'Duty and honour are very important to the Gentry,' explained Jeb.

Henry snorted.

The other boy glared at him. 'To the real Gentry a Pledge is a solemn and binding undertaking: a promise,' he told Verity. He blushed a little as he started to recite from memory: '*Just as my love has turned to hate, my blood will turn on yours . . . That which gave you life shall destroy you.* The Gallant Pledge, it became known as.'

Verity said nothing for a while, then: 'I don't understand what it means.'

'*That which gave you life* is commonly assumed to be the first Original Story,' said a placid voice.

Verity turned round to see that Miss Cameron had came back into the room.

'Your grandfather vowed to make an Original Story that would bring about his wife's death. It had never been done by a mortal before. But he said that it would be: in Ruby's name.'

'But how?' asked Verity.

Miss Cameron went over to stand by the window, with its clear view of the moonlit sea. 'By discovering one of the wellsprings – the secret locations where a story could be told and become reality. Rafe knew that if he succeeded, he could make a story that would kill the Mistress.'

Verity glanced up anxiously at the library clock. 'I need to leave soon,' she said, 'and there's so much I still have to ask. I don't understand why Grandmother is here . . .'

'Rafe sent word that he was returning to Wellow,' said Miss Cameron. 'It seems likely she knows of this, and believes he succeeded in his task.'

'Do you think he has?' Martha asked eagerly.

'Rafe's sheer force of will knew no bounds . . . Your grandmother, Verity, knew that better than most. She would fear his determination accordingly.'

Verity felt a huge wave of relief. Everything she'd read about her intrepid grandfather reassured her that he would know what to do. 'Well, that's all right then. We just have to wait for him.'

'I'm afraid not,' said Miss Cameron sombrely.

Verity's heart sank. 'What do you mean?'

The librarian looked at her intently, as if what she was about to say was of extraordinary importance. 'Because he has chosen you as the subject of the story,' she replied.

'Me?' repeated Verity in shock. 'What do you mean?'

'*My blood will turn on yours,*' said Martha. 'You're Rafe Gallant's granddaughter, Verity. You're his blood.'

'But I can't . . .' She was astonished. 'He wants me

to . . .? That's ridiculous . . . What do I have to do?' she asked eventually. 'What happens in the story?'

'Only Rafe knows the answer to that,' said Miss Cameron. 'All we know for certain – all your grandmother knows – is about the Pledge. The story will take place of its own accord.'

'Take place of its own . . .?' repeated Verity incredulously. After the pressure of the last two days she couldn't believe what she was hearing. 'You expect me to sit and wait?' she demanded angrily. 'But I know her from the book: she steals, and lies, and cheats, and murders. She's in my home. And sometimes' – her voice started to break – 'sometimes I feel as if she'd get rid of me now if she could. The way she looks at me . . . If she finds out I'm at the heart of the story, she'll kill me,' she said simply. 'She'll kill Poppy too, and my father.'

Jeb stood up, his face filled with concern. Miss Cameron said nothing.

'I need to know what's going to happen. Do I have to destroy her? How could I possibly do that?' said Verity, breaking down completely.

Jeb stood in the corner looking pained while Martha and Henry ran to her side. Henry grabbed hold of her and hugged her.

'If Rafe managed to send word,' he said to Miss Cameron, 'why didn't he say what she's got to do?'

'It is not the story you need to fear,' said Miss Cameron gently.

Martha put a hand on Verity's arm. 'We'll be with you,' she reassured her. 'It's your grandmother who's threatened by it. Isn't that right?'

Miss Cameron nodded.

Henry looked at her crossly. 'Stupid mumbo jumbo,' he muttered. 'There's nothing to worry about,' he told Verity confidently. '*You're* a danger to *her*, not the other way round.'

'You have many things on your side, Verity,' agreed Miss Cameron. 'She sees that.'

Verity looked up hopefully. A thought occurred to her. 'Do I have supernatural powers too? Is that how I kill her?'

The librarian smiled kindly. 'No, Verity, you don't have supernatural powers. You have friends and common sense.'

'Oh,' said Verity quietly. 'I think I might prefer to be armed with something a bit more impactful than common sense . . .'

'And friends,' remonstrated Henry, shoving her arm.

Verity turned the strange wooden ball around in her pocket. All at once she felt less daunted. She looked up at Miss Cameron. 'Why are you helping me with this?' she asked.

Miss Cameron paused. 'As the librarian of Wellow, it is my duty,' she said simply.

## Chapter Sixteen

Few in Wellow understood the concept of honouring a commitment better than Daniel Twogood. He had been quietly and single-handedly shouldering family obligations his whole life, and tonight was no different.

The narrow quayside streets and alleys of Wellow's most humble area boasted few lights and dangerously slippery cobbles, so he walked instead of running. His honest, steadfast face was anxious: he had made a decision and needed to act on it. The tiny white terraced cottages crouched on either side of him . . . Mr Twogood steeled himself to begin knocking on doors. There were few in this part of town who would welcome a visit from a Twogood at any time of day, but as he rounded the corner into Catchman Lane he saw the customs man ahead of him, only now returning to his lodgings.

'They used a vacuum,' he shouted out.

Jasper stopped in his tracks. He turned round slowly; inside, he burned with hope.

'The fire and the ice,' continued Daniel Twogood,

slightly out of breath, 'were trapped in two separate vacuums. Extreme heat meets extreme cold and the atmospheric pressure directly around it changes rapidly.'

Jasper's heart was pounding, but his face – as ever – betrayed no emotion.

'I'm telling you because you need to understand that you'll never learn how to control it. And none of us – least of all you – will be safe while it's at large.'

Jasper's heart sank. 'But why make it in the first place?' he asked desperately. 'Why create something so astonishing and then just lock it away from the world?'

'To satisfy his own curiosity,' said Mr Twogood bitterly. 'Once the idea were in Pa's head, he couldn't get it out. Had to make it, just to prove it could be done.

'He were a broken man when I was a lad: never got over seeing the death and destruction he'd brought into the world,' he continued. 'Our family weren't interested in the Gentry business. We just enjoyed inventing. So the first time he saw an actual wreck it broke his heart . . . All those people dying – frightened and alone – on the rocks, with the so-called "Gentry" so eager to get at their possessions, blithely stepping over 'em as they perished. The worst of 'em fighting men as they took their last few breaths – for watches or jewellery they'd taken a fancy to.

'Our family left that night,' he finished sadly.

Jasper stood there without speaking. He didn't know what to say. And anyway, he thought. It would be different. These were more enlightened times. With enough patience he knew he could win Dan Twogood round. Sooner or later he would see sense.

At the bar of the Spyglass Inn, Villainous Usage took another slow, careful sip from the pint in front of him. He was crouching on a stool at the bar, both feet up on the struts, like a rather grey, particularly pungent praying mantis.

Simnel, the landlord, stood on the other side of the bar, wiping glasses with a cloth so dirty they would have been better left alone, and glanced crossly at his unprofitable customer. Like an answered prayer, one of his best spenders walked through the door. Instantly Simnel's manner switched to one of joviality and welcome.

'Seen that customs matey in here lately?' the well-worn regular asked.

Simnel was already pouring a glass of the man's favourite beer, but he shook his head disparagingly to indicate that Jasper Cutgrass had not been in the Spyglass recently, and that it was just as well with him.

The customer laughed. 'Heard he's been plaguing the life out of all sorts of people.'

Simnel tutted and raised his eyebrows.

'But you'll never believe . . .' The man lowered his voice to indicate an item of particular interest. Simnel leaned across the bar to hear better.

'Spoonface Maddox,' his customer continued, 'heard he had a Storm Bringer with 'im. In a *canvas bag*.'

It took a lot to elicit genuine surprise from Simnel, but for once his eyes widened with excitement.

'Did you ever hear the like?' he was asked.

Simnel shook his head with rare and genuine wonder. 'I never did,' he agreed.

'In a canvas bag,' chuckled the man. 'Some people'll believe anything. Next they'll be saying he's been seen with a unicorn.'

Suddenly aware of his rare slip into credulity, Simnel immediately covered his tracks. 'Some will,' he said, laughing in return.

The man handed over his change and took a first satisfying sip of beer.

Meanwhile Villainous was still sitting in the same position, apparently examining his three-quarters empty tankard of beer. But his mind was alive with memories – of the nervous way in which Jasper Cutgrass had handled the custom-made canvas bag that never left his side. And his unseasonably brown skin. Without saying a word, he quietly slipped off his stool, left the pub and headed up the street to a house just a few doors down from his own. It was a long shot, but it had to be worth a try. Mother would be overjoyed if he was right.

Verity, of course, knew nothing of Villainous' plans. But she too was filled with a determination to succeed: Rafe Gallant had placed the burden of responsibility on her and she was going to rise to the challenge.

At first break she and Henry were outside in the playground, huddled together against a wall for protection against the bitter weather. The sky was grey and turbulent. The ice-cold wind cut through their bones like a knife.

'Why do they keep us outside on days like this?' complained Verity, clutching her coat about her more tightly.

'Because the teachers of Priory Bay,' said Henry, jumping up and down to try and get some life back into his toes, 'are of the firm opinion that you can never have too much fresh air. Even if it kills you.'

Martha was approaching from the other side of the playground, clutching an unfeasibly large number of books to her chest.

'Just a few light reads to keep you occupied?' asked Henry innocently.

'I found time to pass by the library this morning,' Martha replied tartly. 'If you applied yourself similarly, Henry, I'm sure you'd be astonished at what you could achieve.'

Henry cheerfully made a very rude sign in her direction.

'There's nothing dedicated specifically to the topic of Original Stories, but there are enough snippets to piece together a picture. Your grandmother created all sorts of stories, Verity, and each one involved her gain – of possessions mostly, but people too . . . the crew of the *Storm*, for example.'

Verity nodded. She pulled out her book and then crouched down to find the right page.

'*The boy*,' she said, finding a section entitled 'Collated Original Stories'.

*The Keeper of the Wind had need of a boy such as him* [it began]. *So she took him from his uncle, who drank, and stole, and beat him. The boy had a sister, but she was not necessary to the Keeper and was killed swiftly.*

*The boy saw only that he had been rescued from the cruel uncle. So he was grateful, and loyal to She of the Wind for ever more. And from that day boys such as he were drawn to the Keeper of the Wind and became her servants.*

'There's a whole chapter of them,' she said sadly. 'They're all so short, but each one involves death or loss for someone.'

'Precisely,' said Martha. 'So the crew of the *Storm* were all stolen as boys: the ship draws them to her. It's how the stories work. Such an ingenious way of recruiting staff.'

'I think you'll find that's slavery,' said Henry tersely.

Martha waved a hand dismissively. 'I know, she's awful. But really very clever too.'

'She's a hateful person.'

'Well . . . that was the other thing . . .' said Martha hesitantly.

'She's not technically a person, is she?' interrupted Verity.

Martha shook her head. 'Definitely not what you would call a person now, no.'

'What do you mean?' Henry asked.

'She was brought to life by a story,' said Martha. 'Legend has it that she can't be killed. She's certainly been alive a very long time.'

Verity felt daunted, but said nothing.

'I suppose your grandfather must have known that,' said Martha. 'That may be why he decided to create a story. Perhaps he thought it was the only thing that would work . . . Equally, though, all the terrible things she's done will have had an effect on her,' she continued. 'Each act of malice or cruelty will have killed a little part of her soul. After hundreds of years she must be . . . mummified really: living, but dead too.'

Verity nodded. 'That's what I saw at Christmas: a skeletal creature. She looked terrifying.'

'So nothing useful on how to kill her?' asked Henry, cutting straight to the chase.

Martha grew more animated. 'Not exactly,' she said. 'But it's believed that ultimately the Keepers will be consumed by the element they control – and at that point held to account for their actions in our world.'

'Sounds grisly,' said Henry, with interest. 'Can't imagine she's looking forward to it.'

Verity shivered. 'She's done so many terrible things,' she said. 'I expect she'll do anything to avoid it.'

It was already the end of school on Friday. Verity headed reluctantly for the school gates, her heart heavy at the thought of another tactics session for the school sailing team. She should have been pleased, she knew, to be selected to crew again. But it seemed unlikely that the other pupils would offer a welcoming reception.

A crowd of girls were gathered at the entrance, huddled around something. Verity wondered what had captured their attention. There was a lot of giggling going on, and a fair amount of hair-flicking too. She realized they were standing in front of a car. Then she did a double take: sitting in it was Jeb. He waved awkwardly at Verity, who became the focus of many keenly interested stares. The group parted like the Red Sea.

'Borrowed Isaac's car. Thought you might like a lift,' said Jeb. 'To the club.'

In the background Verity could hear whispers. She made the mistake of looking up. One girl was saying something to her friend behind a cupped hand. Turning to face Verity, she raised an eyebrow and smiled knowingly.

Verity felt hot and embarrassed. 'Great,' she mumbled awkwardly.

'Best we go then,' said Jeb, who appeared to be finding the whole experience as excruciating as she was. Verity squeezed past a spectator and got into the car, staring intently at the floor as he started the engine and drove off.

'Can you *believe* it?' she heard one girl shrieking at the top of her voice. She turned round. The girls were some hundred yards away, but even at this distance she could make out the palpable air of astonishment . . . and envy.

Verity juggled the wooden ball in her pocket. She giggled. 'They weren't expecting that,' she said. Her good humour broke the ice. Jeb smiled broadly and laughed.

'Anyone'd think they'd never seen a car before,' he said.

He was a good driver: fast, but steady.

'Is it safe for you to pick me up from school?' Verity asked, fastening her seatbelt. 'Won't Grandmother find out?'

'She knows there are people waiting for her in Wellow,' said Jeb, pushing a stray lock of hair out of his eyes, 'and I expect she knows which side you'll be on. Only have to take one look to see you're a Gallant through and through.'

'I meant, isn't it dangerous for *you*?'

'She's beaten the Tempests before.' Jeb gripped the wheel grimly. 'She won't see me as no threat.'

'Do you mean your father, Isaac?' asked Verity.

'My grandfather,' corrected Jeb. 'Isaac's my grandfather.'

'Oh,' said Verity, wondering.

'My pa's dead,' said Jeb. 'Isaac brought me up.'

'Oh, I – I'm . . .'

''S all right – it were a long time ago. When I were a nipper.'

'How did he die?' asked Verity, wishing the car wasn't so noisy that she had to shout every question at top volume.

'Your grandmother killed him too,' Jeb replied with characteristic brevity.

Verity felt terrible, as if it was somehow her fault that

Grandmother was so murderous and hateful. And she felt scared.

'Ain't nothing to do with you,' said Jeb, shifting up a gear. 'She's cruel and vengeful and covetous . . . seems to me it's greed that drives her.'

'So what did she kill your father for?' Verity asked. She would never usually be so blunt, but with Jeb it seemed natural.

'When I was born, apparently he was dead set on going abroad to make his fortune,' said Jeb more expansively. 'Isaac told him to give the Mistress a wide berth, but he must have decided he could handle her.'

'I'm so sorry . . .' Verity didn't know what else to say.

Jeb shrugged, as if to draw a line under the subject. 'So your grandmother won't be surprised to know I've found you. And she won't be worried; won't think I'm a match for her.' He grinned as he pressed his foot to the accelerator. 'But I take after Isaac. So who knows, maybe I'll give her a run for her money . . .'

'You know she's not really my grandmother?' Verity said. 'I mean,' she added hurriedly, 'we're not related by blood or anything.'

Jeb nodded. 'I know.'

'I just . . . I wouldn't want you to think that I might be like her in any way.'

Jeb turned briefly to face her. His green eyes looked directly into hers. 'I don't think that,' he said.

Verity felt herself go unaccountably pink. 'I expect you

know more about my family than I do,' she said, changing the subject.

'Seems that way,' agreed Jeb.

Of course, Verity realized excitedly. Jeb must have the answers to dozens of the questions buzzing around her head. 'Why do you think my father never says anything about my grandfather?' she asked.

'I expect he were still angry about it. He were Rafe's son too. But Rafe just up and left after Ruby died, hell-bent on revenge.'

Verity wondered why it hadn't occurred to her previously. It was funny how so often your parents just seemed to be your parents, rather than real people with their own thoughts and feelings. 'He must have been very hurt,' she said sadly.

Jeb nodded evenly. 'Rafe were always impetuous. But your father were just three at the time.'

'So who brought him up?' asked Verity. She thought of Father, alone and abandoned as a little boy.

'He were passed around a bit at first, from one sibling to another – Rafe had a lot of children before he married Rose – then eventually he settled with his sister, Edie. She were quite strict, were Edie. She had views.'

'No wonder he doesn't like to talk about it.'

'Di'n't make him look too favourably on the Gentry either,' said Jeb. 'Not that he's the only one: there's not much love lost by the Twogoods either.'

Verity smiled, thinking instantly of her sceptical friend.

'Henry will be mad with jealousy when he finds out you're allowed to borrow your grandfather's car.'

'Isaac knew I'd take care of it,' said Jeb simply. 'He knows I'm good at taking care of things.'

When Verity arrived at the club, Miranda Blake was already plaguing the other girls while her parents attended to some essential business in the bar.

'Gallant,' she said with satisfaction as Verity came into the hall. 'So pleased you're here. It's quite the most exciting part when you take to the slipway: everything shakes in such an exhilarating way.'

Verity had both hands shoved in her coat pockets. She gripped the strange wooden ball in irritation. She'd had enough of Miranda's snipes and jibes. 'I'd be careful if I were you,' she said coolly. 'You may be pure poison, but you're still only half the size of me.'

Miranda smiled mysteriously. 'Feeling a bit bolder, are you?' she lisped. 'You are funny, Verity. Only you could take comfort from such a motley gang: Shorty Twogood, that odd girl with glasses you picked up recently – and the Tempests, of all people.'

Verity moved to brush briskly past her – then came to an abrupt halt. On the lapel of Miranda's coat was a brooch – the brooch Grandmother had been wearing on Christmas Day. The image was etched on her memory: enamel centre, dark-haired lady, starlit backdrop, gold frame set with pearls.

'Where did you get that?' she demanded.

Miranda glanced down at it with a superior smile. 'Wouldn't you like to know?' she replied.

'Well, yes,' said Verity carefully. 'That's why I asked.'

She stared anxiously into the little girl's eyes. Could Miranda really know Grandmother? And if so, did she realize what terrible danger she might be in? Verity was no fan of hers, but Miranda didn't deserve to be mixed up in the old lady's plans, whatever they were.

'Seriously,' she said gently, 'are you sure there's nothing you want to tell me? There are things happening in Wellow. Dangerous things.'

'Some of us are popular enough to receive these things called *gifts*, Verity,' said Miranda superciliously. 'If you had any worthwhile friends, you'd know that.'

*There's no point being nice to Miranda*, Verity reminded herself. *She just uses it as an opportunity to put you down.* Watching her move on to her next target, Verity realized that if she were receiving gifts from Grandmother, it probably meant she was reporting back to her too. So now she would know that Jeb had brought her here. A wave of panic swept through her. Who else was in her grandmother's pay? What did she know? Father was already behaving peculiarly. What else was she planning?

Verity was finding the idea of being a character in a live story more than a little unsettling. Did it mean that she wasn't in control of her own actions? Sometimes when she was walking along a street, she would wonder if the steps she took were of her own volition or whether her grandfather's story was driving her along. Now she felt as if everything was closing in around her; as if nothing and nowhere were safe any more.

# Book Three
# SPRING

## Chapter Seventeen

Winter was turning gradually to spring. The first snow-drops had been and gone, and all around Wellow daffodils and crocuses were optimistically poking their heads above ground. Verity couldn't bring herself to share in their hope-fulness. She was finding it increasingly difficult to escape the house and the attention of Grandmother, who seemed determined to keep her close to home and away from her friends.

No sooner had she finished one task than the old lady would helpfully suggest another. Occasionally she would try to sneak out, but she was no match for Grandmother's astonishingly good hearing. Each time she got as far as the door, the old lady would appear silently, like a gust of malevolent wind, with another chore at the ready.

'It's for the best, my dear,' she was fond of saying in a clear voice. And Verity would silently acquiesce, unwilling to leave her mother on her own now that the pregnancy was taking its toll. She was finding movement very difficult, and sleep eluded her.

'Oh, *bother,*' snapped Mrs Gallant in exasperation as she

knocked over the tea caddy. Verity quickly grabbed a dustpan and brush and began sweeping up the leaves from the floor.

'Hurry, child,' goaded Grandmother. 'You can hardly expect your mother to clear up this mess.' Turning to Verity's mother, she added in a cloying tone, 'You should be taking more care of yourself, dear. Go to the sitting room and Verity will bring you a warm drink.'

'It is really very trying that pregnancy makes you so clumsy, when you are least able to pick things up,' fretted Mrs Gallant.

'Try not to worry about it,' Verity soothed, ignoring her grandmother.

Mother sighed, clearly exhausted.

So Verity stayed at home, mindful that her family were unwittingly dependent for their safety on her co-operation with Grandmother. She thought of the baby her mother was carrying and wondered what it would be like. Another brother or sister – she found it impossible to imagine. Sometimes she wished she could be more enthusiastic about the prospect, but it just seemed so hard to grasp.

Fortunately life at Priory Bay had become easier of late. Since Jeb arrived to meet her, many of the girls had become a lot friendlier.

'Never knew you had it in you,' said one admiringly.

The clothes sent by Alice helped too. Her old friend had been so generous that Verity never wanted for stylish new outfits now. Her current favourite was a plaid pinafore dress, which she liked to wear with a cream turtleneck jumper and her black patent shoes. It was silly, she reflected, how much more confident she felt knowing what she wanted to put on in the morning.

Not that being teased at school was her main concern these days: it rather paled in comparison to the prospect of having to defend her family from an evil witch and act out a story she didn't know the ending of.

Verity, Henry and Martha had been spending every spare minute researching the legends of both the Mistress of the Storm and the Keeper of the Wind. Martha was adamant that preparation was going to be the key to success. But it was slow work, and each new reference or snippet they unearthed was more worrying than the last. Verity wasn't convinced it was helping.

'I think your grandmother's scared of you,' said Henry one Friday afternoon as they sat in the library reading room when they should have been attending games.

'She does a very good job of hiding it,' said Verity glumly.

Martha pulled a sympathetic face. 'It must be difficult,' she said. 'But you're actually in a position of power. She's the one Rafe vowed revenge upon.'

Verity nodded. 'But if that involves her death, then I have to kill her,' she pointed out. 'And she's immortal . . . and a lot more powerful than me . . . and evil.'

'Rafe Gallant was a famously clever man,' Martha said. 'He may have put you at the heart of the story, but

I'm sure he wouldn't have planned to just leave you to it.'

'He let Ruby die at sea,' Verity countered. 'And then abandoned my father.'

'The story threatens your grandmother. Perhaps it's simply a case of waiting for things to come to a head. Or for her to do a particular thing that will result in her death — don't you think, Henry?' Martha gave him a swift kick under the table.

'Ow,' he protested. 'What did you do that for? *Ow*. Oh. Er, absolutely,' he agreed, finally realizing what Martha required of him.

Martha patted Verity reassuringly on the back as she got up to put some books back on their shelves.

Verity sighed. 'It wouldn't be so bad if she hadn't got to Father. Often he doesn't seem to know who I am; he's so distant. At Christmas, when she was bullying me on the stairs, it was as if I weren't there.'

'Perhaps she's sent him mad,' said Martha absentmindedly, looking for the correct slot.

'What?'

Martha looked round. 'Oh,' she said, realizing she had piqued her friend's interest. 'Er, well, apparently the wind can send you mad if you're exposed to it too much . . . I'm sure I read that somewhere.'

'Why didn't you say so before?' demanded Verity. 'That must be what she's done.'

'Possibly . . .' conceded Martha doubtfully.

Verity's mind raced. 'Maybe I should get him away from the house?'

'You can't do that,' said Martha, slightly patronizingly.

Henry nodded in agreement. 'You'll just make your grandmother suspicious.'

Verity glared at them. 'Thanks for being so sympathetic,' she snapped angrily, putting on her coat and striding towards the door.

'Verity, I'm sorry. That was badly put,' said Martha anxiously, running after her. 'Promise me you won't try anything dangerous.'

'There's no need to do anything hasty,' said Henry earnestly.

'That's easy to say when it's not your father,' shouted Verity, slamming the red double doors on her way out.

She stormed away angrily, tears streaming down her face. How could they be so insensitive? Neither of them knew what it felt like to be her. She looked back, but neither Henry nor Martha were there. She just wanted something – anything – to be the same as before. If she could make Father normal, things would be better, she knew it.

Verity heard the sound of a car approaching. It was Jeb. Spotting her, he pulled up at the kerb. She quickly wiped her face with a sleeve, hoping her eyes weren't too red.

'You OK?' he asked with a concerned look.

Verity nodded. 'Fine, everything's fine,' she said brightly.

'Things getting on top of you a bit?'

Her lip quivered. Tears pushed at the corners of her eyes.

'Come on, get in,' Jeb said. 'I know a place that'll cheer you up.'

Verity debated for a split-second and then hopped in. She turned her face to the window and let the cold air rush over her. They were heading for the top of the town, then turning carefully and slowly onto a brick-walled track whose entrance she had never even noticed, it was so overgrown.

'Where does this lead to?' she asked.

'The Manor,' Jeb told her. 'Rafe's house.'

Verity felt a flicker of excitement. 'Really? The Manor? It's Rafe's?' she asked, then remembered: 'Miranda Blake mentioned it to me. She said the parties here went on for weeks.'

Jeb smiled. 'Lit up the sky like a beacon, apparently. Torches blazing in the garden overlooking the cliff.'

'Did Father live here?' Verity wondered.

Jeb nodded. 'Until he went to Edie.'

'So who owns it now?'

'It still belongs to Rafe,' said Jeb, steering down a surprisingly weed-free drive.

As he pulled up outside the house, Verity was already enthusiastically opening the car door. She walked eagerly across the lawn. The view out to sea was spectacular.

'It's beautiful,' she breathed, gazing at the clear blue

water, which melded so perfectly with the sky on the horizon. From the top of the uppercliff, it looked like a rippled sheet of silk. Above, one lonely cloud cast a green shadow on the water's surface.

'Wait till you get to the beach.' Jeb pointed to an opening in the stone wall that marked the edge of the garden.

Verity followed him, then gasped as she turned the corner and looked down at a rough-hewn stone path. It had literally been carved into the cliff-face. To her left, dark trees clung to rocks that fell steeply away.

Jeb jumped down in front of her. 'You'll get used to it quickly enough,' he said.

Verity moved a nervous foot towards the first mossy step.

'You can hold my hand if you like,' said Jeb.

Verity realized she was being silly. 'I'm fine,' she told him firmly.

'So how do you know Miss Cameron?' she asked as they made their way down the path.

'She and my grandfather were introduced by your friend Alice,' said Jeb, his voice muffled by the damp rock and trees.

'By Alice?'

They were at the bottom of the steps now. Jeb continued along a dry mud path, obviously confident of where he was going. 'She were a good friend of Rafe's,' he said.

'So she must have known my grandmother?' said Verity, a little breathless as she struggled to keep up.

Jeb stopped at the edge of a bank. Verity could see bright daylight filtering through the overgrown lilac in front of him.

'You'd be surprised what Alice and Miss Cameron know,' he answered simply, then reached out to pull the bush aside.

Verity gasped at what lay before her. She stepped past Jeb to the end of the dune and looked at the sheltered cove. The cliffs towered up on either side, covered in trees so you could hardly see the rock. The shallow sea was clear, fading out to blue the further you looked. The shore was clean yellow sand.

'It's lovely,' she said quietly.

'This was Rafe's beach,' said Jeb. 'It belongs to the Manor.'

Verity looked around in wonder. 'Imagine having this at the bottom of your garden,' she said.

'This was where they found Ruby,' he told her.

Verity looked at him in horror. 'Really? How awful.'

Jeb nodded. 'Isaac said it were heartbreakin'. He was with Rafe when the news was sent. Rafe scrambled down that path and through the woods like the devil was on his tail. My grandfather thought he was going to kill someone – or himself – right there, he looked so crazed with grief.'

Verity stared at the quietly lapping water. 'He must have loved her an awful lot.'

'Yes,' said Jeb, 'he did . . . but the reason he felt so bad were that he was always wrapped up in Gentry business.

She were just a little girl on her own in a grand house full of adults. She went out in her boat because she were lonely. And he knew that.'

'Then he left my father here?' said Verity.

'Rafe were no angel,' Jeb told her.

Verity was troubled. The man in the books she'd spent weeks poring over sounded so thrilling she couldn't help but be enchanted by him . . . and yet . . .

She stared out to sea. It was so peaceful. She breathed in deeply and exhaled slowly. Jeb was right: she *did* feel better here.

'It must have been exciting,' she said wistfully. 'Travelling to all those far-flung places, outrunning enemies on the water, the intrigue . . .'

Jeb grinned. 'My grandfather and Rafe had a rare old time,' he acknowledged. 'Saw a few sights too. Some of the places Isaac can tell you about. They scarcely seem credible.'

Verity glanced at him. 'Wouldn't you rather be doing the same?' she asked. 'Wellow's a bit tame by comparison.'

Jeb shrugged. 'One day . . . But my grandfather promised Rafe the Tempests would stay in Wellow and wait for the *Storm* to return, and I owe a lot to him: he raised me from a child. The least I can do is help him keep his promise.'

He crouched down and picked up a piece of sea glass, worn smooth and opaque from untold journeys in the ocean. 'You know these are called Mistress's tears?' he said.

Verity took the proffered piece of glass and turned it over in her hand. 'Really? Why?'

'It's from an old Gentry tale: we used to say that when a ship went unwrecked, she cried bitter tears of glass that would cut and hurt just like she did.'

'But glass from the sea is always smooth,' said Verity.

Jeb nodded. 'Because the sea heals them.' He stood up and dusted the sand from his trousers. 'It's an allegory.' Verity looked up, trying not to appear surprised at his use of such a long word. 'The Gentry prayer of hope,' he continued. 'That everything can be healed one day – even the Mistress.'

They climbed back to the top of the cliff and wandered slowly across the lawn.

'Would you like to have a look inside?' he asked.

Verity's eyes widened. 'What, really?' she asked excitedly. Then, before he had time to change his mind, 'Yes, I'd love to. How can we get in?'

Jeb shrugged. 'It's not locked,' he said.

Verity stared at him in confusion.

'No one would break into Rafe's house,' he told her.

Verity stood and gazed at the oak-panelled wall in front of her. This was once her grandfather's home. It had been her father's too. Had he played in here? Or read perhaps? To the right was an entire wall of shelves filled with books. With the rays of afternoon light warming the air, it smelled comfortingly of leather and ageing paper. She went over to look at the rich mahogany and brass telescope by the window.

'Nothing's been touched since Rafe left,' said Jeb. 'Just looked after.'

On a bureau stood various framed photographs. Jeb looked at them over Verity's shoulder. 'That's Rafe,' he said, 'on the left, with my grandfather.'

She stared intently at the two people in the picture. Her grandfather, Rafe Gallant. Even though the picture was brown with age she could see he was very handsome. He and Isaac Tempest looked young. They were both laughing – real belly-laughs, she could tell. They were on a yacht.

'Rafe loved racing,' said Jeb. 'Kept so many keelboats he could have had his own fleet.' He grinned.

Verity sighed. So much of her family history was known to others, but not her. She wandered over to a table upon which various maps were laid out.

'Charts,' explained Jeb. 'They show the depth of water, features of the sea bed, things to watch out for when you're navigating.'

Verity carefully turned a large page. Then, just as carefully, put it back again.

'Rafe were meticulous about keeping records,' said Jeb, coming over to the table. 'Didn't need them himself, of course, but he were very particular about the importance of marking things down.'

'Why wouldn't he need them himself?' asked Verity.

'You could set him down in pretty much any harbour

around the world and he'd know as much as the local pilots—' Jeb saw that he'd gone too far with his jargon. 'The experts who are paid to guide newcomers through tricky waters,' he told her.

He tapped a leather-bound volume. 'Not even the Admiralty could match these for detail,' he said proudly.

Verity stared blankly at the unintelligible sheets of paper.

'Knowing the secret routes through waters that were reckoned to be impassable – that was a Gentry skill that made us uncatchable,' explained Jeb.

Of course, Verity remembered. 'Henry told me about this,' she said enthusiastically. 'He said that at Soul Bay there was just one route through the ledge to the shore.'

'That's right.' Jeb smiled and pulled out a large sheet of thick paper from a pile. Verity had a small moment of triumph as she recognized the topography of the local coast. 'Right here,' he said, tracing a zigzag route which she was sure she would never be able to master herself. 'But this is a neat little trick too,' he added. 'See that sandbank . . . ?'

Verity frowned. All she could see was a few random numbers.

Jeb realized his mistake. 'Each figure indicates the depth of the sea bed from the surface level of the water,' he said. 'So when there's a range of ones and twos forming a shape, then you know there's a sandbank under the water. Or leastways something you can't sail through.'

Verity nodded. She understood what Jeb was talking about now: she'd sailed round it often enough.

'Most people think it blocks the sea area off – that you have to go round it, like this,' said Jeb, his finger showing her the route on the map. Then he grinned mischievously. 'But there's a channel, big enough for a small boat . . . right here.' He traced a line along a series of higher numbers written in by hand. 'Lets you cut straight through to Wellow bay, quick as you like.'

Verity's eyes widened. 'Really? But how do you—?'

Suddenly she heard footsteps ringing outside in the hallway. Her face paled with concern at being caught trespassing.

The large brass doorknob twisted and the oversized wooden door swung open to reveal an old man. His face was weatherbeaten and rugged, with green eyes that sparkled beneath thick brows. He looked familiar.

Isaac Tempest came towards Verity, smiling in greeting. 'Miss Gallant,' he said warmly, extending a hand. She shook it. His grip was strong and firm, his palm leathery from age and hard sailing. 'I trust Jeb has been looking after you satisfactory?'

'He's been very kind,' agreed Verity, smiling back. There was something about this old man that was instantly charming.

'Tempests and the Gallants go a long way back,' he told her.

Verity nodded. 'I've heard . . . I've seen,' she added, pointing to the photo.

Isaac looked intently at her face and smiled fondly.

'I was just asking how you find this channel,' she said, pointing to the map.

He smiled. 'A small withy,' he said. 'A piece of willow.'

Verity was astonished. 'That stick near the marker?' she asked.

Jeb nodded. 'The sandbank shifts and changes with the movement of the sea,' he explained, 'and so does the channel. We move the withy as a sign for those who know. You've to keep it to your right . . . Look up to the cliffs on your left and aim for the pepperpot.'

'That peculiar brick lump on the downs?' asked Verity.

'Can't go wrong,' he told her.

Verity smiled wryly. He made it sound easy, but she knew it would be far less simple in practice.

As Verity and Jeb left the room to walk back out through the Manor grounds, Isaac Tempest lovingly tidied away the charts.

'Looks just like Ruby,' he mused to himself. 'Very pretty too, especially when she smiles.' He grinned, thinking of the look on his grandson's face. He could hear steps in the room above him. A familiar tread. The sound of someone else going to the leaded window in the room above.

'Could you drop me off at the library?' Verity asked as they drove down through Wellow. 'I should go back to apologize.'

Now she'd had time to calm down, she could see that her friends were right. She couldn't do anything hasty to help Father. They mustn't let on that Verity knew who Grandmother really was. She had to be careful not to arouse her suspicion.

'They'll understand,' said Jeb. 'They're your friends.'

At the corner Verity smiled brilliantly at him as she prepared to get out. 'Thank you,' she said.

He grinned back, leaning over to open the door for her. 'Weren't a hardship.'

His green eyes caught hers for a second. Verity felt particularly clumsy as she slid out of the passenger seat. She walked awkwardly across the street, unsure whether to look back or not. Jeb watched her for a moment and then pulled himself together. He was being ridiculous.

Verity pushed back through the familiar red doors that led into the main hall. But Henry and Martha were no longer there. As she rounded a corner, she realized that the only other person in the library appeared to be a strange man in a neatly ironed jacket with highly polished buttons. He was sitting quietly in the folklore section, surrounded by piles of books on the Gentry and Rafe Gallant.

Verity stopped short. The man glanced from the book he was reading to his notepad and scribbled something down. Then he stood up abruptly and strode towards the reading room. Why was he reading up on the Gentry and her grandfather? Verity wondered. Did he know something? Seized by a terrible curiosity, she darted over to his table. If he came back, she reasoned, she could say she was interested in them. Which was true.

On the desk was a custom-made canvas bag. It was open. Inside was a maritime gimble holding a glass sphere. It looked as if two liquids were floating separately inside. They seemed to be moving. Verity picked it up, holding it at eye level. A slight breeze ruffled her hair. She gawped in astonishment.

'It took a man of rare talent to make that device,' said Jasper Cutgrass calmly.

Verity swivelled round to stare fearfully at the customs man, who had silently appeared by her side. She wondered how much trouble she would be in for tampering with a Preventative Officer's equipment.

'I shouldn't move too swiftly. It could kill us both,' Jasper continued.

Verity put the gimble down carefully; she wasn't sure what to say. This strange man didn't seem at all concerned, either by this or by the fact that he'd just found her disturbing his property.

'Jasper Cutgrass,' he said, extending a hand. Verity shook it. 'It's a Storm Bringer,' he went on. 'Commissioned by your grandfather's rival, Barbarous Usage. Spinning it gently creates a breeze that radiates out in a wide circle. But the closer the ball is to you, and the faster you move it, the more the local atmosphere is disturbed, causing a violent wind. Holding it at arm's length lessens the effect . . .

That's the general principle at least – I'm afraid in practice it's quite volatile.'

Verity glanced enquiringly at him, and he nodded in answer to the unspoken request. Not many adults would have blithely encouraged a young girl to experiment with something that could blast them both to pieces, but not many adults were Jasper Cutgrass.

Verity held the sphere at arm's length and gently turned it in a circle. As she did so, a light breeze whispered around her. The open pages on the table rustled and flapped. She moved the sphere slightly faster: the wind picked up. The canvas-clad box blew down onto the floor. Verity felt a powerful urge to move the ball faster still – and Jasper was knocked backwards against the bookshelf.

Verity gave a shriek. With great presence of mind, she carefully picked up the box and placed the Storm Bringer back in its gimble before dashing over to see whether Jasper was all right.

'It's difficult to resist the urge to push the boundaries of the device,' he said.

'You know who made it?' she asked.

Jasper nodded. 'Henry Twogood's grandfather was very gifted.'

Verity blinked. Of course. If it was man-made and linked to the Gentry, then it would be their craftsmanship. 'Was it confiscated?' she asked.

Jasper permitted himself a small look of pride. 'Recovered,' he said.

Verity looked puzzled.

'After the death of his daughter, Ruby, your grandfather left instructions for it to be hidden,' Jasper explained. 'Out of reach of mankind. But I found it. It wasn't easy – it took many years of research to discover its likely location in the Indies. But I was convinced it must exist. I have always had something of a . . . fascination with the former Gentry empire.'

Verity looked at the strange man thoughtfully for a second. He must be extremely clever to have pieced together the scant information that had been left behind and used it to locate the last resting place of this Gentry artefact. What resourcefulness it must have required.

'You said it could kill us . . . Is it dangerous?'

Jasper nodded. 'In the wrong hands, yes.'

'Don't you think that if my grandfather was keen for it to be safely hidden away, he must have had good reason?'

Jasper stared blankly at her. 'Such an ingenious device couldn't possibly be left to sit at the bottom of the ocean,' he said eventually.

'Why not, if that's the safest place for it?' Verity asked.

'But there are so many uses for it,' said Jasper excitedly. 'It could change our world in any number of positive ways: as a source of energy, for example. Who knows? And if it's possible for something so small to create storms, then surely there might also be a device that stills the weather.'

'You don't think it would just end up being used to . . . kill people then?'

'No,' said Jasper. 'I would never allow that.'

'And you don't suppose that when you go back to your headquarters and show your commanding officers the Storm Bringer, they might just take it off you?' Verity continued.

'No.' Jasper frowned. 'It's my discovery. I should be the one to control it.'

'There must be a lot of people who'd want to use it but who shouldn't be allowed anywhere near it,' said Verity. 'Even in Wellow.'

Jasper was outraged. 'Don't be silly,' he said firmly. 'No one is going to take it from me without my authority.' Picking up the bag, he closed the box, then buckled it tightly shut. He was obviously very annoyed.

Verity swallowed nervously. She hadn't meant to be so abrupt. It just seemed so obvious . . .

# Chapter Eighteen

Time had passed in a flurry of activity for Villainous Usage. He'd been overjoyed when he realized the *Lady Olivia* could definitely be drawn onto the rocks – until he realized that was just the start of his troubles. The tasks seemed endless: recruiting a suitable crew to retrieve the goods, finding an amenable fence to get rid of them. The negotiations and bartering had taken weeks. It was almost like working for a living.

The *Lady Olivia* was smaller than either of the previous two packet ships Mother had wished to plunder, but still . . .Villainous' sources had promised a cargo of bullion mixed with lucrative and easily sold goods.

Of late, both mother and son had spent many a happy hour planning how they would live on the proceeds.

'No more poky cottage,' Mother had crowed one particularly jovial evening, taking another swig of rum.

'I'll be a man of standing,' Villainous gloated.

She patted his knee heavily. 'That you will, son. Your pa would be proud.'

'Do yer think so?'

'Of course,' she slurred. 'An thish is jusht the start,' she added expansively.

Villainous' eyes widened. He hadn't realized there was more to be done.

'Before we're finished, son,' breathed Mother, leaning in closer to focus, 'the Gentry will live again. But this time' – she flung out an arm to emphasize her point – 'the Usages will be their leaders.' Villainous swallowed nervously. 'And such as the Gallants will know their place,' she spat venomously.

'Just the start,' he repeated anxiously.

At last the fated night was here and all preparations were in place. Villainous stood in front of their one tiny mirror, ducking and bobbing to get an idea of his appearance through the brown spots that betrayed its age. He ignored his churning stomach. This was his fate; his chance to secure Ma's respect and restore the family name. He smoothed down the front of the blue shirt he'd pressed specially. Now he put on his father's old coat. He wanted to look the part.

There was a knock at the door. Villainous clambered down the narrow stairs – each one creaking a different note – and opened it eagerly. A hard-faced woman in clean but well-worn clothes rushed in.

'I can't say when he'll notice,' she snapped as she lifted her cape to reveal a custom-made canvas bag. 'He never seems to let the blessed thing out of his sight. I had the devil's own job, I can tell you.'

Villainous dropped a bag of coins into her outstretched palm. 'I'm not paying you any more,' he said.

The woman scowled. 'You'd best be quick with it, is what I'm saying,' she said. 'I don't want to lose him as a tenant. He pays regular as clockwork.'

Villainous took the box out of the bag and eagerly extracted its contents. He held the mysterious glass sphere up to eye level. The fire and ice swirled within. Just having it in his hand made him feel more powerful – little wonder, given how many lives it could take. A flicker of doubt darted through his mind. He pushed it aside.

'It'll be back by midnight, as we agreed,' he said.

The woman glowered at him and turned to leave. 'Midnight at the latest,' she said irritably.

The Usages walked slowly up towards Soul Bay's grassy clifftop, Mother wheezing and coughing with the effort. She was still laughing at the thought of Jasper's naivety.

'Did he really think he could bring it back to Wellow safely?' she cackled.

'I allus remembered you sayin' – wherever the Twogoods took it must have been fierce hot on account of how brown they was when they got back.' Villainous nodded proudly. 'Soon as I heard Simnel talking of it, I remembered. He seemed proper scared of what was in 'is canvas bag.'

'You did good, son,' Mother told him.

They were near the top now. The leader of Villainous' recruits approached, ready to begin. Villainous drew himself up to his full height and repeated his instructions. The man nodded curtly at each point, then left abruptly for the path that led down to the shore. Villainous felt better. It wasn't so difficult. The man accepted his authority. He could do this.

Thirty minutes later he stood at the top of Soul Bay cliff, staring dumbstruck at the scene of carnage. On the sea below, the *Lady Olivia* pitched and rolled like a tormented beast. A shrieking, howling wind was blowing directly in to land, building up a giant surge that crashed violently onto the rocks. Even through the storm he could hear the hopeless cries of a crew who knew they were about to die.

The *Lady Olivia* had not carried many passengers, but those unlucky few with a berth were now on deck, having thrown on whatever clothes were to hand. Now, praying for salvation, they clung to anything they could find that might prevent them from being tossed like rag dolls into the raging sea.

The *Lady Olivia* was cruelly close to the shore, but it seemed that nothing could save her. The other wreckers waited with stony faces, their hearts hardened.

The waves poured mercilessly over the deck. Draining back with a fearsome pull, they clawed at a passenger, whose scream seared Villainous' ears. Mother stood next to him, gripping the Storm Bringer in her doughy hand. She had immediately become an expert. Its exhilarating power coursed through her veins.

'Her cargo is ours. Oh, son,' she exulted, holding the glass sphere jubilantly aloft, 'you have done us proud with this.'

Villainous looked out to sea. His mind raced as he watched a woman gripping the rail and trying to hold onto her young son. She was blue with cold. Villainous could hear the boy's sobs – the abject fear in them – and the woman's last desperate declaration of love for her child. Villainous had done many terrible things, but he'd never actually killed before. He'd hadn't realized it would be like this. Their cries filled his head.

'Mother, stop,' he begged. 'Please stop it. I've changed my mind. I don't want the cargo. We don't need it.'

Mother stared at him scornfully. The Storm Bringer's force throbbed within her. 'Are you soft in the head?' she snapped. 'This sorry hulk is just the start for us—'

'I'm afraid I can't let you do that,' a voice shouted across the dark, windswept downs.

Mother looked up in surprise and irritation. Out of the driving rain stepped Jasper Cutgrass. In his neatly ironed uniform and carefully polished buttons, he looked very out of place against the wild landscape.

'What the hell are you doing here, customs man?' she snarled contemptuously. She raised the Storm Bringer in her grubby mitt, preparing to unleash its full fury.

Jasper raised a hand. 'By the power invested in me as a Preventative Man, I order you to cease your activity and return the stolen item immediately.'

Mother laughed at him. 'Your power? *Your power?* I think I know whose power I'd lay money on. Couldn't even find anyone to help you, could you? No one willing. That tells you everything you need to know about the lie of the land in Wellow, *customs man*. I'm Gentry, born and bred. And what we say goes in this pl—'

But Jasper was to learn no more about Mother's perceived position in Wellow society. Instead, her eyes rolled up in her head and her tongue lolled from her mouth as she slid to the ground, cushioned against any significant damage by the heavy layer of fat that protected every bone.

Behind her stood Daniel Twogood. He was holding a large and heavy spade above his head. In his other hand was the Storm Bringer. That would put paid to any hope of an easy life in Wellow, he thought to himself grimly.

As he held the Storm Bringer still, the writhing ocean calmed. The *Lady Olivia* gradually rolled and pitched herself back to an even keel. The skies cleared of clouds. Stars could once more be seen twinkling down on the fortunate passengers, who were picking themselves up in wonder.

'You idiot,' Mr Twogood shouted. 'Are you happy now?'

Jasper stood on the cliff-top in silence: he didn't know what to say. 'They shouldn't have stolen it,' he protested.

'That's your answer, is it?' Daniel Twogood turned and started to stride back across the downs, Jasper hurrying after him. 'Leave the likes of the Usages to decide what happens in the world? You should not have brought that thing back here – let alone think of making more.'

Villainous knelt on the muddy grass, holding his mother's head in his lap and patting her cheek as she came to. He stared at her anxiously, all traces of cunning and guile wiped from his face; all that remained was the worried look of a child who yearned for approval.

'It'll be all right, Muvver,' he said, heaving her up. 'We don't need the cargo. Not at that price.'

Mother dusted down her skirts and looked at him as if only just noticing he was there. Villainous cowered instinctively.

She slapped him across the face with every ounce of force she could muster. 'You're no son of mine,' she bellowed. 'How could you let them just walk away with our destiny?'

The force of her blow knocked him to the ground. He'd been used to worse in his time. In his head the pleas of those in peril of the sea still rang faintly. He knew now that he could take no part of a fortune snatched from the hands of dying men.

Mother turned away angrily to call off the crew.

In the early hours of the morning Jasper read the same line from his book for the fifteenth time and took another sip of water. He shifted uncomfortably on the bentwood chair and blinked repeatedly. Rubbing his eyes would only make them worse. He dared not sit on the bed.

Daniel Twogood had left now, but Jasper had nowhere else to go, and no way of leaving Wellow until daybreak. So he kept his vigil; waiting in his clean but bare room for the sun to creep above the horizon. Then he would begin the long journey to the other side of the world.

'Do you understand why it has to go back?' Daniel Twogood had asked.

Jasper had nodded. 'This time it must be hidden where no one can ever recover it,' he agreed.

Despite himself Mr Twogood's fingers had lingered admiringly on the polished finish of the sphere. Then he reminded himself of the burden the Storm Bringer had placed on his family.

Jasper got up and walked over the warped floorboards to his tiny window. He pushed it open as far as it would go to let in the cold night air, breathing deeply to refresh himself. Looking down across the street, he saw an unexpected figure striding across the cobbles. He stared in astonishment. What could that person be doing here at this time of night? His disbelief doubled as the figure stopped outside the front door of his lodgings, looked up and then beckoned to him.

## Chapter Nineteen

The start of the weekend was as beautiful and bright as the previous had been stormy and dark. A new dawn, with possibilities. But unfortunately, for many in Wellow the weather was to be no guarantee of a happy outcome.

In the Gallant house, Verity opened her eyes to the rose-patterned wallpaper of her room. Even though the curtains were drawn she could tell it was very early. Day was breaking and the birds in the tree outside her window were busily telling each other off.

She lay still under the covers as, guiltily, she remembered the row with Henry and Martha. She pulled on some clothes, tucked the smooth wooden ball into her pocket, crept downstairs and left the house. The town was so still at this time of day. It only took a few minutes to reach Henry's house, and she soon secured his attention with a few carefully aimed stones.

He opened the back door in his pyjamas, rubbing his head. 'Couldn't sleep?' he asked.

Verity shook her head and followed him in.

'I expect it was the worry of falling out with your brilliant friend,' he said, making for the kettle.

Verity grinned, relieved to have been forgiven. 'Probably,' she agreed. 'Sorry,' she added.

''S all right,' said Henry, spooning out tea from a tin. 'It's a lot to deal with.'

Verity looked gratefully at him. 'I don't know what I'd do without you.'

'I think it's pretty clear you'd be in a terrible state,' said Henry, mock-seriously.

Verity laughed.

'Why don't we go sailing?' he suggested. 'We could get Martha and take *Poor Honesty* out for a spin. She's never been sailing before, has she?'

Verity thought longingly of a day on the water. She could almost smell the breeze now. It would be lovely to forget her worries for a few hours.

'We must have read every book ever written on your grandmother and the Gentry,' Henry went on. 'Well, Martha has. Anyway, it can't be good for you, all that paper.'

'A morning couldn't hurt,' Verity conceded. Perhaps it would bring inspiration on what to do about Father? Right now a few hours of freedom seemed worth the risk of Grandmother's wrath.

'Mum could make sandwiches,' said Henry as Mrs Twogood came downstairs in a quilted dressing gown, rollers still in.

'A nice trip out,' she said approvingly. 'Get a bit of colour back in your cheeks.'

Sadly the new day had brought only a grey pallor to Mother Usage's complexion. She groaned as she lifted her head from the table. The Spyglass Inn swam slowly into view. Drinking away the disappointment of last night had come at a price.

Fellow wreckers were strewn around the bar. One snorted and looked up, a congealed piece of chicken stuck to his face. Mother ignored him and heaved herself upright. She stumbled to the door and let herself out. Time to look for that idiot son of hers.

The unmistakable thud and clatter of the cottage door alerted Villainous to her return. He'd been washed and dressed since before the sun rose. He looked cleaner and tidier than he had in years. But there was something else about his appearance that had changed. His posture was different: he was standing straight, not loping or slouching. He moved with a quiet . . . dignity almost: yes, it was a dignity of sorts. Stealing the Storm Bringer had been a baptism of fire indeed.

Inside, Villainous shrank. It takes more than one night to wipe out a lifetime of fear. But he was determined to plough a new furrow.

'Here he is. The great hero of the hour,' Mother sneered as she dragged her mass into the room.

Villainous said nothing.

'You're a sorry excuse for a son,' she snapped.

He nodded. 'I know you think that,' he said. He didn't cry, because the tears had been beaten out of him years ago. But it still hurt. She may have been a terrible mother, but she was the only one he'd got, and now she was lost to him. He had to change; she never would.

Verity, Henry and Martha anchored *Poor Honesty* in Soul Bay, then sat enjoying the sandwiches Mrs Twogood had made. The breeze was gentle and the sun was shining. It was a beautiful day. Verity closed her eyes and let the sea air wash over her. The smell of the ocean refreshed her like a tonic. The warm spring light bounced off the waves. It had been a lovely trip. What a brilliant idea to go sailing.

'Just what we needed,' said Henry, beaming.

Martha's freckled nose wrinkled with genuine pleasure. 'It's lovely out here,' she said. 'I can see why you enjoy sailing so much.'

Verity smiled warmly at her friends. 'I really appreciate it,' she said earnestly. 'Your help, I mean. I know it hasn't been easy . . . I know *I* haven't been easy.'

Henry grinned in reply. 'You've been a right pain in the bum. But if this isn't what friends are for, I don't know what is.'

'Absolutely,' agreed Martha.

Verity gazed happily out at the view. All the colours today were so vivid: the terracotta orange of the sandstone cliffs, the azure sky, the emerald sea. It was beautiful. She wished she could spend the rest of her life out here. She wished they could sail away right now, and never come back.

She looked at the harbour. In the distance she could just make out the dots of various moorings. 'There are a lot of boats milling around,' she said, frowning. 'Is something happening?'

Henry turned round to look. He watched the vessels ferrying to and fro. There was a distinct pattern to their movements.

He fumbled quickly in his pocket, pulling out a pair of mini binoculars to scan the horizon. 'They're ferrying goods to the *Storm*,' he said urgently. Verity and Martha didn't understand. 'The ship is preparing to leave,' he explained.

Verity's mouth opened in astonishment. 'That can't be good,' she said.

In Wellow itself, Mrs Gallant was under no illusions that things were not as they should be. She gripped the kitchen table. Her stomach clenched in another agonizing contraction.

'This isn't right,' she puffed anxiously when she could finally speak. 'It's too early.'

Her aged guest appeared silently at the door. 'Not everyone has your patience,' she said grimly.

'How kind' – Mrs Gallant glanced at the bag in her mother-in-law's hand – 'of you to pack some things for me.'

'This way, Felicity,' said the old lady as she steered her out of the house, leaves skittering around her in circles on the path.

Mrs Gallant staggered on her arm, the pace too quick for her. 'Where is Tom?' she asked anxiously. 'Where are Verity and Poppy?'

'*How could I have gone on a sailing trip?*' Verity gasped. She was racked with guilt. The familiar pressure was bearing down on her again. 'How could I leave her alone with my family? What's she up to?'

'I'm sure it will be fine,' soothed Martha. 'Perhaps she's just decided to leave.'

'I don't think that's very likely,' said Verity, a sense of panic rising within her, 'do you?'

'Let's just get back to Wellow,' said Henry with more confidence than he felt.

Verity sat at the tiller in a horrified daze. This was like a waking nightmare. Henry had already leaped into action, tuning the sails to get the best speed from the wind.

'Jump over here and sit your body out,' he shouted to Martha. 'We need the dinghy to be as flat as possible.' He looked around anxiously. 'Let's get going. We have to go round that whole sandbank.'

Verity stared at him. A memory flashed through her head. She scanned the waters. There it was: the withy. 'We can take a short cut through it,' she shouted.

Henry stared at her in horrified disbelief. 'No we can't. We'll get stuck.'

'Jeb told me about it,' she explained. 'It's a Gentry route. See the withy? We have to keep it to the right and head straight for the pepperpot. It'll save half an hour easily.'

'Verity, my family have been sailing these waters for generations. We were Gentry too, remember?' Henry pointed out.

But Verity didn't have time to argue. A feeling of calm authority took possession of her. She moved the tiller to point *Poor Honesty* in the right direction.

'Martha, ease that sheet,' she instructed; 'that rope there, let it out a little – we'll reach, so it'll be faster.'

Martha stared desperately, first at Verity and then at Henry. She registered Verity's determined face and did as she asked, letting out the sail to take more wind and pick up speed.

'What do you think you're doing?' Henry demanded, trying to grab the tiller. 'Father will go mental if we ground his boat.'

'We won't.' Verity pushed him back with a strength born of desperation. 'We can get through. It's shorter and quicker. Look at the speed we're picking up already. Henry, we *have* to do it,' she pleaded.

They were at the withy now. Just a simple stick of willow Jeb had attached to a weighted float. Verity looked up at the cliff, searching for the pepperpot. She corrected the position of the dinghy, her heart in her mouth. The channel was so narrow. The centreboard started to scrape against the sandbank.

'Damn, damn, damn,' cursed Henry as he reached across to pull it up. 'The tide's going out,' he shouted. 'We're going to be stuck here.'

Verity shook her head vigorously, as if to shake even the possibility from her mind. She scanned the water on either side. She could see the yellow of the sandbank below the surface. There were a few yards to go now. Her chest was tight. She could hardly breathe. They *had* to make it.

'*We're through*,' bellowed Henry in astonishment, slapping the side of *Poor Honesty* in amazed relief.

Martha whooped with joy.

Verity beamed. 'We did it.'

'You've got the nerve of the devil,' announced Henry, shaking his head in disbelief.

Verity grinned mischievously. 'Let's get a move on,' she said. 'We haven't finished yet.'

Neither – unfortunately for her – had her mother. The cottage hospital at Wellow was a maelstrom of activity. Mrs Gallant focused on an area of wall in an effort to ignore the pain. It had been such a long time since she'd last given birth and she was on the point of collapse, exhausted and frightened.

'Almost there,' encouraged the midwife. 'You're doing really well . . . keep going.'

In another room the nurses huddled together anxiously. 'Still no sign of the father,' said one with concern. They heard steps – hard, confident steps. A sharp gust rattled the door.

'Ah, Mrs Gallant's mother-in-law,' said the most senior, a slightly bovine lady. 'I really do think it would be as well to fetch Mr Gallant.'

The old lady raised an imperious eyebrow as she appeared in the doorway. 'Why exactly?'

'Your daughter-in-law is tired,' explained the midwife. 'Having her husband here might lift her spirits.'

'I am the child's grandmother,' said the old lady haughtily. 'Who better to attend than me?'

The midwife opened her mouth to start a new line of attack, then looked up. A primal bolt of fear shot through her. 'Of course,' she said.

As the door blew shut behind her, the old lady smiled quietly. This was almost too easy. Why had she troubled herself for so long about that idiot child Verity? There was no one here to stop her. All she had to do was wait for the infant to be born and take it. Suddenly the bleating mew of a newborn baby came drifting through the walls. *It was here.*

Time to leave.

Verity's heart pounded as Henry moored the dinghy to the jetty of Wellow harbour.

'She'll be OK here for a bit,' he panted.

The quay was bustling with onlookers who had heard the *Storm* was leaving. Verity, Henry and Martha got off *Poor Honesty* and climbed up a nearby ladder for a better vantage point.

Verity scanned the crowd anxiously.

'Over there,' shouted Henry, first – as ever – to spot the target.

Grandmother was on the other side of the quay, clutching a bundle to her chest. Abednego was assisting her into a small rowing boat.

'Look who's with her,' exclaimed Henry. 'Miranda Blake is in the boat too.'

'The brooch . . .' said Verity. 'The brooch – it *was* Grandmother's – I think Miranda's being sort of paid by her,' she explained.

'Well, Blake's met her match this time,' said Henry.

'It doesn't make sense . . .' Verity frowned. 'Why would Grandmother just leave – so easily – after all this time?'

She belted along the jetty, possessed by an overwhelming conviction that something was wrong. She scrambled up another small ladder to the quay and pushed her way through the crowd. Her heart was beating so fast it hurt. It was like wading through treacle: trying to get past all these milling people who were completely oblivious to the drama playing out in front of them.

'Easy, girl, you'll get your chance for a look,' said one man, not unkindly.

'Grandmother,' Verity shouted as she ducked and

shoved, mindless of how rude people thought she was. 'Grandmother, where are you going?'

Abednego had already put the oars in the rowlocks and was preparing to cast off. Verity saw Miranda taking the bundle from her grandmother. It seemed to be moving. Suddenly her blood ran cold.

Miranda turned, looking at Verity with cool disdain. 'Meet your new sister,' she lisped contemptuously, holding up a tiny new baby.

'My sister?' gasped Verity, horrified. 'But it's too early . . . it's not due yet . . . a *sister*? I've got another sister,' she gabbled, overwhelmed.

'That's what I said,' replied Miranda. 'Are you deaf?'

'Hand her to me – please,' Verity shouted desperately as the reality of the situation sank in. 'You're both in terrible danger. Take the baby and get off the boat now.'

'I'm sure it's a wrench, Verity,' the little girl said crisply, 'but in the better kind of families it's very normal for children to be brought up by elder relatives.'

'She's taking my sister,' Verity shouted angrily from the quay. She stared beseechingly at Abednego. 'Why are you helping her?' she asked. 'Don't let her take my sister away.'

Abednego said nothing as he untied the mooring rope, his face furrowed with sorrow.

Verity couldn't understand it. Why had he given her the book if he wasn't prepared to help now? She jumped down to the jetty, readying herself to board.

'Abednego,' Grandmother barked, her anger rocking the boat.

He picked Verity up as if she were as light as the foam on a wave, holding her firmly, ignoring her struggles. Verity no longer cared what physical danger she might be in. She pummelled and kicked, prised and wriggled, but it made no difference. Abednego tucked her under his arm and climbed up a short ladder to the quay. Grandmother and Miranda laughed at the sight.

Verity didn't know what to do. She was crying, her breath coming in ragged gasps. She looked around frantically, but Henry and Martha were nowhere to be seen, lost in the crowd somewhere.

'Miranda, you've got to help me,' she screamed, her voice raw.

The girl stared at her. 'Such a fuss,' she sighed.

At the top of the ladder Abednego placed Verity deliberately on the quay. She tried to dart round him, but his powerful frame stood in the way of both the jetty and her sister. He leaned down to hold her with both muscular arms. Looking into his face, Verity started, for she realized that his eyes were wet with emotion.

'I cannot help you more than I have done,' he said in a low voice.

Verity's heart fell. That was it then. She couldn't fight her way past him on her own. She stopped struggling and simply watched as Abednego got into the boat and cast off.

'Looks like she's finally seen sense,' said Miranda smugly.

Grandmother smirked and held firmly onto the baby. 'Goodbye, Verity,' she said.

The sea breeze caught Verity's hair, whipping it into her eyes and obscuring her view as the boat drew away from the quay.

# Chapter Twenty

Verity stood there, her tear-streaked face blotchy and red, watching Abednego row towards the *Storm*. Grandmother still clutched her baby sister while Miranda Blake simpered and smirked.

The old lady cast one final, triumphant glance in her granddaughter's direction. Verity felt a wave of fury overwhelm her. Every snipe and jibe, every barbed comment and cruel act came flooding into her head. What a witch. What a loathsome witch. Why was she letting her just row away?

Verity jumped down to the jetty and ran as fast as she could towards Henry's dinghy. The anger burned in her chest, eliminating all fear, all reason. Who did that wrinkly old prune think she was? She wasn't going steal her baby sister without a fight.

As she quickly adjusted the sails and readied *Poor Honesty*, Verity wondered where her parents and Poppy were – what could possibly have happened to them? – but she firmly pushed aside her fears. She unclipped the tiller extension from the rudder to sail singlehanded and sheeted in the mainsail to draw some wind into it. The boat started moving and she steered away from the jetty. Verity sheeted in the jib and fixed it in its cleat, keeping her eyes fixed on Abednego. *I cannot help you more than I have done*, she thought to herself bitterly. He'd done nothing.

There were many eyes watching Verity's progress. On the other side of the quay Jeb pushed through the crowd towards Isaac. 'She's not going out there alone, is she?' he asked anxiously.

'She can do it,' his grandfather replied.

Meanwhile, on the tender, Grandmother was looking back towards the quay. 'Let her follow if she likes,' she sneered as she spotted the little wooden dinghy with the red sail setting out behind them. 'She'll find it hard to keep up with her weight.' Miranda let out her best delicate tinkle of a laugh.

Abednego's progress was swift, but Grandmother saw that, despite what she'd said, Verity was gaining on them rapidly, leaning out as far as she could: the flatter the boat, the quicker she would go.

'What an annoying little mosquito she is,' muttered the old lady.

Miranda put on her best smile. 'Too stout to be a mosquito surely?' she asked coquettishly.

Grandmother smiled and patted the girl's thin cheek. 'This will send her back to shore . . .' she said.

On the horizon a squall appeared. The sky within it was

dark and menacing, casting a shadow on the sea's surface. The waves directly beneath it were choppy and flecked with foamy white. 'Oh, how clever.' Miranda clapped her hands in delight.

'Just a little something to frighten her,' Grandmother muttered to herself.

The watchers on the quayside saw the squall. They saw Verity let off both sheets with calm efficiency so the sails flapped loose. *Poor Honesty* stopped.

'She's not moving to face the wind,' a man near Isaac gasped.

'No,' Isaac agreed. 'I expect she plans to sail through it.'

More and more people were gathering on the quay as word rippled through the crowd.

'Excuse me. *Excuse me.* Mind out. Coming through. Move to the left, will you?'

Jeb couldn't see Henry yet but there could be no mistaking his voice. Sure enough, the sandy-haired boy soon appeared from behind a scowling spectator.

Henry ignored the man's huffs. 'I need your boat,' he gasped to Jeb, slightly out of breath. 'Verity's got mine.'

Jeb wondered what this small Twogood thought he could possibly do against the might of the Mistress. There'd been no Original Story about any Henry. 'You can't go out there. You'll drown.'

'The only person who's in any danger of drowning is Verity,' insisted Henry. 'She's the one on the water. And I'm her friend. I have to help.'

'The story is about Verity,' said Jeb. 'I don't like it any more than you do, but that's who Rafe chose.'

Henry had had enough of all this hocus-pocus for one day. 'I don't care if Rafe's story says we all sit here and have a picnic. I'm going to help her,' he said firmly. 'Now, can I use your dinghy or not?'

Jeb stared at the determined slant of Henry's chin. The boy was right. To hell with Rafe Gallant and his story. 'Fine,' he said, 'but I'm coming too.'

Verity moved into the centre of the boat and crouched as low as she could, gripping onto both rudder and gunwale. The squall hit the boat with a vicious bang. *Poor Honesty* pitched and heeled violently. Everything flapped furiously. The sheets tugged through the blocks like frantic snakes. The noise was hellish.

She'd never sailed in conditions like this before, but there was no time to panic. She looked up at the burgee – the little flag at the top of the mast – to check the wind direction. She knew the sensible thing to do would be to face into the wind and let the sails loose. But there was no time for that. She had to try and get through the weather. The boat was working itself round to face the squall. She partially sheeted in the mainsail to draw in just a little of the wind – not too much or the boat would heel and capsize.

Verity steeled herself to sit out as far as she could. It was terrifying. The main sheet was still flapping violently. The jib was flying loose. She needed a little power from that small front sail too, if she was to make progress. But the sheet that controlled the jib was dangling over the side of the boat, dragging uselessly in the sea, and she didn't dare move to retrieve it. It made the boat a lot less easy to steer and the tiller far heavier, but she didn't have a choice.

Cold salt spray was whipping in Verity's face, stinging bitterly. Each time the dinghy pitched she saw the sea rear higher than the boat, threatening to swallow her with every roll.

Grandmother was burning with anger at Verity's audacious defiance. Miranda seemed thrilled by the sport of it, leaning over to get a better look. The old lady glared at the dinghy, and the wind increased in intensity.

The crowd on the quayside could see its effect and watched *Poor Honesty*, silent and fearful.

'*Come on*, Verity,' Isaac breathed.

On the jetty, Jeb jumped nimbly into the dinghy and grabbed the rudder. 'I'll helm,' he said. 'She's a bit temperamental.'

'Fine,' said Henry as he untied the painter. He looked up to see Martha climbing awkwardly down the metal ladder to the gangway. 'You're not coming with us,' he told her, pre-empting anything she might have to say on the subject.

'Don't you need more weight when the weather's choppy?' Martha asked, still heading towards them.

Henry frowned at her. 'One day trip does not make you a sailor,' he said bluntly.

Martha clambered over the gunwale and sat down obstinately.

'You're just going to get in the way,' he insisted.

'Are we going to go out there and help Verity or sit here arguing about it?' she asked.

He cursed under his breath. Jeb shrugged.

'You ready?' Henry asked him. Jeb nodded in reply, so Henry stood on the gunwale and gave a hefty shove against the jetty to push off.

Jeb steered expertly away from the quay, filling the mainsail with wind while Henry busily sheeted in the jib. Jeb noticed that Henry didn't look even slightly scared; just purposeful and determined.

'I'm sorry I called you a Twogood turncoat,' he blurted out unexpectedly. Henry looked up, surprised. 'Your grandda saw what the Mistress was,' Jeb continued. 'But it took Ruby's death for Rafe and Isaac to realize.'

Henry blinked. 'I expect I've been quite snotty to you too,' he admitted.

'For a little 'un you don't give much ground,' Jeb agreed.

'Six older brothers,' Henry explained. 'Does wonders for your determination.'

In the depth of the squall, the thought of every malicious dig and jibe made by Grandmother spurred Verity on. She had to get her sister back. She sat out a little more to gain speed.

'I – will – not – turn – back,' she muttered to herself,

gritting her teeth against the freezing cold and peering blindly through the wall of spray.

The rowing boat had reached the *Storm* now. Grandmother was helped aboard, snapping angrily at her crew – taking her temper out on whoever was nearest. The impudence. The sheer defiant insolence of that idiot child. Her temper – always thinly stretched at the best of times – snapped.

'It will be worth the risk to be rid of you,' she hissed, throwing both her arms out again in the direction of the dinghy.

The squall intensified. A new gust of wind blasted the mainsail. Verity mustered all her courage and sat even further out of the boat in a last-ditch attempt to keep her righted. But she was just one girl in a boat meant for two. The dinghy reached tipping point and Verity realized she just didn't have enough weight. As the boat pitched onto its side, she hopped over the gunwale and onto the centreboard.

She was now standing precariously on the half-capsized boat while its sails floated in the water. The wind howled. To right the dinghy, she would have to pull with all her strength and lift the sopping wet sails – heavy with water – out of the sea. The waves crashed around her as she heaved on the main sheet.

'I – will – not – turn – back,' she repeated to herself. 'I – will – not – turn – back.'

The mast came up to vertical, moving faster as it righted itself. Water streamed off the sails and rigging onto Verity. Fast as lightning, she stepped off the board and over the gunwale into the sopping wet hull.

In the harbour everyone cheered and clapped for the valiant little girl.

'She's not out of the woods yet though,' said Isaac Tempest.

A man appeared at his side. His once handsome face was now lined and scored; his blue eyes burned with anxiety. 'Do you think I've done the wrong thing?' he asked.

Isaac shook his head, but couldn't hide his concern as another massive gust of wind hit the dinghy. *Poor Honesty* didn't stand a chance: her sails were wet, her rigging was sopping. She was far too top-heavy. This time she turned turtle, taking Verity into the sea with her.

Henry, Jeb and Martha were making good progress. With three of them on board they were able to keep the dinghy on an even keel. Martha leaned out dutifully, her eyes scrunched tight shut. She'd found it was the best way to avoid feeling very, very sick. The little boat was planing now: juddering and thrumming with the effort of going at her maximum possible speed.

A man on the quay spotted the three children. 'Ain't that Jeb Tempest? And the Twogood nipper with some other lass?' he exclaimed.

A shimmer of excitement spread through the crowd. 'They're going to help her,' someone shouted. 'Must be her pals.'

Out in the dinghy, Henry stared in amazement at the squall – a tight ball of weather – surrounding Verity and the upturned boat. 'She's turned turtle,' he shouted to Jeb. 'I don't think Verity can right her.'

'It's no use sailing into the squall,' Jeb called back. 'The Mistress will have us all then.'

Henry had no intention of giving up. 'We'll have to throw a sheet to her and pull her out,' he yelled back. 'Outrun the squall. Think you can go that fast?' He turned round and grinned, unable to resist a small dig.

Jeb smiled. 'Just watch me.'

Verity gasped with shock as she fell into the choppy water. It was bitterly cold. *Poor Honesty* bobbed about, finally stable. Verity scrabbled at the wet wooden hull, trying to pull herself out of the water. Her feet kept kicking under the boat, making it difficult to gain any purchase, but she still managed to get a hold.

Immediately another wave hit the dinghy and knocked her off before she could climb onto the upturned hull.

Then the squall seemed to intensify. Verity gasped again. The cold was like a punch to the chest. She thought frantically of Henry's instructions. Why hadn't she paid more attention to him? Then she remembered. Scrambling around the upturned boat, she looked for a loose sheet to throw over the hull. Success. Flinging it across, she swam round to the other side, coughing and spluttering as the waves buffeted her. Verity grabbed the rope and used it to haul herself up onto the hull again. She clung to the centre-board and tried to catch her breath, shuddering with cold.

She knew she didn't have the strength to swim beyond the squall or right the boat again. Now she could see Jeb's dinghy approaching. Henry was there, waving and shouting something she couldn't hear . . . but he'd never get through. Grandmother would see to that. This was it. Grandmother had won. She was going to die.

On the quay the crowd were silent. They could see that Verity was exhausted. Isaac Tempest stood there quietly, his pipe hanging from his fingers. His companion clutched anxiously at his silver forelock. 'What if they can't—?' he moaned.

'They're coming for her,' Isaac insisted, his eyes fixed on Jeb's dinghy.

Verity saw Henry leaning out of the dinghy, bellowing something at her – but she couldn't hear him. He looked so desperate and frustrated.

The events of the last six months flashed through her mind. How strange that it had all started with Abednego's arrival and it should finish with him so near at hand. I *cannot help you more than I have done*, she heard him saying.

As she clung onto the upturned boat, soaked to the skin,

Verity's consciousness threw out a desperate series of memories, like shutters opening up one by one.

'*The eye of the storm*,' said Henry in the reading room. '*The calm at the centre of the gale.*'

'*Surely there might also be a device that stills the weather*,' Jasper speculated in the library.

'*The Storm is coming*,' said Abednego once more as he took something from his pocket and placed it on top of her book. She remembered the infinite stillness in her room.

Verity's mind made the final connection. She knew now what Abednego had meant. Still clinging to the boat with one hand, she rummaged in her sodden pocket for the strange wooden ball he had given her with the book. It was there. Verity pulled it out and held it tightly. She mustn't drop it. She pushed and pulled at it – the eye of the *Storm* – grimly trying to remember how she'd opened it before.

She was now lying with her whole body curled around the centreboard, her hands scrabbling at the ball. All at once the seal opened. Her heart in her mouth, Verity spun the marble centre around in its casing, praying it would work. The curious eye turned to face her.

In an instant the squall disappeared. All was calm.

On the quay the people cheered and applauded. Amongst them men were shaking complete strangers by the hand and women were dabbing at their eyes with hankies.

On Jeb's dinghy the three crew members hugged each other in jubilation. Henry exhaled with relief, then gave a weak smile. 'Didn't think she was going to make it there,' he said in as jokey a tone as he could manage. Jeb watched thoughtfully.

'The eye of the *Storm*,' Verity shouted, elated. She jumped up, standing recklessly on the hull. '*It's the eye of the* Storm,' she repeated.

On the *Storm*, Grandmother gasped. 'It can't be . . .' she hissed. 'How could . . . ?' She was livid. 'How did she get that?' she howled. 'The thieving little guttersnipe.' All self-control lost, she reverted for a second to her natural shape. Her death's-head face, her petrifying skeletal limbs, the unmistakable odour of decay . . . all were revealed.

Miranda took a careful step towards her, still clutching the bundle that was Verity's new sister.

'Why don't you rest for a while?' she soothed. 'Surely your crew can deal with a nuisance like her on their own?'

Grandmother glared balefully at Miranda for a second and then acknowledged the point. 'Abednego,' she bellowed in a gale-blast of fury. Her captain looked up in acknowledgement. 'Set sail now,' she ordered, striding across the deck towards her cabin. 'You will notify me of any attempts to board.

'Let her try if she wishes,' she muttered, taking one final look out to sea. 'It will save a task later.'

# Chapter Twenty-one

Henry, Jeb and Martha sailed up to Verity. Henry leaned out of the boat to help pull her in.

'It's the eye of the *Storm*,' she shouted out. 'It brings calm.'

'Don't stand on an upturned hull, you idiot,' Henry scolded. 'You'll fall in again.'

Verity was riding high on a surge of adrenalin. She jumped into Jeb's boat, making it rock and sway.

'Easy,' he warned.

'Did you see me?' she babbled. 'Did you see? I think I did quite well really. I tried to remember everything I'd learned.'

It was the final straw for Henry. 'Yes, we saw you,' he snapped. 'Trying to sail through a *squall*: it was a ridiculous thing to do.'

Verity stopped in mid-flow. Then it hit her. She had nearly died. Henry grabbed her and gave her a hug. She held onto him and sniffed. 'Thanks for coming to get me,' she said.

Henry let go. ''S all right.'

'I still have to get to the *Storm*,' she added tentatively, in case anyone thought they could talk her out of it. 'I know it's dangerous, but I've got to.'

Jeb, for one, had no intention of talking her round. He scanned the *Storm*, trying to see what was happening on deck. 'Can't spot the Mistress,' he said, frowning. He stared up at the ship's soaring masts and spars. There were crewmen climbing expertly up the shrouds. A man near the top unfurled the first gigantic square of cloth. They heard the ripple and crack as it filled with wind. Others were doing the same across the rigging.

'They're preparing to set sail,' Jeb said anxiously.

'She's got my sister,' panicked Verity. More sails were dropping across the square lattice of rigging. The crew went busily about their tasks on deck.

'They're not paying any attention to us,' said Henry. Taking command, he turned to Jeb. 'Tack now,' he said. 'I think we can make it.'

Jeb moved the rudder to swing the dinghy in the direction of the *Storm*.

'You take the jib,' Henry instructed Verity. 'Martha, you and I will have to sit out: we need as much speed as possible.'

Martha just nodded. She was too scared to say or do anything now that they were in the middle of the wide, open sea and at the mercy of Verity's grandmother.

Verity felt sick with worry as the dinghy began to pick up speed. The *Storm* looked impenetrable. Suddenly they heard an order relayed across her decks.

'They're weighing anchor,' shouted Jeb.

The dinghy was racing along now, water splashing over the gunwales. Verity was still sodden from the capsizing of *Poor Honesty*. As they sped across the water, the wind chilled her to the bone. But all that mattered was getting to the *Storm* before she set sail; getting to her baby sister in time. The *Storm*'s best anchor clanked up out of the waves with a groan.

'We're not going to make it,' she fretted.

At last they were gaining. As they approached, the *Storm*'s hull rose above them, dark and forbidding. A stray Jacob's ladder was dangling down, swaying with the increasing movement of the ship. Jeb set a course straight for it.

The dinghy was soon right up against the *Storm*, completely dwarfed by the huge ship, still apparently unnoticed.

'Your grandmother will probably be in the cabin suite,' shouted Henry above the slap of the waves. 'There's a chance we could sneak in and steal your sister back.' He tried not to think about the many, many flaws in this ridiculously simple plan.

Verity stared in horror at the swinging rope ladder. She couldn't climb that. Henry was already reaching for it, apparently undaunted. With a leap he grabbed it and hopped up a few steps. He leaned back down for Verity. 'Take my hand,' he instructed.

Verity didn't have time to think. She jumped, reaching

for Henry with one hand and the rope ladder with the other.

'Don't look down,' Henry shouted as they swung to and fro against the hull.

Jeb got up to follow her. 'No,' said Henry commandingly. 'You stay here.'

'And let you board on your own? No way.'

'You can't leave Martha here with the boat,' said Henry with authority. 'Verity's best chance of rescuing her sister is if one of us acts as a decoy and the others wait here to get them back to shore.'

'So let me board the *Storm*,' Jeb shouted.

Henry shook his head in reply. 'You're nearly a grown-up. They'd show even less mercy to you than they will to me.'

Verity closed her eyes. The waves were sucking and swirling around the massive ship. The cold was closing in on her.

Jeb started to argue the point. 'There's no time for this, Jeb,' Martha interrupted. 'Verity needs to get moving. She's freezing.'

Jeb stared helplessly at her. He didn't like it, but she and Henry were right. At least if he stayed here there'd be a chance Verity might escape.

'You can't plan to stay on the *Storm* alone,' he said finally.

Henry grinned. 'Obviously I'll expect you to come back for me – once you've got Verity and the baby home.'

*　　*　　*

Verity would never know how she made it up that precarious rope ladder. It was like scaling the walls of a fortress. Her hands were numb, scarcely able to grip. But Henry kept encouraging her.

'Not much further,' he said, looking down at her once more, smiling confidently.

Poking her head above the edge at last, she saw the vast wooden deck stretching out ahead of her. The imposing grid of masts and spars towered for hundreds of feet into the air. Even through her fear Verity couldn't help feeling thrilled. The *Storm* was breathtaking.

She pulled herself up beside Henry. The two of them stood there, silent. The ship was vast and unbelievably noisy, but it was still astounding that no one had noticed their arrival.

'That's the cabin suite,' Henry said in hushed tones, pointing to a door. 'If I run to the other side of the deck and make a commotion, you might get a chance to sneak in.'

A few yards in front of them a crew member reversed towards them, apparently intent on swabbing the deck. The two stowaways watched the flamboyantly dressed man with his gold jewellery and vivid silk scarf. What should they do? How could they get past him?

But the sailor solved their dilemma for them. Dropping his mop, he swivelled round and grabbed both of them by their collars. He held them close and leered at them; he smelled of spiced oil, stale rum and sweat. 'Come to rescue her?' he asked.

Verity's heart plummeted. They had got no further than the rail.

'Thought you'd just saunter aboard and take her back?' Holding them both with one hand, he smacked Henry across the ear with the other.

The sight of her friend being hurt sparked Verity's temper. She was furious – at her own stupidity, at their helplessness. 'Leave him alone,' she shouted.

The sailor raised an eyebrow. 'Some of the Gentry spirit there,' he said. 'We'll have to see if we can beat it out of you.'

Verity struggled to free herself, but the man just held them tighter still and lifted his other hand again. 'Don't think you'll get any special treatment just because you're a girl,' he spat.

Looking up, he shouted for help. 'Hey, lads. We've got callers.'

Within seconds a small gang had gathered around the two children: they dropped down from above; they appeared silently from each side; one jumped over the rail of the quarterdeck in his eagerness not to miss out.

Verity and Henry looked around silently at the hard-looking, weather-beaten crew. Assembled together, they were an intimidating sight. Henry tried very hard not to recall all the stories he'd heard about the crew of the *Storm*.

'Very touching,' said one sailor, 'coming to rescue your baby sister.'

'Do you know what we do with unwelcome guests?' added another, reaching out to stroke Verity's cheek as she instinctively flinched away from his touch.

'Shall we kill them now or wait for the Mistress?' asked the man in the silk scarf.

'We could slice the girl quick and save this one for fun,' someone suggested, staring aggressively at Henry. 'Always fancied bringing the Twogoods down a peg or two . . . tearing them off a strip.' The man mimed a cutting action then a whipping flick to make sure his meaning was clear. His colleagues laughed nastily.

Henry stared at the threatening man. 'Do your worst,' he muttered – and immediately received a punch in return. Verity felt sick at the sound of the sailor's knuckles coming into contact with Henry's body.

'Oh, we will,' he reassured Henry – who still refused to look cowed. Verity's mind raced with fear. What had she been thinking? They'd walked straight into Grandmother's lair. She was going to die; Henry too. And it was all her fault.

The *Storm* was now straining and swaying in the water: with her sails filled, she was held only by the lesser anchors. But all activity had ground to a halt as more of the crew gathered around Verity and Henry.

A silent shadow fell over them. Verity looked up. It was Abednego. Her heart jumped into her mouth. Whose side was he on? Perhaps only his own. He made his way through his men, who melted away to let him past.

Dressed in his embroidered coat and dark brown trousers, he stood there, towering over the two children. Seconds passed. 'I ordered you to set sail,' he said to his crew.

'They're stowaways, Cap'n,' said one man uncertainly, thrown by their leader's unexpected reaction.

'You will leave them to me,' said Abednego. There were a few disgruntled mutters, but he silenced them with one look. 'Do you question me?'

Not one of the men ventured a word more. Verity held her breath in suppressed hope.

Suddenly the door to the cabin suite slammed open violently. 'What is this *commotion*?' shrieked a venomous voice. The crew looked up in alarm. The Mistress must have sensed the disturbance – like a spider detecting vibrations at the outermost reaches of its web. The old lady's mood had clearly not improved. 'I said I was to be notified,' she barked.

The crew leaped into action, immediately busying themselves with their tasks.

Miranda kept pace with her benefactress. 'Would you like me to hold the baby for you?' she asked, keenly aware of how important it was right now to remain in the Mistress's good graces. 'It must be very tiring for you.'

The Mistress was in no mood to be charmed by anyone, but the crying brat was doing nothing for her nerves. She shoved the tiny bundle towards Miranda, who held the infant warily at arm's length.

The old lady had reached Abednego now. It took her just a second to absorb the scene and come to the correct assessment.

'*You*,' she shrieked, turning to face him. '*You* gave the Gallant child the eye.' Her disbelief was palpable. '*After all I've done for you*,' she breathed, with an ice-cold draught of fury.

Abednego turned to face her, steeling himself to do so without fear. He had been preparing for this moment since he first sat on the floor of the library in Wellow and saw his own life in the book. Nothing she could do to him now would be any worse than the damage she'd already wreaked. He pulled the cherished peg doll from his pocket as witness.

'You killed Abigail,' he said. 'You killed my sister. You didn't save me. You took me because I was useful and killed her because she was not.'

The Mistress of the Storm was – for once – slightly taken aback. 'I–' she started.

'You made it an Original Story: fated to happen over and over again. It was in the book, *your* book.'

The Mistress stood there staring at Abednego: the one man who had shown unswerving loyalty to her all these years was fighting back. 'Where did you find it?' she spat. 'How did you get a copy?'

Abednego ignored her. 'You must not take this child,' he said. 'No more stealing children. No more killing children.' A single tear rolled down his noble face.

The Mistress's temper was rising. She was not used to insubordination and it did not appeal to her now. 'I asked where you found the book,' she demanded. 'Who told you?'

The dark giant watched her carefully but said nothing.

His Mistress snapped. Her fury at this act of defiance was incandescent. '*Who – told – you?*' she hissed. A frozen wind threaded around him like a snake. 'I am still your Mistress, boy,' she added, leaning in a threatening manner towards the straight-backed and stony-faced Abednego.

'I do not owe you any further allegiance,' he said. 'You lost that when I discovered the truth.' As if to demonstrate this, he went over to a locker. Lifting the lid, he revealed the hiding place of an extremely surprised and rather sheepish-looking man in a neatly pressed navy blue uniform with very shiny polished buttons.

'Mr Cutgrass,' gasped Verity, and Henry gawped openly.

Jasper stepped out of his secret cubbyhole. He was carrying a custom-made square bag on his shoulder. He stared at the assembled crowd. Even he could see that this was going to cramp his plans for stowing away. That, he reflected, was the problem with mysterious visitors such as Abednego. You never knew what they were going to do next.

'A customs man?' roared the old lady. '*A – customs – man?*'

It was too much for her. She could no longer control her emotions, and no longer wished to. It was time to revert to her natural form.

With a deep breath and an exhalation that reeked of decay, she allowed her transformation to take place. The air was rent in two and she was replaced in one hot, dusty blast of fury by a scarcely human creature. Still shrouded in robes, the figure paused, head bent over. The assembled group stood watching silently, fearfully, as it looked up to reveal itself fully.

All the soft tissues of the face were gone; in their place was only blackened and papery skin from which all moisture had been removed: you could clearly see the skull beneath. The cuffs and edges of the clothing offered small glimpses of bones that were similarly mummified. The breath issuing from the monster was hoarse and ragged. A gritty wind swirled around it.

Verity gasped, instantly recognizing in the creature the angry features of her grandmother.

# Chapter Twenty-two

The crew stepped back a little, well aware that such a change did not bode well.

'Enough of this defiance,' said the cowled figure in a grating, hollow voice. 'It is time . . .'

Verity shuddered.

Most people, when faced with the natural form of the Mistress, collapsed in terror. But not Jasper Cutgrass. To think that the Mistress of the Storm really existed, just as Abednego had explained . . . he reflected. It was astonishing.

Henry was stunned. So the book had been right. All the terrible things this woman . . . creature . . . had done — they'd killed her soul, piece by piece.

'She's damaged her soul so severely, she's scarcely alive,' whispered Verity.

The creature laughed — a scraping, jarring sound that set the teeth on edge. Verity stared at the atrophied figure. Even though it had scarcely any features left, she recognized that look of scorn.

'So convenient,' rasped the Mistress, glancing at the tiny bundle in Miranda's arms. 'I can both prevent Rafe's Pledge to destroy me *and* restore my youthfulness.'

Verity stiffened. The hairs on her arms prickled. What was her macabre enemy planning? Her baby sister moved a swaddled limb and snuffled.

'She is your mother's third daughter,' said the Mistress. 'Surely, little bookworm, that must mean something to you . . .'

Verity looked at her in horror. '. . . *but this time she chose to tell a tale of terrifying cruelty,*' she said, reciting the words from memory.

As she continued, the Mistress of the Storm began to say the words with her: '. . . *of how each would be sacrificed. That they would die, so she might have longer life. And from that day on it was a bitter blessing to bear a third daughter.*'

'You're going to drink her blood to rejuvenate yourself,' Verity realized, aghast.

The Mistress tilted her head in a self-satisfied smirk, unable to resist the opportunity to gloat. 'Poor Rafe,' she said. 'So clever usually, but I don't think he intended the story to end like this.'

Verity reeled. Somewhere amidst the fear it occurred to her that she should try to keep her enemy talking. 'How could you know it would be a girl,' she asked, 'before she was born? Boys are no good to you.'

The Mistress stared triumphantly at her. 'I could hear it,' she announced. 'I am the Keeper of the Wind.'

Verity's mind started to race. 'That's why you couldn't kill me until now,' she realized. 'Because if you did, she wouldn't *be* the third daughter . . . but you must have wanted to.'

The Mistress glared at her. 'Oh, I did,' she snapped. 'What an irritation you have been to me, with your books . . . and insolence. But it has been worth the wait. Now I can revive myself, and then kill you to make sure Rafe's story never comes about.'

'And you think we're just going to stand around and let you get on with it?' demanded Henry angrily.

The Mistress laughed. Extending a withered finger, she beckoned towards a cabin door. With a clatter it swung open to reveal Verity's father. He looked as if he hadn't slept for days. The man Verity had once known as the very essence of composure stood before her with bloodshot eyes and scarecrow hair. His head bobbed and jerked sporadically. He didn't appear to recognize them at all.

Behind him he was dragging a large sack. As he untied it, Verity gasped in horror. In it was her sister Poppy, gagged and bound. Even from this distance Verity could see that she was bruised and trembling with fear. Her heart turned over.

'What do you think you're doing?' shouted Henry, outraged.

Spinning back round, Verity glared at the merciless creature. 'How could you hurt her like this?' she demanded. 'And what have you *done* to my father?'

'Being tormented by the wind can drive even the

strongest of men to insanity,' the Mistress said smugly.

Verity gasped: so Martha had been right. 'You've been controlling him . . .'

'A heady combination of desert and polar breezes.' The Mistress chuckled at her own cruel ingenuity.

'Well, no more,' said Verity angrily. She knew exactly what to do. Scrabbling in her pocket, she found the eye of the *Storm* and opened it. Her father looked up from his stupor. He seemed confused. Verity ran towards him and closed his limp fingers over the wooden ball. It was as if a mist had cleared from his eyes. Focusing on his daughter for the first time in months, Tom Gallant gazed in shock at her, and then at his surroundings.

'You won't do this to him any longer,' insisted Verity, tears running down her face.

The Mistress stared calmly at her. 'That is your choice,' she said. 'It can only protect one of you. Not both.'

Verity swivelled round, brushing a tear from her cheek. 'Do what you like,' she snapped. But as she spoke the words, a peculiar sensation enveloped her. A baking hot wind was whipping around her. At the same time tiny cold darts of a freezing draught pricked her skin. Her vision blurred and then re-formed. She felt sick and disorientated, maddened and hideously uncomfortable. Was this what Father had endured these past few months? Verity couldn't imagine how he had borne it.

'*That which gave you life shall destroy you* – that's what Rafe pledged,' screeched the Mistress. '*My blood will turn against yours.* How dare he? I gave him everything he sought and that was my repayment?'

'You killed his daughter,' said Verity, struggling to get the words out but determined to say them. 'My aunt.'

'She was an annoyance,' said the Mistress dismissively. 'You remind me of her a great deal. His blood . . .' She sniffed. 'Well, if there is none of his bloodline left at all, that will be the safest thing for me.'

Verity's head throbbed. The torment was over-whelming, making every thought an effort; the tiny spikes of cold grew increasingly agonizing. But it was Abednego who responded by grabbing the bag from Jasper's shoulder. In a second he had removed its contents.

'He found the Storm Bringer,' he said, holding aloft the glass globe.

Jasper was outraged. 'What are you doing?' he demanded. 'That is the property of the Revenue.'

'You broke many rules when you charmed this for Barbarous Usage,' said Abednego angrily. 'But now it will be your undoing.'

The crew of the *Storm* leaped away from their captain. Some were standing by the rail, as if preparing to throw themselves into the sea. They might not have seen it in a long time but they knew what the Storm Bringer was and what it could do.

'You don't have the nerve.' The Mistress tilted her desiccated head in defiance. 'Use it, and it will kill everyone.'

'It will destroy only you,' said Abednego, raising his hand to shake the mysterious glass globe. The crew took another step back. 'It is part of you; you are part of it. If you collide, both will disappear.'

The Mistress fixed Abednego with her terrifying gaze. 'You should be sure that it will work, boy. If I live, I shall not rest until I have punished you.'

Abednego hesitated. A trace of doubt flickered across his face. He knew the Mistress's bent for cruelty better than most.

She smirked and leaned out to take the Storm Bringer from Abednego's hand . . . Too late.

Focusing every ounce of will and determination, Verity had already steeled herself to take action. This was it: her chance to fulfil the Pledge. Forcing her hands to reach out, she grabbed the mysterious Storm Bringer from the captain.

Years later, she could still remember that moment as if she were experiencing it afresh. It was as if she were outside her body looking down on the deck of the *Storm*, watching herself in silent slow motion.

Around her she was aware of Jasper throwing out an arm – too slowly – in an effort to stop her. She saw Miranda Blake, with the baby in her arms, coolly weighing up the situation; Abednego turning, startled; Henry, running towards her, shouting something she couldn't make out. She could see the raddled, desiccated creature that was the Mistress cringing.

And then she saw her own overwhelming confusion as the Storm Bringer was lifted gently but firmly out of her hand. The terrible dry pricking heat lifted.

'That is not how the story ends, Verity,' said a familiar voice.

'Alice,' exclaimed Verity, stunned, as she turned and recognized her friend. 'What are you doing *here*?'

The old lady's inquisitive pink face looked exhausted. For the first time in her life Verity noticed the deep lines and wrinkles. Alice turned to face the wasted cadaverous creature in front of her.

'Oh, Aure,' she said softly. 'What have you let yourself become?' Her voice was filled with love, disappointment and regret.

The Mistress hissed. 'I don't need your pity, *sister*,' she said, managing to fill that one word with a world of contempt.

Verity and Henry gasped in shock.

'How . . . ?' Verity asked incredulously. How could Alice be the sister of that . . . that thing?

Alice looked ashamed. 'What must you think of the deception?' she asked.

Verity didn't know what to say.

'All I can tell you is that my love for you was genuine – whatever it must look like now.'

Verity swallowed awkwardly. She knew that. Of course she knew it. Why would Alice think otherwise?

Alice walked towards the Mistress. 'You will not take the baby,' she said. 'I won't let you.'

The Mistress was furious. 'How dare you interfere again? You see how she uses you all?' she barked, staring around.

'I know what you did, Aure,' said Alice, briskly switching to the real reason for her presence. 'I know what happened to our sisters.'

In a day of unprecedented shocks, this was the most startling revelation of all for the Mistress. She stared at her sister with undisguised horror.

'You have to come with me now,' Alice told her.

'I shall do no such thing,' snapped her sister, desperately trying to recover her composure.

Alice reached out with sympathy and love. 'This is how it finishes, Aure,' she said.

The Mistress gave a guttural screech of frustration and anger; suddenly arid sand-filled air blasted the onlookers' faces. With a movement so swift it scarcely seemed possible, she snatched Verity's baby sister from Miranda's arms. Verity shrieked in horror. The creature that was the Mistress opened its terrifying maw, preparing to feast on the infant's blood.

Each thing after that happened so fast that it was impossible to be sure what was taking place. But Verity saw Alice at the Mistress's side with the Storm Bringer. She saw the two struggling. They made such a strange contrast: the terrifying creature whose skin was as black as its soul, and the frail-looking old lady with delicate pink cheeks who was evidently a great deal stronger than she appeared.

Then Verity found herself holding her new sister. The world froze. The tiny baby was so perfect. Her pink rosebud lips were slightly apart beneath her snub nose. Her blue eyes opened and they seemed to look at Verity with the wisdom of ages. Verity was overwhelmed with love. She had never expected to feel like this.

Then came an earth-shattering explosion. The deafening crack and boom of the blast ripped the air. A tremendous force shook the *Storm*, knocking her crew and all her unexpected guests off their feet. Verity thudded to the deck as Henry flew across to protect her and the baby.

The *Storm* hadn't been readied for such a blow. The great ship pitched and yawed frantically. Everything not battened down flew through the air or rolled across the deck. The rigging smacked and thwacked against every neighbouring piece of wood. Verity clung grimly to the baby and to Henry, her eyes tight shut.

Eventually the swell subsided and the *Storm* settled. Verity opened her eyes to see a scene of devastation. The Mistress was gone; the grandmother – who had never been her grandmother – was no longer there.

She looked around: Henry was there; Poppy and her father were safe, on the other side of the deck.

'*Alice*,' screamed Verity, staring in horror at the space where her old friend should have been. She ran across the deck clutching her sister. Henry followed her, his face creased with concern.

'She was too close, Verity,' he said sadly. 'Whatever Alice

did caused some kind of explosion. She couldn't possibly have escaped the blast.'

Of all the people Verity had expected to lose today, Alice had not been one of them. 'You're wrong,' she yelled desperately at Henry. 'Not everything has a logical explanation.' Tears started to roll down her cheeks. She ran to the side of the deck and looked over the rail. Henry tried to take her arm.

'You're wrong,' she repeated with a sob, jerking herself away.

Henry grabbed hold of her more firmly this time, saying nothing. He held her and the baby in his arms.

Verity wept, the tears hurting as they welled up in her eyes, her chest tight. 'She can't be gone,' she cried, the words raw with grief. Henry stroked her hair silently while her baby sister mewed and wriggled in her blanket.

Abednego came over and placed the eye of the *Storm* in her hand. 'I do not believe Alice is dead,' he said.

Verity looked up at him, her face red and swollen. Instinctively she knew he was right. She felt calmer. 'Why did you give this to me?' she asked.

'I am not sure,' he admitted. 'Perhaps I hoped it would be the start of my penance for my time as a servant of the Mistress.'

Verity turned it around in her hand. 'I'll miss the peace it brings,' she said, handing it back to him.

Abednego shook his head, his high cheekbones glinting

in the sun. 'No,' he said. 'It soothes the weather, but not the spirit.' He stared thoughtfully at her. 'What you felt was within yourself. It is yours to keep.' And he wrapped her fingers around it.

Verity stood beside her father as they prepared to leave the *Storm*. He leaned on her slightly: after so many months of torment it would be a while before he was fully recovered. In the distance they could see the watching crowd still milling about on the quay, presumably desperate to know what had happened. Henry and Jasper helped Poppy gently over the side and down into Jeb's waiting dinghy. Martha had boarded the *Storm* to help and was carrying the youngest Gallant sister for now.

'Your family are animals, Gallant,' spat Miranda Blake as she shoved her way past, carrying handfuls of jewellery she had liberated from the cabin suite. She knew she couldn't go back to her mother empty-handed.

'We came to rescue you, you poisonous girl,' shouted Henry indignantly. 'Well,' he conceded, 'not you specifically . . . but *still*.'

Verity looked furiously at Miranda. Her family and friends had nearly been killed, the woman she'd trusted all her life had turned out to be the sister of her worst enemy . . . and had now disappeared once more. This stupid girl felt like the least of her worries at the minute.

'I did warn you about her,' she told her. 'And anyway, she's gone now.'

# Chapter Twenty-three

The miraculous disappearance of the Mistress seemed to have broken down all normal barriers and put everyone in a celebratory mood. Isaac Tempest was waiting at the quay to help Tom Gallant home, and things had progressed quite naturally to an impromptu gathering.

Martha was assisting Henry in making large pots of tea and great mounds of sandwiches in the Gallant kitchen. He knew all about the correct procedure for large family get-togethers.

Mrs Gallant was sitting on a sofa feeding her new baby, whose beautiful eyes were clamped shut, her cheeks pink. She didn't quite understand why her husband had arrived looking so dishevelled, or what had brought so many people to their home right now. He had started trying to explain something about his stepmother and the baby, but it hadn't made any sense.

'And it's all thanks to Verity,' he had finished proudly, patting their eldest daughter on the shoulder.

'Well, that's nice, dear,' she had replied dutifully. She was sure she would hear about it later.

At the moment Verity's father was manfully welcoming everyone into his house with quiet good humour. He looked a little frail. 'So pleased you could make it,' he could be heard saying to each and every guest in turn.

The customs man, meanwhile, had matters of a more urgent nature to attend to. Jasper Cutgrass turned once again at a brisk half-run into a familiar street.

'Shouldn't you have left by now?' Daniel Twogood demanded as his head appeared round the front door. Then he glanced at Jasper's side. The custom-made canvas bag was no longer there.

'It's gone,' said Jasper happily. Dan frowned. 'An elderly lady claiming to be the Mistress's sister caused it to impact against her – the Mistress, that is,' the customs man explained, 'and both disappeared.'

Mr Twogood nodded slowly as he absorbed this information. 'Colliding with each other: that could annihilate both . . . or remove them at least.'

Daniel Twogood detected a certain elation emanating from this curiously unreadable man. It occurred to him that *he* was not feeling as he normally did, either. He looked in astonishment at the customs man. The Twogood family burden was his no more. The terrifyingly dangerous instrument his father had made was no longer a threat to the world. He grinned. 'Well I'll be . . .' he said, stepping out onto the path. 'Gone, eh? That's a turn up for the books.'

Jasper was so excited he was swaying slightly from side to side. 'Completely disappeared,' he agreed. 'No one can use it now.'

Daniel Twogood patted him approvingly on the arm. 'A good day's work there, nipper,' he said.

Jasper Cutgrass smiled broadly.

And the widow's son – what of him? In the tiny front room of the Usage cottage Villainous closed the front door, took off his boots and put them on the mat. It had taken no small amount of earnest persuasion, but next week would be his first as an apprentice at Lapp and Muster.

'You'll be the oldest they've ever had,' Mother would sneer when he told her.

He went into the kitchen and took up where he had left off, cleaning and mending each part of their home. In the months and years to come it would gleam like a new pin. What else is there to do in the long dark hours of the night? There was no prospect of sleep. Sleep brought no rest.

For Verity – who had never expected the *Storm*'s arrival – everything was now very different. She remembered the day – a lifetime ago – when a lonely little girl walked through the red double doors of Wellow library and encountered a tall stranger.

'Rtyy goo'f say s'm'self,' said Henry, his mouth full of corned beef sandwich. Verity tipped her head to one side in enquiry. 'These sandwiches,' he explained, 'are pretty good. Even if I do say so myself.'

'Pleased to hear it.'

'Well, it was hungry work, all that sailing and running around. It's no wonder I'm starving.'

In the background Martha was discussing myths and legends of the Gentry with Isaac Tempest. Verity was sitting on the floor next to Poppy. She gave her another hug.

'Careful,' laughed her sister, already back to her usual sunny self. 'You'll wear me out.'

Verity grinned. Poppy hugged her back. They didn't need to say any more.

'What an adventure.' Poppy grabbed a jam sandwich. 'And what a relief that Grandmother's gone. She was terribly hard work.'

Jeb Tempest walked awkwardly into the sitting room, long hair tied back and head down. Verity jumped up, hoping to put him at ease.

'I've come to say goodbye,' he announced, rather formally. Standing in the middle of the room being stared at by various females and Henry was very far from his ideal platform. Verity looked at him quizzically, a little wrong-footed by his propriety.

'I'm taking off for a bit,' he added, to make it clear that he wasn't just going home for afternoon tea.

'Oh,' said Verity, not sure what to say. She tried not to look disappointed.

Jeb shuffled uncomfortably on the spot. 'We've kept my grandfather's promise to Rafe, you see,' he began. 'I'm free now to leave Wellow; see something of the world.'

Verity nodded. 'There must be lots of places you'd like to see,' she said sympathetically. She could certainly understand how he felt.

'There are.' For a moment Jeb forgot both his audience and who he was talking to. 'So many things my grandfather's told me about.'

Verity smiled. 'Well, that's absolutely brilliant.'

Jeb allowed himself a brief glance at her face.

'I'm very envious,' she continued. 'But you've spent quite enough time waiting in Wellow for other people.'

Jeb looked down at the floor again. 'I was happy to do it,' he said quietly.

Verity hoped desperately that the burning sensation she could feel on her cheeks was not visible.

Henry got up, evidently of the opinion that this compelling dialogue had gone on for quite long enough.

'And you've got Henry to look after you,' Jeb pointed out. 'They don't come any more reliable – or honourable – than him.'

'That's true.'

'Verity doesn't need looking after,' said Henry. 'She's more than capable of taking care of herself.'

Jeb grinned. 'Yes, she is,' he agreed.

Verity shoved Henry in a silent reminder that this was not a very gracious acceptance of an obvious compliment.

'I couldn't have reached Verity without you,' Henry acknowledged reluctantly.

'I know you won't see it as a good thing,' Jeb told him, 'but there's true Gentry spirit in you.'

Henry nodded. 'And there's less of it in you than I thought there would be,' he replied, shaking Jeb's hand, completely and blissfully unaware he'd just won a battle he had no idea he was fighting.

Verity went out into the garden to see Father. He was sitting on a bench, looking tired. She took a seat next to him. He smiled welcomingly at her.

'Just having a little rest,' he explained.

They sat together in companionable silence, enjoying the last rays of late afternoon sun.

'I'm so sorry, Verity,' he went on, holding his daughter's hand. 'I should have told you about your family heritage. Not left you to hear it from others . . . And then, when I really needed to, I couldn't,' he continued sadly.

Verity smiled reassuringly, not sure what to say.

'I should have been stronger,' he said, his voice breaking.

Verity frowned. 'How could you have overcome that?' she asked. 'It must have been unbearable.'

'I'm so proud of you,' Father told her.

'I had some help,' Verity pointed out.

Mr Gallant looked lovingly at his daughter. 'You can tell a lot about a person by their friends,' he said, 'and I think yours reflect very well on you.'

Verity smiled, feeling a little glow of happiness inside her. 'I'm glad you like them,' she said.

'I realize now that we should have let you enjoy your childhood more,' Mr Gallant said sadly. 'We were just worried that you'd . . .' He trailed off. 'I was so angry with your grandfather for leaving, I tried to wipe out the Gentry past – pretend it never happened. I cast aside everything from that life . . . but you were terribly brave today.' He smiled proudly. 'It made me see that there were many good things about the Gentry originally: courage, spirit, enterprise. You displayed all of those. And I promise I will try to live up to that heritage for you in the future.'

Verity hugged her father, holding him as if she never wanted to let him go.

Later, in the library, Miss Cameron took out her personal copy of *On the Origin of Stories: A Disquisition*. The book was not bound. It was loose-leaf, and far bigger than the volume Abednego had handed to a little girl on Steephill Cove. It also credited an additional editor: Hodge, Heyworth, Helerley . . . and Cameron.

Beside her stood a man, his once handsome face lined and scored, though his blue eyes burned. The librarian turned to show him a new section. The words *Verity* and *Gallant* could be seen in the title. He looked at it proudly. '*Without love I am nothing,*' he said. 'That is what you taught me.'

'What would you be if you honoured your child's memory with hate?' she asked.

Rafe nodded to acknowledge the truth of it. 'This is better,' he agreed. 'An Original Story that shows how every child who is alone or out of place will find the friends they need, and the love they deserve. Verity's tale.'

Miss Cameron smiled.

'A nobler way to make good what I owed to Ruby and Tom . . . to all my children,' he added sadly. 'What must you have thought,' he asked, 'when I appeared on your doorstep that night – half crazed – and thrust the book into your hand?'

'You were grief-stricken,' said Miss Cameron. 'To lose a daughter . . . and then find your own wife was so much more than you had realized.'

'I was a fool,' said Rafe briskly. 'To know what she could do – to profit from her ability to control the wind – and not consider what else she might be capable of.'

'The book makes it very clear,' Miss Cameron told him.

Rafe nodded. 'When she murdered Ruby, I couldn't bear to have one thing of Aure's in the house. I went to her room to throw out every last trinket. And there it was. It took just a few pages to realize at last; to understand her capacity for cruelty . . . and the means by which she staved off death . . .

'How did you know I would come to doubt my thirst for revenge?' he asked.

'I didn't,' said Miss Cameron. 'But it takes a long time

to travel to the other side of the world . . . and back again.'

Rafe laughed wryly. 'All that way to learn that the place I sought was here in my home town.'

'Many stories begin in Wellow,' Miss Cameron replied impassively.

'It must have seemed a terrible burden to Verity when I returned,' Rafe said regretfully. 'To be told that she was charged with avenging Ruby's death; with killing Aure.'

'She will understand when she finds out the truth,' said Miss Cameron. 'Look what she has helped to create: a story of love and friendship that can be repeated over and over again throughout the world.'

'And now Aure is gone . . .'

Miss Cameron said nothing.

'It was a neat trick,' he went on admiringly. 'Everyone knew the words of the Pledge – *that which gave you life shall destroy you* – but you turned them into a new story, a second story.'

'I simply told a tale of protection.' Miss Cameron ignored the compliment.

Rafe nodded. 'One which told how, if the Mistress murdered another child to prolong her life . . .'

'. . . the result would be her own death,' finished Miss Cameron.

'If she hadn't tried to use the third daughter for sustenance she'd be here still.'

'Perhaps so.'

'Where is she now?' Rafe asked hesitantly.

'Alice saved her, I believe,' said Miss Cameron. 'Anyway, your story – the first story – is spoken. For every child like Verity, it is there. It is original, and it will happen again and again – the friends they need, and the love they deserve when they are alone or out of place. A fitting epitaph for Ruby.'

At six foot three, Abednego cut a lonely figure on the quarterdeck of the *Storm*. He stared silently at the bright green ocean.

The first mate approached warily. 'Tide is turning, Cap'n,' he said. 'Time for us to make our way, I reckon.'

Abednego stared at him in confusion. 'The Mistress of the Storm is gone,' he said. 'We no longer belong to her – you are all free to leave.'

'You're our captain,' said the first mate simply. 'Always have been, still are. Shall I give the order?'

Abednego watched as a solitary figure in a neatly pressed navy blue uniform with very shiny polished buttons rowed determinedly across the water. 'Not yet,' he said.

# Book Four
# SUMMER

## Epilogue

The walk to Soul Bay is beautiful on a fine day. But to reach it you must first make your way down a precarious set of wooden steps, put there who knows how long ago or by whom.

You step across the sweetly scented grass downs, through the ancient woods carpeted with dense ferns and damp rich moss. Finally you see a knotted rope strung across the last piece of muddy cliff. It stops all but the most determined from making their way to the warm shingled beach.

At the bottom is a small wooden bridge – more a set of planks really – perched over the trickling stream that eventually seeps into the sand long before it reaches the sea.

A young girl is sitting on the bridge. Tall for her age, she wears her long brown hair loose; it strays wildly in all directions. Her happy, shining face, with pink cheeks and dark, dark eyes, wavers constantly between pretty and very plain. Her feet are bare and her forehead has a smudge of dirt on it.

Next to her, a sturdy, sandy-haired young boy is hauling up a length of string tied around various scraps of meat and bone.

A crab is clinging for dear life to the end of the string. He extracts it and puts it in a bucket with the others they've collected. The girl is swinging her legs and laughing at something the boy has just said.

*Not everything in life turns out as we would like. But things can change.*

A man stands at the top of the wooden steps. His once handsome face is lined and scored, but his blue eyes burn. He is watching the two children: it is as if he is trying to commit every last detail to memory. He seems consumed by conflicting emotions: pride, happiness, sorrow, loss.

A cloud of vanilla tobacco wafts through the air. The man smiles and turns round to greet the faithful friend approaching him.

'It was well done, Rafe,' says Isaac Tempest.

Rafe Gallant stares into the distance for a second. He says nothing. He seems unable to speak.

Isaac looks fondly at his companion. 'A wise woman,' he says, 'once told me that to love is to act with purpose, for the happiness of all.'

Rafe nods.

'Shall we go down?' Isaac asks.

'No,' says Rafe thoughtfully. 'Let them have their day in the sun.'

The two friends turn to leave. Above them the sky is a clear and vivid azure, save for one lone cloud – unnaturally dark for this weather – that scurries, scowling, across the blue.

## *Acknowledgements*

I once read somewhere that being an author requires an unnatural level of single-mindedness. Certainly the process of writing this book involved securing the help of many other people whose time and effort I'm sure could have been spent far more enjoyably.

My heartfelt thanks therefore go to Victoria and Rachel for being my first readers. To Catherine and Claire for offering hope that it might be worth finishing the first draft. To Bella, Hannah and David for giving Verity a home, and a clearer voice. To Melissa and Georgie for reading the final draft. To Jim for checking that nothing very stupid had been written about sailing, ships or dinghies (any remaining errors are entirely my fault and not his). And to Jenny for allowing her gardening time to be interfered with. But finally, and most importantly of all, to the Wray boys – Lou, Joe and Ben – without whom there would be no reason to write.